T0194224

STANDING NAKED IN PUBLIC

By Karli Keefe

authorHOUSE®

AuthorHouse™
1663 Liberty Drive
Bloomington, IN 47403
www.authorhouse.com
Phone: 1-800-839-8640

First published by AuthorHouse 3/10/2011

ISBN: 978-1-4567-5306-1 (e)
ISBN: 978-1-4567-5305-4 (sc)

Printed in the United States of America

Any people depicted in stock imagery provided by Thinkstock are models, and such images are being used for illustrative purposes only. Certain stock imagery © Thinkstock.

This book is printed on acid-free paper.

CHAPTER 1

"I HATE RED CARPET events," Kate professed. "Another ten minutes before this phony shitfest begins."

"Come on girl, you're bringing me down. I love working these gigs. Stop complainin'," Andre, a security guard for the Academy Awards, said as he wiped droplets of sweat from his forehead with a cocktail napkin. "I just wish it wasn't so fuckin' hot out."

"How on earth can you love this? Everyone is so fucking phony. And please don't get me started on those vultures," Kate said, motioning her head toward the frenzied crowd of photographers gathered by the red carpet entrance to the Kodak Theatre at Hollywood and Highland.

"Wait a minute. Aren't *you* the paparazzi?" Andre asked, raising his eyebrow.

Kate was irritated by Andre's insinuation. "You know I'm not like them. Look at them. They're blood-thirsty maniacs."

Andre laughed, "I knew that'd get you going."

"Ha. Ha. Very funny," Kate snickered. She looked at Andre and wondered if anyone would dare try to pummel their way through his six foot ten inch, three hundred pound powerhouse body. He was a rock solid human security wall.

A man's voice blared from Andre's walkie-talkie. "Yo, Andre. Where are you?" the man asked.

"Over by the press area. Why?" Andre seemed annoyed that someone was questioning his whereabouts.

"I need you to cover for me up front for a minute," the man requested.

"Be there in a sec," Andre replied. He turned to Kate and said, "This will only take a few minutes. Don't worry. I've got your back. Squeeze into the press crowd. As soon as you see me, get my attention. I'll make sure you get a front row spot."

"You're definitely coming back this way, right?" Kate was concerned Andre wouldn't return in time to help her secure an unobstructed view of the red carpet. After all, he did abandon her at the Emmy Awards last year.

"I promise I'll take care of you. I'll find someone to cover for me," Andre assured her as he adjusted his crooked bow tie.

"You owe me for disappearing at the Emmy's. I was stuck in no man's land. I only had one money-shot that day," Kate reminded him in a demanding, yet teasing tone.

"Are you ever gonna live that down? You know there was a security breach—no—a death threat I had to respond to."

"Well, who is to say that won't happen again? Huh?" Kate loved teasing Andre.

"You're driving me nuts, Kate," Andre said as he began to push his way through an excited group of onlookers to make his way to the front gate. "I promise I'll hook you up," he hollered back to Kate.

"Just keep an eye out for me," Kate yelled back to him. She glanced at her Cartier tank watch and realized she'd better start heading over to the press area.

God I hate doing this. Why do I subject myself to this torture?

Kate asked herself. This was Kate's least favorite thing to do—photographing celebrities at their phoniest. She wasn't like the other photographers. The other photographers, or rather, the "paparazzi", loved the Academy Awards so much you'd think they were having an orgasm every time they clicked their cameras. Kate felt a world apart from her colleagues. She was probably the only celebrity photographer who hated the Academy Awards—and every other red carpet event.

As she approached the rear of the press corps, Kate reminded herself of the large sum of money she'd get for today's photos. It was a tight race for Best Actress and photographs of any of the five nominees would fetch a high bid.

Photo editors salivated over the opportunity to purchase Kate's photos. She possessed a talent for capturing celebrities' better sides on print. Some celebrities were beautiful in person and on film, but appeared mediocre on print. Mediocre photos didn't sell magazines. Beautiful photos of beautiful people sold magazines; unless of course it was a deliberately hurtful article about celebrities with cellulite or celebrities sans makeup.

Kate never hesitated to capitalize on her talent for producing exquisite, eye-grabbing photos. She made it very clear to editors that she owed no allegiance to any particular publication. This gave her carte blanche in negotiating the sale of her photos. Photo editors knew it was all about the money for her and if she had a price in mind, they knew enough to give her what she wanted or she'd surely move on to the next tabloid that would purchase them.

Though it was her most profitable area of expertise, Kate hated the fact that photographing celebrities had become her career. Photojournalism, the kind that impacted society and changed the world, was her true love. She'd much rather be in a third world country reporting on a human rights issue or photographing an endangered animal in need of saving than photograph the wealthy and famous. However, photojournalism didn't exactly pay the bills, provide for a nest egg, or afford Kate her taste in designer clothes, shoes, and accessories. The only photojournalism assignments that paid well were those that would endanger her life, like wars, natural disasters, or terrorism.

Though Kate longed to donate all of her time and effort to worthwhile causes, she'd become very comfortable and spoiled since making the Los Angeles area her home and photographing celebrities her vocation. Over the past two years, Kate had become increasingly reliant on the large sums of money she earned. She was able to travel anywhere, buy nice things and still have money left over to sock away in retirement and savings accounts. She loved the money, but despised the work that accompanied it.

Kate often fantasized about the day she would have freedom to devote all of her time to "saving the world". Her life would be close to perfect. Fortunately, that day wasn't too far off. In a few years she would be financially able to practice photojournalism full-time, thanks to her prudence in the area of saving money. She wouldn't be wealthy or "set for life" by any means, but comfortable enough to quit photographing artificial people against artificial backgrounds. She'd get the hell out of L.A.

The only thing missing from her life plan was a partner to share in her dreams. Three weeks ago, Kate broke up with her girlfriend of five months, Tami. Tami turned out to be an obsessive, jealous, control freak who Kate added to her list of psycho ex-girlfriends. Kate was beginning to think she may never find her soul mate and often wondered if such a woman even existed. Since breaking up with Tami, Kate thought about completely giving up on her search for true love. She wondered if maybe she was meant to be single and alone.

Earlier, Kate thought about staying home and blowing off the Academy Awards. She really wasn't up to working in this pandemonium. She knew she'd regret blowing off this moneymaking opportunity, so, to her disdain, was standing on the sidelines of the red carpet entrance to the Academy Awards, fighting with the other photographers for a front row position. It was always a pushing, shoving, obscenity-yelling match amongst the paparazzi at these high profile awards shows. Miraculously, once the celebrities began strutting in, everyone settled into their best behavior, like uniformed school children fearing their headmaster's approach.

Fortunately, Kate often had an "insider" looking out for her on the red carpet to assure her a front row spot. Kate worked very hard in developing and sustaining key relationships. Schmoozing with editors, publishers, agents, and publicists secured her very beneficial alliances on the red carpet. Plus, it didn't hurt that she was a tall attractive blonde or that the majority of her colleagues were obnoxious jerks.

Kate was standing in the far rear of the press area when she spotted Andre. She yelled out his name as loud as she could to get his attention.

Andre quickly spotted Kate and held up his finger making a "wait a minute" signal as he spoke into his walkie-talkie.

"Oh, great, wha d'ya know this guy too?" a paparazzo standing next to Kate asked in a nasty tone. Kate didn't recognize the disgruntled photographer. He, on the other hand, must have remembered her from a previous event and wasn't pleased that she was about to get special treatment again.

She ignored his comments. She was accustomed to the jealousies and backstabbing this profession spawned.

"Open the line," Andre commanded of the frenzied group of paparazzi standing directly behind the makeshift miniature hedges, separating the press from the red carpet area.

Kate gleefully observed Andre taking control of the situation. In an apparent act of united protest, none of the paparazzi moved, opting to ignore Andre.

Incensed by their defiance, Andre raised his voice and said, "If you don't move, I can have every one of you escorted to the back row, or removed entirely. Now move!" Andre was good with scare tactics.

Kate squeezed her way through four rows of photographers but came to a standstill behind two men in the front row. Andre came to her rescue and motioned for the two photographers to move to the side to open a spot for Kate. The two photographers obliged, moving to each side as far as they could, showing their disapproval of Andre's authority by rolling their eyes at each other. Once they repositioned themselves, Kate was able to situate herself in the front row.

"Thank you, boys," Kate said, mockingly, to the two photographers next to her.

She gave Andre a wink to thank him.

He returned with a wink of his own and exited the press area to assist with the sudden influx of celebrities.

Kate was introduced to Andre through her contact at Variety. Andre immediately took a liking to Kate, telling her he appreciated how pleasantly different she was from the rest of the Hollywood press. Andre also had a crush on Kate. Rather than possibly ruin her red carpet connection, Kate never mentioned her affinity to women when he asked her out on a date. She declined, simply telling him she was seeing someone, which she was at the time.

"I guess it doesn't matter that we were here first," Tony, a short and stocky balding paparazzo standing to her left, said.

"You're such a fucking kiss-ass Kate," William, a pencil

thin, greasy haired paparazzo standing to Kate's right, spewed.

"It's not that I'm a kiss-ass. It's that I'm not an asshole," Kate replied.

"No, William. She's got tits and we don't. He obviously prefers tall blonde bimbos," Tony spat.

"Too bad he's not gay. If he let me blow him, I'd have a permanent front row spot," William said in an overtly effeminate tone.

"I highly doubt that, William. You always reek of dirty wet socks," Kate mumbled. She looked at her watch and realized she had only a few minutes to set up before the celebrities began corralling into the erratic press area.

She ignored the rest of Tony and William's nasty comments. She had more important things to do, like focusing on getting her equipment ready. Kate could care less that William and Tony were bothered by her ability to weasel her way into the front of the line at the last minute. It was a cutthroat profession where one had to do what one had to do to get the job done.

It was a much hotter than normal March day in L.A. The air was thick from smog and humidity. Sweat dripped from Kate's brow and her long, thick curly blonde hair began to frizz from the humidity, weighing heavily on her neck. Kate felt the heat of the sun scorching into her scalp. Luckily she never went anywhere without a hair tie, which she retrieved from her black dress slacks and used to secure her hair into a ponytail on top of her head.

Kate had turned thirty that week, but looked years younger. From an early age, people told her she should model. She had perfect, chiseled facial features and high cheekbones. Her near perfect rosy complexion never required makeup. She rarely applied anything more to her face than lip-gloss and mascara.

The only thing about her body she wanted to change was her breasts. Most women would die to have her perky, 36C breasts. Her ex-girlfriends loved them, but they made her feel like an implant-filled Playboy model.

Kate looked stunning in a form fitting Armani suit, which consisted of a white pant and blazer set with a silk black button down shirt and silver scarf. Kate hated getting dressed up, but the Academy Awards imposed a black tie dress code on the press as well as the attendees.

Feeling uncomfortable as her suit clung to her sweaty appendages and torso, she regretted not buying the full length black spaghetti strap gown she tried on at Fred Segal's the day before. At the time, she didn't want to invest in a $2,000 gown she'd probably wear once or twice.

The intense heat and humidity reminded her of her recent trip to Central America. While loading film into her old, beat up Nikon—her tried and true camera that she refused to upgrade to digital—Kate began to daydream about the animals and the people she encountered there. She wished she was still there, taking photos in shorts, a tank top and flip-flops.

Her daydream was short lived when Tony the paparazzo, very loudly, began shouting in her ear, "Angela, Angela. Over hear love!" He was trying to get the attention of Angela Moore, who was entering the red carpet area. Angela was nominated for the Best Actress Oscar for her portrayal of the brilliant, yet tragically suicidal poet, Anne Sexton.

Like a trained beauty pageant queen waving from a float, Angela sauntered onto the red carpet and waved to the press and crowd of fans.

Kate fumbled to get the lens cover off of her camera. "Damn it," she cursed aloud. She didn't want to miss getting photos of Angela.

Angela was now standing directly in front of Kate, posing and pivoting to show off every angle of her body for the cameras.

"Finally," Kate sighed in relief when the lens cover popped off. She immediately began clicking away.

Angela, with dark brown, near-black hair and piercing ice blue eyes, eerily resembled Sexton. She was wearing a vintage Valentino violet gown that accentuated every curve and feature of her body. A huge, flawless, pear shaped diamond, most likely a Harry Winston bauble, hung slightly above her breasts, which peaked out from the plunging neckline of her silk, flowing gown. Her long, dark mane caressed the middle of her bare, open back.

Kate admired the beautiful woman standing before her and thought, *my God, she is so perfect, so beautiful; it's hard to believe she's real. What I'd give to suck on those full, pouty lips.*

Angela repositioned herself and distended her right leg slightly to accentuate the slit in her dress, highlighting her long, perfectly tanned leg.

"Is it true you and Jason are trying to have a baby?" William shouted. Angela was married to Jason Saunders, one of the hottest actors in Hollywood.

Tony followed by yelling, "What's the real reason you're taking a break from making movies?"

They are so stupid. Like she's really going to answer your stupid questions? Kate thought. *These idiots really do make the rest of us appear to be insensitive, brainless vultures.*

In a loud whisper, Kate could hear William tell Tony, "Ask her if she's a lesbian. I dare you."

"Yeah, right. Are you completely out of your mind? She'll never let me photograph her again. She already hates me for that night outside The Ivy." Tony was referring to a highly publicized incident in which he ambushed Angela and Jason as they exited the restaurant. Tony accidentally knocked Angela to the ground after he aggressively pushed his way through a crowd of celebrity-watchers to photograph the couple as they exited the club. Jason, in turn, punched Tony in the face and was later arrested for assault and sued by Tony. The charges against Jason were eventually dismissed. However, Tony's lawsuit is still pending.

Angela ignored the intrusive questions thrown her way by the paparazzi, simply choosing to continue posing in silence and smiling her wide, perfectly white pearly smile. She would save her interview responses for the television reporters.

Still clicking away, alternatively turning the camera to take both horizontal and vertical shots, Kate wondered if the rumors were true—that Angela Moore was a closet lesbian. Some of the tabloids labeled her marriage to People magazine's "Sexiest Man Alive" a sham. Jason was frequently linked to other women and Angela had, in the past, been seen on numerous occasions with a famous lesbian writer, Kristan Daniels. However, when Kristan and Angela were confronted about ever having had an affair, both women, along with their publicists, vehemently denied the rumors and haven't been spotted together since Angela and Jason married over a year ago. Jason further insisted in interviews that he and Angela's marriage was rock solid. The lesbian rumors were just par for the course compared to the thousands of other rumors the tabloids dreamed up for the high profile couple, which included such headlines as, "Angela seeks sperm donor: Jason impotent!" and "Jason and Angela have threesomes to save marriage".

Kate thought about the upcoming photo session she would be doing with Angela. Vanity Fair magazine contracted with her as the lead photographer for an upcoming magazine spread on the actress. Kate jumped at the opportunity to photograph Angela Moore.

Her contact at Vanity Fair couldn't believe Kate didn't

bitch even once about the assignment. Usually, Kate moaned and groaned to her Vanity Fair contact, Melissa, about up close and personal celebrity photo assignments. However, this was a photo shoot with Angela Moore. Kate didn't care if Angela turned out to be like all the other celebrities she photographed, ordering the makeup artist around, complaining about the lights being too hot, or having a fit because her sandwich was made on the wrong type of bread. No, none of that behavior would matter. Kate was getting paid to drool for an entire day.

In the five years she'd been photographing celebrities, Kate had never been star struck. She had never experienced even the slightest crush on a celebrity, until she photographed Angela at an Independent Film awards soiree. There was definitely something about Angela. Kate would get butterflies in her stomach every time she saw her, whether it was in person or print. She never shared details of her secret crush with anyone. She was embarrassed about feeling this way about a celebrity. She viewed the crush as immature and a sign of pathetic weakness.

Angela's publicist gently tugged at Angela's elbow to let her know she needed to move on. Angela turned away from the press area and began walking toward the broadcast journalists, who were conducting live interviews. Kate could see Angela joining her husband, Jason, who was already being interviewed by a television reporter.

What on earth does she even see in him? Kate wondered, surprised by the pang of jealousy that arose in her gut. *Well, he is a handsome man.* She reasoned. *I'll give him that much. But, if what the tabloids say is true, he's a louse and certainly undeserving of Angela.* Kate realized what she was saying to herself. I *can't believe this. I'm actually jealous of Jason Saunders. But, like the rest of the world, I want to fuck his wife.*

Kate turned her attention to one of the other Best Actress nominees, continuing to photograph, stopping only to unload and reload film. After she depleted ten rolls of film, Kate replaced the lens cap on her camera, gathered her bags and exited through the rows of photographers. She didn't wait for the last of the nominees to arrive. It was too hot. She felt like she was going to pass out and couldn't wait to get inside her air-conditioned BMW SUV.

"Damn, she pushes her way in, then leaves before it's over," Tony complained, wrinkling his nose and making a nasty face in Kate's direction.

"She's *such* a bitch," William added.

Kate pretended she didn't hear them. They didn't deserve a reply from her. As Kate made her way to the parking lot, she delighted in the fact that she knew these photos would be some of the best she'd ever taken at a red carpet event. She sensed the success with every click. It was an intuitive gift she had. When she took a bad photo, which was a rare occurrence, she knew it long before the film would be developed. There were so many factors other than lighting, like the subject's hair and makeup, the film speed, etc. There was a definite aura that needed to exist. This day was right on the mark. Although the heat was uncomfortable, it would add a steamy quality to the pictures.

CHAPTER 2

A NGELA FELT LIKE she'd stepped into a hot oven as
she exited the comfort of her air-conditioned limo.
The thick, humid heat weighed heavily on her. She worried
that her hair would soon droop and frizz from the heat, but
then remembered her hairstylist applied so much hairspray
and anti-frizz serum; nothing could permeate it, not even
the worst L.A. humidity. As she stood on the red carpet,
performing her fake waves and poses, she couldn't help but
think about how incredible this moment was. She was living
out her dream. She was a movie star and an Academy Award
nominee. It was hard to believe just seven years ago she was a
broke, struggling theatre actress living in a crappy apartment
in New York City.

The opportunity of a lifetime came her way when Angela landed a leading role in a small off Broadway theatre
production in lower Manhattan. By shear coincidence, one
of the biggest producers in Hollywood, Ted McNeil, was
in attendance during a matinee performance. Seated in the
front row, Ted was under the impression he was at the play
of his nineteen-year-old lover, Guy. He patiently waited for
his beloved new boy toy to take the stage and perform. To
his dismay, Guy never appeared on stage. About halfway

through the production, Ted finally realized he was in the wrong theatre, at the wrong play.

He would've left as soon as he realized his error, but was captivated by the lead actress's performance. As the curtain closed for the intermission, Ted scrambled to locate the playbill he had earlier tossed to the floor. He had to know who this incredible actress was and, most importantly, had to meet her.

He leafed through the playbill to locate her name. "Angela Moore", he read quietly to himself. "Angela, today is your lucky day my darling," he said under his breath.

Backstage, after the performance, Ted congratulated Angela on an incredible performance and asked if she'd be interested in going to L.A. to audition for a minor role in an independent film he was producing. Ted rarely ventured from his usual productions, which were big budget action movies. This independent film was a special pet project. Angela thought he was kidding at first or that he must be some lunatic pretending to be someone important in the hopes of getting laid.

Only after she witnessed the other actors trying to vie for his attention did she realize this really *was* Ted McNeil. *The* Ted McNeil was handing *her* a ticket to her dreams in the form of a playbill, which had his secretary's contact information scribbled on it. Angela no sooner accepted his invitation to audition, than Ted quickly disappeared to search for his boy toy Guy.

The next day, Angela called Ted's secretary. It took three attempts as Angela forgot about the three-hour time difference. By 8:00 a.m. Pacific time, Ted's secretary finally answered the phone. She instructed Angela of her itinerary: the flight, ground transportation, reservations at the Chateau Marmont and audition information. Apparently, Ted called her the night before and instructed her to get moving on this ASAP.

That evening, Angela was on a direct flight to L.A. to the audition that would become the launching pad for her now successful acting career. Angela won the role of a down-on-her-luck welfare mom who goes back to college and becomes a famous doctor. She would later receive accolades from both critics and peers. "Angela Moore—the next Meryl Streep," one said. "Where have they been hiding this incredible actress? Angela Moore's career will definitely be one to watch," another wrote.

After her successful debut, Angela was offered a minor role in Ted's next big action production. Her career was taking off and she was living rent free in Ted's sprawling estate located in the Hollywood Hills. Ted had grown quite fond of Angela. Though he preferred the romantic company of young studs, he fell in love with Angela's spirit. They became best friends.

Angela appeared content and hopeful on the outside, but hid a heart wrenching loss on the inside. What Angela gained in showbiz opportunity, she lost severely in love.

Prior to her trek to Hollywood, Angela had been content on living out the rest of her life in New York City with her partner, Julia. Angela never dreamed of leaving New York. Her goal was to become a famous Broadway actress, not a movie star. Angela and Julia planned on spending the rest of their lives together in New York City.

They met when Angela was acting in a dinner theatre troupe, Angela's first paid acting gig since arriving to the city from her home town in upstate New York. It was love at first sight when she met Julia, a very tall auburn haired New York University student waitressing at the dinner theatre. Angela and Julia became inseparable friends. However, the more time Angela spent with Julia, the more she wanted to hold her, not as a friend, but as a lover.

One evening while they sat on the couch at Julia's apartment watching a movie, Angela took the risk of revealing her true feelings to Julia.

"Julia, this is really uncomfortable for me and I'm not sure how to say this but," Angela paused and took Julia's hand into hers. "I'm really attracted to you," she blurted.

Julia, who had never been with a woman before, pulled her hand away and said, "I don't know what to say Angela. This is definitely weird for me. I don't think I'm into women."

Angela lunged forward and began kissing Julia. Julia pulled back a little, but then succumbed to Angela's kisses. They spent quite some time kissing and exploring each other's mouths. Angela, who was extremely turned on, reached up under Julia's shirt to caress her breast.

"Stop." Julia jerked her body away from Angela and leaned back to the opposite side of the couch. "This is freaking me out a little."

"It's ok," Angela tried to assure Julia.

"I'm really confused right now." Julia folded her arms. "You're beautiful and I'm definitely attracted to you, but it's just kind of weird."

Angela reached her hand out, attempting to caress Julia's hair but Julia stood up and said, "Please Angela, go home. I need time to figure this all out."

"Ok Julia, I'll go home. But, please don't let this ruin our friendship." Angela gathered her sweater and pocketbook and left Julia's apartment. She felt rejected and ashamed.

A week went by and Angela hadn't heard from Julia. Angela presumed she scared Julia to the point where their friendship was now over. Angela felt embarrassed, but angry too. *Did she not feel what I felt when we kissed? How could she not want this?* Angela wondered.

Eventually, Julia called and invited Angela to come over to her apartment to talk.

When Angela entered Julia's apartment, she was surprised to see a candlelit dinner with two place settings at Julia's kitchen table. "What's the occasion, Julia?" Angela inquired, tossing her coat onto Julia's couch.

"It's to celebrate our first night together," Julia said, smiling. She gently grasped Angela's hand, leading her to the table.

"I thought you were never going to speak to me again. I was so worried," Angela confessed.

"Well, I thought about it and realized how much I love you and want you as weird as it may feel," Julia said, pulling the dining chair out for Angela to sit down.

Angela remained standing and pulled Julia into her. "Julia, there's nothing weird about us. I promise you," she said, leaning in to kiss Julia.

The kiss was tender at first, but grew harder as the two women voraciously submerged their mouths and tongues into one another. Dinner was all but forgotten at that point.

"I just can't believe I'm doing this," Julia said, breaking their embrace to lead Angela to her bed.

"I'll make sure you won't regret it," Angela whispered as she toppled onto the bed with Julia.

The two women hurriedly undressed each other until they were both naked. Though Angela was thin and petite, she was attracted to tall, voluptuous, shapely women. Seeing Julia completely nude made Angela feel extraordinarily horny. She trembled as she explored and caressed Julia's curvaceous, soft body with her mouth and hands.

Angela relished having Julia's naked body underneath her. Her ample breasts felt warm and supple against Angela's small breasts and frame.

Never one to be patient when turned on, Angela didn't

hesitate to plunge her fingers inside Julia's hot, wet pussy. Angela forced her fingertips into Julia's soft, silky wall, focusing on her pleasure spots, while rubbing her clit with the pad of her thumb. She suckled on Julia's hard nipple while thrusting her fingers into Julia's moist fiery walls, harder and faster. Angela could feel her own clit swell, engorged with excitement.

Julia pulled Angela's head up from her breast to kiss her, then grunted and panted her way to an explosive orgasm. Julia and Angela held each other tightly, kissing so ferociously it was animalistic.

Angela was so turned on she knew that once Julia touched her, she'd be cumming.

"I want to taste you. Can I do that?" Julia asked.

"Are you crazy?" Angela couldn't believe Julia—her Julia—was about to go down on her. "Of course," she murmured. Within minutes, Angela experienced an earth shattering orgasm as Julia teased her clit with the tip of her tongue.

Within days of their romantic tryst, Angela moved into Julia's Greenwich Village apartment. As time passed, they talked of a commitment ceremony, children, and spending their lives together. They often talked about their hopes and dreams for their future together. Angela would be a huge Broadway star and Julia a social worker, helping the homeless.

For three years they struggled, living in Julia's tiny one room studio, barely getting by financially. Julia worked as a waitress and attended NYU fulltime, while Angela worked as a bartender at a local bar in Greenwich Village and auditioned for plays and musicals. They were poor, but madly in love with each other and hopeful of the future.

The beginning of the end came when Ted offered Angela her breakout role, taking her far away from Julia. The two women committed to making the long distance relationship work. Julia promised Angela if her career started to take off, she'd move to L.A. to be with her. In the meantime, she'd be there for Angela no matter what and no matter how far apart they would be from one another.

After Angela moved to L.A., they kept in touch by phone calls, texting and emails. Julia visited Angela on the west coast several times, taking advantage of Ted's generosity to pay for her airline tickets. However, as time passed, Angela sensed something was changing in Julia and their relationship. Julia became distant.

When Angela's first movie had been released, Julia accompanied Angela to the premiere. Everything seemed fine that evening, but it was clear the next day that not everything was fine.

Out of nowhere, Julia informed Angela she hated L.A. and demanded that Angela return to New York. "This wasn't part of our original plan, Angela," Julia said, sitting in a cab in front of LAX airport.

"What are you talking about? Julia, you have to think about the opportunities out here. You'll get used to it," Angela pleaded. "The weather's perfect. Plus, Ted will help you find a job after you graduate next month."

"This isn't what I want." Julia had made up her mind a long time before this conversation. "I can't leave New York and I can't stand this long distance relationship."

"I thought all you wanted was me?" Angela felt like her life was slipping away from her.

"Of course I want you, Angela. But my life is in New York. New York is what you wanted—what we wanted." Julia began to cry.

"Honey, things change. My love hasn't. Let's finish this discussion when you get back to New York. I know we can work this out." Angela pulled out a tissue from her purse and blotted the tears dripping onto Julia's ivory cheeks. They sat in the cab, hugging and weeping.

Julia boarded the plane and left L.A., never to return. In the following days and weeks, their phone conversations grew shorter and less intimate. Angela knew something was wrong.

Her suspicions that it was over were confirmed when Julia called to inform her that she had fallen in love with a man. He was a medical student she met at a party thrown by a fellow NYU student. Julia tearfully confessed to Angela that she wasn't in love with her anymore.

Angela was devastated by Julia's decision to break up. Even worse, Angela couldn't believe Julia fell in love with a man. She couldn't imagine her Julia with another person, especially a man.

Angela grew despondent and suicidal. She wondered how she was ever going to survive without Julia in her life. Weeks went by where all Angela seemed to do was sob uncontrollably day and night. One night, while Ted was away on vacation in Fiji with a young Swedish hunk, Angela opened the medicine cabinet in the master suite bathroom and pulled out a new disposable razor from its plastic bag.

She placed the razor on the floor and began smashing it with a hammer Ted kept in the kitchen until the razor blade separated itself from the disposable shaver's casing. Angela hammered so hard that a portion of the marble tile shattered, causing spider web-like fissures.

Angela sat on the cold bathroom floor alongside the enormous Jacuzzi bathtub and held the blade over her wrist. The master suite bathroom was decorated completely in white. Everything in the bathroom was white; the fixtures, the towels, the countertop, the cabinets, even the marble tile and bathroom rugs were white. It was a stark, blinding, bright white—everywhere. The room reminded Angela of a giant sheet of blank copy paper, without as much as a dot of ink on it. Angela hated the intensity of so much white. She had been meaning to buy a bright colored throw rug and matching towels, but never did get around to it.

She envisioned the blood from her severed artery spurting lines in every direction, splattering the tub, the white paneled walls, and the bathroom rugs. Red droplets would be everywhere. She would paint the bathroom with her despair. There would finally be color in the bathroom and her pain would be lifted forever. She toyed with the razor over her wrist, allowing it to occasionally scratch the surface of her flesh, causing tiny paper cut wounds.

Minutes turned into hours as she sat there, dazed over whether to cut deeper. Angela thought about how the police would find her lying there, covered in her own blood. Her family would be devastated.

She arose from her sitting position, staring at the blade now resting in the palm of her hand. For what seemed like an eternity, she contemplated whether to cut or not. She squeezed the dull side of the blade between her thumb and index finger and placed the sharp side on her left wrist. She pushed the blade into the flesh until a few drops of blood rolled off her wrist onto the white bath mat. Just as she started to cut her wrist, she lifted the razor.

She couldn't do it. After that day, Angela was determined to recover from this breakup. With a new, high profile career to worry about, Angela eventually accepted the fact that Julia breaking up with her was probably better for her acting career. She ultimately forgave Julia and gave her blessing. A year and a half later, Angela had recovered enough from the breakup to attend Julia's wedding to the medical student, who is today a successful cardiologist. Angela still talks to Julia, now the mother of four, a few times a year.

Ted helped Angela heal. He became her best friend and

mentor. He helped her win roles and taught her the ins and outs of Hollywood. Three years after their initial introduction, Angela would repay Ted for his kindness by caring for him as he died from AIDS. Angela took care of his every need as he became bedridden, dying, over the course of six months. It was a harrowing loss for Angela. Ted was the only person she trusted in Hollywood. She felt abandoned and lost.

Immediately following Ted's death, Angela began working nonstop, never taking a break between films. By staying busy and distracted, she didn't have to feel the pain.

Never during the time they were together did Angela or Julia ever imagine Angela would someday be an Academy Award nominee. Angela thought about how simple her life had been when she lived with Julia. Her sexual preference really didn't matter. Most importantly, she had her privacy, which certainly wasn't the case today. Now, her entire life was on display for the world to see. As far as the public was concerned, she was not a lesbian, bisexual or curious.

After she posed for photographers near the red carpet entrance, Angela joined her husband, Jason, as he gave an interview for the E! Television reporter. The reporter quickly turned her attention to Angela. Jason was as famous and in demand as she, but this was her night to shine. Jason had been the focus of attention in recent months for his Emmy win as a lead actor in television's number one hit comedy show and recently renegotiated his salary, making him one of the highest paid television actors. Angela lost out on the Golden Globe a few months ago and wanted the Oscar more than anything.

Actually, what Angela wanted more than anything was to get a divorce from Jason and live happily ever after with the woman of her dreams, whoever she was. Unfortunately, that just wasn't going to happen. Angela made the difficult decision of playing it straight for her career's sake. There was too much stigma in Hollywood around being gay. It was cool to be bisexual, but being a full-fledged lesbian could potentially damage her career. It was all a crapshoot. Fans were fickle. You just never knew when they'd root for you or throw an egg at you.

Angela decided that love would have to come last in her life and her career as a successful actress would come first. It would be the price to pay to continue being one of the highest paid and most in demand movie actresses in Hollywood.

"Hi Angela. Congratulations on your nomination," the E! reporter said, shoving the microphone under Angela's chin.

"Thank you," Angela said with a huge smile. *What, did she get another face lift? Ugh she looks like a strange breed of cat.*

"I was just talking to Jason about you."

I bet you were, you gossiping freak. "Oh yeah? All good I hope," Angela let out a fake giggle.

"Of course. He said you are the most beautiful woman here tonight and that whether you win or lose, you will always be a winner in his eyes."

Boy, you sure laid it on tonight, Jason. "He's so sweet. Thanks honey," Angela said, looking into Jason's eyes. *If this reporter ever knew the truth about us, her face would probably crack.*

"She's the love of my life," Jason added.

"And you are mine," Angela said, feeling a bit nauseous over the act they were putting on. Angela's publicist whispered in her ear that it was time to proceed to the next television reporter. "Sorry, but it's time to go in. Bye," Angela concluded the interview with cat-lady, pulling Jason's arm to follow her.

"That was an over-the-top performance, Mr. Saunders," Angela whispered to Jason.

"That's why I make the big bucks, babe," Jason whispered back.

"What's with, *I'm* the love of *your* life?" Angela commented out of the side of her mouth. "Puhleaze," Angela hated when Jason went overboard with fabricating their love for each other.

It wasn't that she didn't love Jason. She just wasn't romantically in love with him. He was her best friend—the masculine brother she never had as her brother, Joe, was an effeminate, gay drag queen.

The truth was that their marriage had been a charade from the very beginning. Jason learned early on that Angela was a lesbian. They were never a couple in the traditional sense. They never had sex or even kissed passionately. They agreed to marriage for unconventional reasons. Their publicists introduced them and then schemed for them to get married. "It would help your careers," they insisted. "You'll be *the* Hollywood power couple."

On a whim, Jason and Angela drove to Las Vegas and got married. Angela couldn't bring herself to lie to her family and have them participate in the media circus farce that would have been their wedding. Jason and Angela sent photos of their wedding at the Chapel of Love to the press and her parents, who were devastated that Angela didn't get married in the Catholic Church.

Then the media blitz began. It was the biggest story that year. Hollywood's most eligible bachelor and bachelorette marry. Kissing in public was an uncomfortable, yet necessary part of their publicity ploy. They committed to never using their tongues. It was difficult at first to kiss for the cameras, but they got used to it. It was like kissing a family member.

Jason agreed to marry Angela for the instant publicity as well as for the simple fact he could still screw around. Jason was a player. He was irresistible and had no desire to settle down and have a family. Upon first meeting Angela, Jason saw her as a hot piece of ass. Soon, however, their relationship developed into something much bigger than the typical fuck 'em and leave 'em relationships he was accustomed to having with women. He came to the conclusion long before he met Angela that he would probably never meet a woman he'd want to have as his wife. All of the women out there, besides Angela, were good for one thing—sex. Angela was his best friend. She was the sister he never had.

Angela agreed to marry Jason for the publicity too. She also married him to get over her recent breakup with her lover, Kristan, and convince the world the rumors that she preferred women weren't true. Plus, Angela was no dummy. She knew that an Angela Moore-Jason Saunders union would be a huge deal for the tabloids and other Hollywood fodder.

Neither Jason nor Angela ever imagined the magnitude of success their marriage would bring to their careers. They quickly became the most influential Hollywood power couple. The public couldn't get enough of them. They were constantly on the covers of tabloids and requests for pictorials and interviews streamed in. Since marrying, each of their salaries had quadrupled. Movie and television offers piled in.

To the outsiders who had the privilege of knowing their marriage was a sham; it appeared to be a rather bizarre situation. As bizarre as it seemed, their "marriage" was turning out to be a very profitable business arrangement.

Inside the auditorium, Angela patiently sat through two and a half hours of awards, bad jokes, the honorary Oscar presentation and entertainment. Finally, the nominees for Best Actress were being announced. As Angela heard her name, she squeezed Jason's hand tightly. Angela's portrayal of the poet, Anne Sexton, was critically acclaimed worldwide. She won the Screen Actor's Guild Award and a Cannes Film Festival Award. She wanted this Oscar badly.

The previous year's Best Actor winner opened the envelope and read, "And the winner is…"

Angela clenched Jason's hand harder and said a silent prayer.

CHAPTER 3

KATE ALWAYS LEFT red carpet events early for two reasons. First, she couldn't stand the small talk between her rival photographers. One of them always managed to corner her with, "Can you believe so and so wore that?" In reality, Kate didn't give a rat's ass if every star in Hollywood arrived in burlap sacks. Kate wasn't like the other photographers at that event. She was a photojournalist and humanitarian. She just happened to be trapped by this profession for her own selfish, materialistic reasons.

The second reason she always left these spectacles early was to avoid traffic. It was a bitch trying to get through the security and the ungodly number of limos. Kate hopped into her Honda CRV and turned the air conditioning as high as it would go. Almost immediately, the vents blasted ice cold air. Kate adjusted the vents so the frigid air would blow directly on her. It was invigorating and relieving.

Angela got a lot of flak from her hybrid-driving friends over her SUV, though it was pretty good on gas. Kate would argue that she had no choice but to drive a 4-wheel drive SUV for photographing in rough terrain and hauling all of her photographic equipment. She did, though, feel a pang of guilt every time she filled her gas tank. They say conservation has to start at home and she felt bad that she wasn't doing her part to conserve the world's oil supply.

Kate reminisced about her trip to Central America, as she waited to exit the parking area. Eight months ago, she was on a dream assignment, playing pro-bono photojournalist in Belize.

An international power company was planning to build an energy producing dam and would need to flood the Macal River Valley, a pristine tropical rainforest, ruining the habitat of endangered and rare species, including the scarlet macaw, howler money and jaguar. Ancient Mayan monuments would also be threatened. The corporation countered the environmentalists that energy produced from the dam would drive energy costs down and improve the overall standard of living for Belizeans.

Kate's photos and articles of the environmental crisis were picked up by the Associated Press and published around the world, igniting worldwide protests against the corporation. The bad publicity incited threats by consumer groups to boycott the corporation's subsidiaries. Due in part to her efforts, the dam project was halted indefinitely. Kate became an environmental hero amongst her peers and environmental organizations.

Her mother, Sharon, a conservationist and veterinarian, alerted Kate to the Belize crisis.

"Kate, brace yourself, because I have *the* assignment for you", her mother exclaimed on Kate's answering machine. "Better than that tiger poaching assignment. Call me."

Kate had just arrived home from a horrible date with a woman she met on the Internet. It turned out that her date looked nothing like the photo she emailed and was in fact an unemployed alcoholic who repeatedly abused the wait staff at the restaurant they spent their date at. It didn't surprise

Kate at all. She didn't know anyone with as many bad dating stories as she.

After listening to the message, Kate said a prayer out loud for this to be an assignment that would take her far away from LA for some much-needed respite. She had enough money saved for a working vacation and never had difficulty securing travel assistance from organizations like Green Peace or The Sierra Club. Plus, for the first time in months, her calendar was clear—no events, pictorials, or cast shoots.

Kate didn't hesitate contacting her mother. *Better than the tiger poaching assignment?* Kate wondered.

Kate's photos of the illegal tiger poaching trade were picked up around the world. She was even interviewed on a segment of 60 Minutes. She had taken two months off from photographing celebrities and devoted all of her time and energy to exposing the slaughter of tigers in India and the trade of tiger products in China and Japan.

Her efforts helped force the Indian government to crack down on tiger poaching. In addition, the United Nations' Convention on International Trade in Endangered Species called on Japan to ban the tiger trade.

"Hi mom, how's it going?" Kate asked.

"Belize's rain forest is being threatened by a first-world corporation. No one is covering the story. I thought of you and they could really use your help. There was a journalist covering it, but he fell ill with a horrible bout of dysentery. It looks as though they will break ground next month." She went on to give Kate the details and who to contact at the environmental organization involved in the campaign to preserve Belize. Kate excitedly jotted down all of the particulars.

"Of course I'm interested. In fact, I'd leave now if I didn't need sleep." It was only eleven o'clock at night, but she had gotten up at 5:00 a.m. that day to begin setup for a photo shoot of a popular sitcom cast. Kate had to shoot between takes, as the cast was extremely difficult and spoiled, refusing to pose for publicity photos on their own time. Jason Saunders was the worst behaved of the bunch. He had a near temper tantrum when he found out he had to sit for photos in between takes.

The shoot didn't end until almost 6:00 p.m. She hadn't even had the time to go home and freshen up before her nightmare date. It had definitely turned out to be a very exhausting and disappointing day. That all changed, though, after speaking with her mother.

Before hanging up, Kate's mother asked if she was seeing anyone yet.

"Not yet. In fact, you wouldn't believe the horrendous date I just went on. Dating in L.A. is horrible." Kate was so grateful her mother was supportive and accepting of her being a lesbian. Kate's father, Richard, was another story. He had hoped it was a phase his daughter was going through when, at the age of seventeen, Kate came out to her parents.

"I thought you should know. I'm a lesbian," was all that she said that evening at Sunday dinner with her father and brother. Her little brother said nothing as his jaw dropped along with his dinner fork. Her father's reaction wasn't exactly approving either. He, too, dropped his fork and, clearly flustered asked, "Can we talk about this after dinner?"

Later, Kate called her mother, who was working in Australia.

"Hi mom. I felt the need to tell dad and Marcus I'm a lesbian. I guess that means I just told you as well, doesn't it?" Kate was crying and a bundle of nerves, hoping her mother wouldn't dismiss her as her father had.

To Kate's delight, her mother couldn't have been more supportive. "Oh darling. I love you. You know this doesn't change anything. Don't you? I just want you to be happy," Her mother went on to relate her own philosophical monologue about love and the insignificance of gender.

"What about dad?" Kate asked, interrupting her.

"Does it really matter? Kate, you will be finishing school in a month. Then you can do whatever it is you want to do. If you want to join me, you are welcome to do so. Just hang in there and finish school," she assured her.

"I hate it here. I wish I didn't have to live here," Kate protested, in tears.

"I'm sorry Kate, just finish school and I promise I will fly you here," her mother said.

Kate felt reassured, but resented the fact she had to remain in cold Massachusetts with her father. Kate and her father never did talk about that coming-out day ever again. In fact, her father still greeted her occasionally with "Seeing any lucky fellows?" or "Meet any nice guys lately?" Kate would roll her eyes and count the days to when she would be joining her mother in Australia. It disappointed Kate immensely that her father refused to acknowledge or support her sexual preference. On the other hand, she was grateful to have her mother's support and, over time, her younger brother Marcus'.

Marcus, four years Kate's junior, had even set her up on a few disastrous blind dates when she'd visit him in New York City, where he now lives. Marcus' problem was that every time he met a lesbian, he felt compelled to play matchmaker for Kate. After the last setup, in which Kate's date arrived in a real fur coat, a major faux pas for animal lover Kate, she informed her brother to never involve himself in her love life again. Plus, it didn't make sense for him to set her up on blind dates with women living in New York since she lived on the opposite end of the country, and had no desire for a long-distance relationship.

Kate was born and raised in the Cambridge, Massachusetts area. Her father taught English at Harvard University,
while her mother worked as a veterinarian not far from their
home. It was a rather normal upbringing for Kate. From
the day she was born, Kate lived with her mother, father,
and brother in the same home. That was until the summer
Kate turned sixteen, when her mother moved out and swiftly
divorced her father.

Kate and her brother had always shared with each other
that they didn't understand why their parents were together.
They were very different people. Kate's mother, Sharon was a
free spirit, while Kate's dad, Richard, was uptight and cranky.
When she wasn't working as a veterinarian, Sharon dedicated
her free time to traveling the world, assisting animal rights
organizations in saving endangered wildlife. Richard, on the
other hand, preferred to stay at home with the kids and
putter around his garden or read a good novel. Apparently,
according to Sharon, their relationship began as love struck,
college sweethearts who enjoyed the same music, movies,
and books. They had a lustful beginning, but over time they
found themselves enjoying less of the same things.

A month prior to Sharon's departure from the Ashford
home and marriage, Kate arrived home early from school,
ill from cramps caused by her monthly cycle. As she hung
her raincoat on the wall hook in the narrow foyer, she heard
strange noises coming from one of the upstairs bedrooms.
She tiptoed up the stairs and could hear what sounded like
her mother moaning. Kate approached her parents' bedroom
door and pushed it slightly ajar so that she could peer in.

She couldn't believe what she saw. In fact, it was probably
one of the most horrific sights she'd ever seen. Her mother
was bent on all fours on the bed getting fucked from behind
by a man who was clearly not Kate's father. The man was
trim and had a full head of hair, unlike her father, who was

overweight and bald. Kate stood there in disbelief and shock. Seconds later she could hear the young man utter, "I'm gonna come Margie." Kate watched as he pulled out his humongous cock and splattered a white liquid much thicker than urine all over her mother's back. His cock frightened Kate. It was enormous. It wasn't like the tiny, shriveled cocks of the boys she dated from school. She started to gag.

Kate involuntarily dropped one of her schoolbooks she had been holding. Her mother heard the book crash onto the hardwood floor and immediately turned around. Kate met her mother's eyes, which were wide with shock.

Kate quickly ran to her bedroom in horror and disgust.

Sharon immediately put her bathrobe on and ran out of the bedroom to console Kate, who was lying face down on her bed, sobbing.

"Kate, it's not what you think," she said, desperate to make things better. Sharon attempted to put her hand on Kate's shoulders. Kate flinched and moved to the other side of the bed.

"Then what was it? How could you do that to daddy?" Kate demanded, yelling into her pillow.

"I guess you should know. I am leaving your father. We'll be divorcing. He's known for quite some time. We are simply waiting on the paper work and the right time to tell you and your brother. It has been over for a long time. Kate, I just can't try to make this work any longer. We aren't in love with each other anymore."

Sharon didn't look forty-two. She was very attractive, resembling the redhead actress Julianne Moore. While it was true that Kate often wondered what her mother saw in her father. He was so drab, so boring. To see her mother with this young man, thrusting and spewing juices over her mother, was utterly shocking and disgusting.

Kate turned around to face her mother, "So, what, are

you in love with that pervert in there? What's wrong with you?"

"Yes. I have very strong feelings for Arthur. He's certainly not a pervert, though. Please know that. You were supposed to be in school. Why are you home?"

"It's my house, too. I'm sick, if you even care," Kate shouted.

Sharon started to stroke Kate's hair in an attempt to show her concern. "Your father and I agreed it was ok to see other people since the marriage is over for us."

Kate shooed Sharon's hand away. "Can't you go somewhere else? That was disgusting seeing you and him. I want to puke." Kate arose from her bed and ran to the bathroom, retching into the toilet.

Sharon followed her daughter into the bathroom. "Here," she said as she handed her a towel. "I might as well tell you now. I'll be leaving for an assignment next month in Madagascar. I've been commissioned to offer my veterinary services to help save an endangered lemur colony. I won't be returning to Cambridge after that. I've decided to dedicate my career to the field with an international focus."

Over the next week, Kate gave her mother the silent treatment. She couldn't get the horrible image of that day out of her head. It was all too much for Kate—the divorce, the sex scene and the reality that her mother would be leaving for Madagascar and not returning home. *How could she abandon her and Marcus? What type of mother does that?* She wondered.

Kate realized there was no way she could stay in Cambridge that summer. The thought of spending the summer with her father and brother was unthinkable. They were so boring. Though she was disgusted and angry with her mother, her disdain for spending the summer in boring Cambridge outweighed the ire she felt for her mother. Though she felt betrayed by her, Kate wanted to spend the summer with her mother.

Kate began scheming of ways to convince her mother to allow her to go to Madagascar with her. She decided she'd use her mother's mistakes to her advantage. Kate knew her mother suffered tremendous guilt for the graphic scene Kate witnessed and hoped that guilt would impel her mother to allow Kate to join her.

Kate pitched the idea to Sharon to bring her with her to Madagascar. "It would help mend our relationship," Kate told her. Guilt-ridden, Sharon obliged to the idea of her daughter joining her that summer and the two hugged.

Though Kate resented her mother, and did everything she could to avoid her once in Madagascar, she secretly admired her mother's dedication to tracking and caring for the lemurs. The grey, black, and white lemurs were beautiful monkey-like creatures with mesmerizing bright amber eyes, erect ears, and long, furry striped tails. It horrified her to discover that since humans arrived on the island of Madagascar, approximately 1,200 to 1,500 years ago, 16 species of lemurs had become extinct, due to habitat destruction and hunting. Their habitat was constantly being destroyed for farmland and logging. Because the soil was so inadequate, the land was often abandoned after several years of cultivation and more rain forests were cleared.

Kate fell in love with the people of Madagascar and, in a way, couldn't blame them for destroying their ecosystem. Madagascar was one of the poorest countries in the world, where seventy percent of the population lived below the poverty line.

The camp's lodging and plumbing was primitive. Kate and the others resided in huts built of flattened bamboo pieces woven together. There was no running water and buckets were the only option for bathing. This didn't bother

Kate at all. She adapted well and quickly forgot about the luxuries she left behind in Cambridge.

Kate's mother, always mixing education with pleasure, gave Kate the assignment of photographing her team's field project, since Kate's maternal aunt Susan had recently given Kate a new and very expensive 35mm Nikon camera for her birthday.

Aunt Susan was Kate's favorite of all her relatives. Susan had spent her career photographing famous rock and punk bands, like The Clash and The Sex Pistols and was now photographing U2 on tour. Her photographs were often printed in Rolling Stone and she would soon become an influential catalyst for the creation of the popular British rock magazine "Q".

While her aunt vacationed with Kate's family for a much needed rest from traveling with the Rolling Stones, Susan tutored Kate on how to use the new camera she'd given her. Kate practiced by taking pictures of classmates and Harvard's campus. Now, for the first time, she would be able to use the camera on a real field assignment. Unbeknownst to her, as she spent her days and evenings photographing, this would be her first of many photojournalism achievements. Her photos of the lemurs, people of Madagascar, and of the project's team would be included in an issue of National Geographic.

It was also the summer Kate had her first sexual experience with another girl. Her name was Eve. Eve's parents were Christian missionaries residing in the same camp as Kate and her mother. When Kate first met Eve she felt a flutter in her heart and stomach, which confused her, since the object of her affection was another girl. Kate had always had secret crushes on girls back home at school, but dismissed her feelings as a phase she must've been going through. As the hot days went by, Kate found herself lying on her cot at night fantasizing about kissing and touching Eve.

Eve was from England, a year older than Kate, and the most beautiful goddess Kate had ever seen. She had very long hair which was a beautiful shade of strawberry blonde with platinum blonde highlights bleached by the scorching Madagascar sunlight. Her eyes were as green as shamrocks and skin tan with faint freckles that covered her petite frame and angular face.

Eve's parents kept her busy by having her assist them during the day. Kate was busy following her mother's team around, taking photographs. Once it was night, however, the two girls were inseparable. They'd play backgammon and chess and talk about life back home. They would often sleep together in Kate's bungalow. Kate's lust for Eve grew every day. She would lie on her cot at night, pretending to be asleep, desperately thinking of a way she could seduce Eve. It was torture to not act out on these intense feelings.

One night, Kate and Eve were sitting on a blanket on the floor of Kate's camp bungalow, chatting. Eve surprised Kate by asking her if it would be all right to practice kissing boys with her. Kate felt her panties get wet and her area "down there" began to pulsate, which had never happened when she was with a boy. The only other time she felt that thumping in her crotch was when she discovered her father's secret stash of Penthouse magazines. She'd sneak into her parent's room to look at the pictures of naked women and read the raunchy sex stories. The photos of naked women and sex stories would turn her on to the point she'd have to seek relief by rubbing herself to climax.

Her heart raced as she voiced her approval and leaned forward to initiate her first kiss with a girl. At first, they pecked lightly at each other's lips, hesitant to delve their tongues inside the other's mouth. Both girls trembled with excitement and fear. Their kisses were juvenile and awkward.

Kate pulled her lips away and asked, "Have you ever French kissed a boy?"

"Yes, once. But the boy forced his tongue down my throat and I gagged. Have you?" Eve asked.

"Yes, and had the same experience. Boys are terrible kissers," Kate giggled. She brushed the top of her hand across Eve's cheek very gently and said, "Let me try with you."

"Ok", Eve said, trembling.

Kate delicately kissed Eve's pink, moist lips and slowly inserted her tongue until it met Eve's. They played with each other's tongues, cautious as to not be too forceful or enter too deeply. As their kisses grew more intense, Kate realized she had never felt this turned on before. *Why hadn't she ever felt this way with a boy?* She wondered. It was as though her entire body was on fire.

She embraced Eve and carefully nudged her backwards to rest her back on the floor. With Kate's entire body now pressing against Eve's, it was obvious to both young women they had passed the threshold of "practice kissing" and had entered into something illicit. They stayed up for hours kissing, but were too nervous to go any farther.

After several nights of "practice" kissing, Kate got up the nerve to touch one of Eve's breasts. At first, Eve gently nudged Kate's hand away. Eventually, Eve gave in to Kate's fondling. Kate reveled in exploring Eve's body. The pulsating grew stronger between her legs as she caressed Eve's breasts and buttocks. Eve was the first to venture her kisses to areas of the body other than the mouth. Kate could feel her pulse beating out of control in her private area as Eve tickled her breasts with her tongue.

Several weeks passed since their first kiss. Finally, in a moment of very heavy petting, Kate put her hand over Eve's special place. Eve moaned as Kate very gently stroked her clit through her cotton panties. Kate, prepared for Eve to push her way, hooked her middle finger under Eve's panties and slid it into her vagina. To Kate's delight, Eve didn't object. Instead, she kissed Kate's cheek and told her it felt good.

Kate's finger was now deep inside the softest thing she'd ever touched. It was softer than the finest silk. She removed her finger and began rubbing Eve's clit. Kate knew how to rub herself to the point of cumming. She hoped it would produce the same result for Eve. Kate rubbed faster and faster, until Eve spasmed in delight. She bit into Kate's neck as to not make any loud noises, which could awaken her parents. Eve immediately dove her fingers into Kate, causing her to release a quiet screech in ecstasy. Eve stroked Kate in the same manner she had done to her. Kate was so aroused she came almost immediately.

The two girls made love to each other every night after, bringing each other to orgasm.

Kate felt like she was in heaven when she and Eve made love. Kate had never experienced an orgasm with another person before, only through masturbation. It was the most magical thing on earth. None of the boys back home in Cambridge made Kate feel the way she did with Eve. Eve's slightest touch sent lightning bolts through Kate's entire body.

Occasionally, Kate would feel a tinge of shame and confusion around her feelings for Eve and the sex they had been having. She'd watch the male lemurs have vicious "stink fights" with each other to woo the female lemur. The males, who had scent glands on their wrists and chest, would rub their tail along their wrists. Then they'd face off, waving their tails held high over themselves. The smelliest tail would win.

Watching this breeding behavior often led Kate to

wonder if what she was doing was very wrong. Was this unnatural? She wondered. She didn't witness lesbian or gay behavior amongst the lemurs.

What was reassuring to her was that the female lemurs were extremely dominant. One female usually dominated the troop of adult males and females. Kate decided to ignore her confused thinking. How could something that felt so incredible be wrong?

Neither of the girls wanted their intimate adventure to end. However, it was late August and Kate had to return home to finish her last year of high school. Eve had to stay behind in Madagascar with her parents, who home schooled her. Kate fought with her mother over wanting to stay in Madagascar with her. Her mother felt a tinge of guilt about sending Kate back home, but decided it would be best for her daughter to have a normal life and attend school with other kids her age in a structured school environment. Kate hated her mother for this. Her heart was broken. She knew she might never see Eve ever again.

"I love you so much, Eve," Kate wept as she hugged Eve prior to boarding the plane.

"I love you too. You'll write to me every day, right?" Eve was also crying.

"Of course. My mom said I might be able to visit during the holidays." Kate wanted to kiss Eve good-bye, but Kate's mom loomed behind Eve. Kate whispered in Eve's ear, "I love you, Eve."

"I love you, too, Kate," Eve murmured.

The two girls wrote to each other almost every day during the first few months that followed their physical separation. Then, a month before Kate was to travel to Madagascar for Christmas holidays, she received a disturbing letter from Eve. Eve wrote that she was forced to confess their affair to her parents after her mother read a pile of Kate's letters to her. Eve, obviously brainwashed by her parent's strong religious beliefs, informed Kate that what they had done was very wrong. Eve quoted passages from the Bible and told Kate "homosexuality is an abomination". She told Kate that this would be her last letter, since she didn't want to go to hell. Kate wrote back trying to reason with her, but to no avail.

Kate fell into a deep depression and decided there was no way she could return to Madagascar after Eve's rejection. She cried often. Her body ached for Eve's body, her lips, her touch, and her love-filled letters. It felt as though someone had died or a part of her was gone forever. To make matters worse, she felt uncomfortable sharing her plight with anyone. She was sure no one would understand. She felt alone, stranded on her own island.

Eventually, Kate recovered and had flings with other lesbians when she'd sneak off by train to dive bars in Boston. On occasion, she'd find straight girls at school who were willing to experiment, but it only happened if the other girl was drunk. Kate fooled around with a few boys, but hated their fumbling hands and the way they'd insist on sticking their dick in her mouth.

For Kate, photography became an excellent diversion to recover from losing Eve. Instead of joining her mother in Madagascar on holidays, she traveled with Aunt Susan to photograph the Red Hot Chili Peppers and Radiohead. Kate consumed herself in her photography. The love she lost in Eve reappeared in her photography. While her fellow students practiced musical instruments, did ballet, or played a sport, Kate was taking pictures of everybody and everything around her. Her camera went with her everywhere then and now.

CHAPTER 4

ANGELA COULDN'T BELIEVE her ears. She didn't win. The presenter at the podium didn't say her name. She was devastated. She wanted to cry, but knew that wasn't the appropriate thing to do at the Academy Awards. Imagine that. Crying over losing the Oscar broadcast around the world. Instead, she fought back the tears, smiled and clapped for the winner. The remainder of the ceremony was a blur. She couldn't remember time passing so slowly in her life.

Following the last award, for Best Picture, Angela informed Jason she wouldn't be joining him at the post awards party they had planned to attend. She confided to him that she was just too upset over losing. He, in turn, reminded her that it wouldn't look good if she didn't show up—that people would think she was a poor sport.

"Who cares? I don't want to go. I want to go home" Angela whined, clenching her fist while stomping her foot.

"You're acting like a Goddamn Scarlett O'Hara. Get over it. The after party's important. You know that. Please just go…for me?" Jason pleaded.

Angela felt like smacking him. She hated this side of Jason, when his ego ruled over his ability to be compassionate. Making matters worse, not only was she upset about not winning, she had horrible cramps. Earlier that day, her period began to flow just as her makeup artist, Maxwell, was putting the finishing touches on her face. Maxwell had his work cut out for him to conceal the many blemishes and acne mounds that developed because of that time of the month's hormone overload. To show her appreciation, Angela gave Maxwell a $500 bonus tip after he transformed her face into flawless, glowing perfection.

"Why? To play pretend? I'm sick of it, Jason. It's bad enough that we have to be these phony assholes for our jobs, but this marriage thing, too?" At that moment, Angela felt like hopping on a plane and fleeing to a deserted island, or to her brother's apartment in lower Manhattan. She wanted to get out of Hollywood. She was resentful and bitter over not winning. She was also angry that she didn't have a real life partner to console her. She felt as though she had no one in her life to turn to, someone who truly understood and supported her. She wished she had a real spouse, someone who would hold her in her arms until she felt better and make passionate love to her.

"What do you want me to tell people?" Jason asked. "You know, why you aren't at the party?"

"I don't care what you tell people, Jason. Make something up. I am not going to the after party. Tell everyone I have a stomach flu. No, wait a minute. The press will say I'm pregnant. Here's what you're going to say. Tell everyone my throat is sore and I probably have strep. It was a miracle I made it to the awards ceremony at all. My doctor ordered me to stay home. I'm on antibiotics," Angela instructed.

"Ok, Angela, whatever you need to do. But I must say I *am* disappointed in you."

"That's harsh. You know, for once in my entire career, I'm doing something to take care of me. It really sucks that you don't get it." Angela's face was bright red with anger.

Jason changed his tone. "Hey, Angela, I'm sorry. We'll

talk about it tomorrow. O.k.? Go chill and take care of yourself. I'll handle it," Jason said, trying his best to appear compassionate.

"Thanks, Jason. We'll talk tomorrow." Angela's ire left her face.

"I love you. I'm sorry you didn't win. You deserved to win," Jason said, hugging her.

"Yeah, well the Academy didn't," Angela grumbled in his ear, but accepting the hug.

"Fuck the Academy."

"Maybe if I'd done that I would have won," Angela said sarcastically, with a smile.

"There's always next year."

"Will you arrange my limo? I don't feel like doing anything at this point."

"Only if you give me another hug," Jason reached his arms out.

Angela responded by reaching her arms forward and embracing Jason's waist.

"You'll be o.k. Just don't wait up for me," Jason said as he released his embrace from Angela's back.

"Maybe you'll get lucky," Angela winked, giggling. Angela wanted nothing more for her "husband" than for him to be happy. Apart from his man-slut personality, he was a great guy. She loved hearing Jason's sexual conquest stories. Her favorite was the time he slept with a woman who was into S&M. She poured candle wax all over Jason's body, including his penis. He ended up so badly burned that he couldn't get an erection for a week.

Unlike Jason, Angela hadn't even had a single one night stand since marrying him. She was too paranoid of the press finding out. According to the press, Jason cheated on Angela all the time and she was a lesbian. Although this was the absolute truth, Angela and Jason denied these reports and insisted people would do anything, make anything up, in an effort to ruin their marriage.

Once Angela was in her limo, she grabbed her cell phone from her tiny gem-encrusted purse. *I can't believe I lost. I feel like the biggest fucking loser. I should call someone, but whom?* Angela thought. The first person Angela thought of calling was her closest friend and confidante—her sister Mary. She was the only one in her family besides her brother who knew Angela was a lesbian and that her marriage was a farce. Mary was very supportive of Angela, the majority of the time. However, Mary often gave her opinion that Angela needed to stop living a lie, find a woman, and be happy.

Angela decided not to call Mary. She could use the consoling, but didn't want to hear about how she should live her life, though Mary was almost always right when it came to dishing out advice.

So who to turn to?

Angela had few female friends in her life. She considered her sister to be her best friend. Every other relationship she had with a woman was superficial, like those she had with her publicist or agent, or random actresses with whom she'd worked. She hadn't had a lover or girlfriend in over a year and missed the intimacy and friendship she shared with her last lover, Kristan. Suddenly she longed for Kristan.

Reluctantly, she decided to dial Kristan's phone number. She hadn't spoken to Kristan since their breakup over a year ago.

CHAPTER 5

"HERE KITTY, KITTY. Where are my little angels?" Kate called for her two cats, Snowy and Mitzy, while opening the door to her modest two bedroom cottage she rented in Malibu. It was oceanfront property with a balcony that overlooked the ocean. Kate lucked out with the rental. The cottage was owned by a very wealthy friend of her mother's. Having recently inherited the property, the owner hated Malibu and spent most of her time in England and Australia. Kate rented the cottage for half of what similar rentals were going for in Malibu, making the cottage one of the motivators for Kate to remain in the L.A. area. Besides the rent being cheap, the sunsets were magnificent and her celebrity neighbors were hardly ever around.

Snowy, an entirely white shorthair with bright blue eyes, greeted her as she headed for her dark room to unload her film. Kate had to quickly develop the rolls of film so that she could scan them and email samples to photo editors. She often thought about going to digital photography. The few times she'd tried digital, the photos were of mediocre quality—too flashy and grainy. No matter what filters or lighting she used, she could never achieve the same effect she accomplished with good old 35mm film. Plus, she felt as though she would be "cheating" if she went to digital. She wouldn't be a real photographer if she used digital.

Mitzy, a fat tabby, leapt on to the dark room table to greet her as she laid out all of her film rolls from her canvas tote. She paused to pet Mitzy, who by now was purring very loudly. She loved her cats. They served as her companions and sources of comfort. Snowy meowed at Kate's feet. Then she realized they probably had no food left in their bowls.

Kate scooted her cats out of the dark room and went into the kitchen to replenish their bowl, which was indeed empty. The two cats ravaged the food as the last pellet landed in the bowl. Kate noticed the red light on her answering machine was flashing to indicate there was a message. Kate walked over to the answering machine and saw the number twelve blinking. She hesitated to press the playback button. She feared all twelve messages were from Tami.

Kate had changed her cell phone number, but hadn't gotten around to changing her land line yet. It was a pain in the ass calling every contact in her address book to let them know her number changed. Hopefully this would be the last insane ex-girlfriend for Kate and the last time she'd have to change her phone number.

Kate pressed "play" and sure enough, it was Tami's voice. "Kate, we have to talk. I'm in love with you. I'm sorry I was a jerk. Please, you have to call me. I love you. Call me tonight. I need to hear from you."

The next three messages were also from Tami, sobbing for Kate to call her. The fifth message was from her friend Marisol. "Kate, you have to call me. Victoria left me. She left a note and all of her things are gone. Please call me," Marisol sounded desperate.

The next six messages were hang-ups. Kate reviewed her caller id. They were all from Tami. *How do I get myself into these messes?* Kate thought. *She seemed like the perfect woman—beautiful, intelligent, caring, great in bed. At least that was when we first met. Now she's gone absolutely psycho on me. If this continues, I'll have to file a restraining order against her.*

Tami seemed perfect—for the first month or so. Soon she showed another side—an obsessive, paranoid, jealous, and controlling side. After they dated for a few months, Tami began questioning Kate about every woman in Kate's life and career. When Kate would be on an assignment or visiting with friends, Tami phoned and left messages every half hour. One day, Tami threatened to kill herself if Kate didn't call her back. Although Kate felt bad for Tami and still had feelings for her, she knew she had to let her go.

She really didn't feel like dealing with Tami's phone calls. She had to develop her rolls of film. On the other hand, she had to make time for her best friend, Marisol, who sounded like a train wreck.

Kate dialed Marisol's cell number. The phone rang five times, and went to voice mail. At the prompt, Kate left a message. "Are you ok Marisol? I'm worried about you. Call me as soon as you can. I'm here for you and love you."

She hung up the phone and returned to the dark room. She very carefully began removing the film from the film cans and secured them on the film reels to be immersed later in the chemical solutions.

Kate began setting up the photo paper and poured the chemical solutions into the basins. She retrieved a film reel and began the developing process. The image of Angela Moore slowly appeared through the clear liquid. So far, it looked like the perfect full length shot. She picked up the photo with her tweezers and attached it to the suspended string to hang dry. The next photo was a bust shot close-up of Angela. Kate could feel her blood flowing to her private area. Usually in control of her feelings, it frustrated Kate that she got turned on so easily by the mere sight of Angela.

Kate thought about the upcoming photo shoot with Angela and wondered how she'd be able to compose herself while in the same room with her. She envisioned herself acting like a bumbling idiot. Kate thought about her vibrator. Once the film was developed, she would go into her bedroom and pleasure herself. Unfortunately her needs would have to wait. The paparazzi were a cutthroat bunch—one in which you snooze, you lose. She couldn't think about masturbating right now, it would have to wait until later.

CHAPTER 6

ANGELA PANICKED AS Kristan's phone began to ring. She had no idea what she would say if Kristan answered the phone. "Hi" was the only thing that came to mind. Angela panicked, decided to hold off on talking to her and pressed the red "end" button.

"Sorry to bother you Ms. Moore. I just wanted to let you know that traffic's pretty bad. Don't plan on being home for at least forty-five minutes," her personal driver said through the limo's intercom.

"Great. What else is new?" Angela responded, sarcastically. "Thanks Bobby, I'm going to lie down. Please don't disturb me unless it's important."

"Yes Ms. Moore," he replied.

Angela reached behind her seat and opened a compartment behind the leather seating. She retrieved a small feather pillow and neatly folded blanket. She turned off her cell phone, laid her head down, and thought about the first time Kristan and she met.

Not long after Ted McNeil died of AIDS, Angela injured her back while performing a stunt on a movie set. She was prescribed painkillers and muscle relaxers and became instantly addicted. She quickly discovered that not only did the drugs take away her physical pain; they numbed her emotional pain too. If she thought about the loss of Ted and Julia, she'd pop a pill. If she got stressed over work, she'd pop a pill. If she was breathing, she'd pop a pill. The pills lifted her from her stressful world and plopped her into a nice, fuzzy, safe cloud.

At one point she was popping over thirty pills a day and had prescriptions all over town. Often, her doctors would refuse to refill her prescription. On these days, Angela would hook up with a drug dealer-to-the-stars who would get her whatever she needed, on the fly and delivered.

Her addiction became a major interference when she started nodding off on movie sets and throwing tirades when she'd run out of pills. On one occasion, the director of a film she was starring in held a personal intervention with Angela. He warned her that if she didn't clean up her act, she'd be out of a job. She thought he was overreacting and continued to pop pills, nod off on the set and have abusive mood swings to the dismay of the movie crew. She never did get fired. The movie was too far into production to replace the lead role. It would cost millions to bring another leading actress on board. Therefore, everyone including the director, tolerated her drug usage and, when needed, rearranged production to meet Angela's needs.

Angela knew she should cut back on her pill usage, but couldn't understand why she couldn't take them in moderation. It frustrated her that she had no control over her addiction and virtually no willpower.

The last day she used drugs she had gone to her dealer's apartment in Venice Beach. With her prescriptions depleted and no doctor agreeing to refill them, she needed something to stop the insidious cravings. Angela's dealer wasn't returning her calls, so she put on her platinum blonde pageboy wig and sunglasses and headed for Venice.

Angela knocked on the dealer's door. "Who is it?" a man with an unfamiliar voice called out.

"Is Lenny here?" she yelled into the door, trembling and dripping of sweat from withdrawal.

"Naw. He's in Cancun", the man answered in a rough, scratchy voice.

Cancun? Since when do drug dealers go on vacation? Angela thought. *How dare he. I'm in pain and he's off sunning his ugly ass.* Not knowing who this man was on the other side of the door, Angela's gnawing intuition told her to turn around and split. She only dealt with Lenny—no one else. As always, her cravings ruled over her instinct.

"I need something. Lenny usually takes care of me. You think you could help me out?" Angela desperately pleaded.

The door opened and a very thin, sickly looking man with long stringy dirty blonde hair motioned for her to enter the apartment.

"So *who* are *you?*" Angela asked in an overtly snobbish tone.

"I'm Lenny's brother, Chuck. I'm crashing here while he's gone." Chuck looked like one of those long-haired rockers from the eighties but without the eyeliner, lipstick and big hair. Maybe he had been an eighties metal rocker back in the day. He had to be pushing forty. It was quite possible. Who really cared, Angela decided. She pulled out a chair and sat at a card table situated in the middle of the living room. The high-rent apartment smelled of rotten garbage, which completely made sense, since the place was a pig sty and the kitchen garbage was overflowing onto the littered kitchen floor. Chuck definitely wouldn't win the Good Housekeeping award.

"So what're you lookin' for?" he asked as he took a drag of a freshly lit cigarette.

"Percs, Vicadin, whatever you got", she eagerly blurted.

"Wait a minute. Let me go see if he's got anymore left," he said, leaving the room and entering one of the bedrooms beyond the kitchen.

A minute later he returned with a bag of pills. Angela began to salivate. "Here ya go," He handed the bag to Angela, drool spilling from the corner of her mouth. "That's gonna be $500."

"Five…Hundred…Dollars? You're out of your mind," Angela protested as she marveled at the bag that would soon end her pain.

"Hey, there's 'round fifteen Oxies in there. That's a bargain."

"What's an Oxy?"

"They're better than Percs. You never had an Oxy? They're the best thing 'round."

"They better not be ibuprofens."

"Believe me. These ain't no ibuprofens."

Angela held the baggy up to the light and counted the pills. "There are only twelve pills in here. And you want five hundred dollars? Lenny charges me that for fifty percs. I'll give you two hundred," Angela tried to negotiate.

"Un uh," He shook his head. "You're nuts, lady. These pills go for fifty a pop on the streets. If you don't have five hundred, I'll sell you a couple. But I can't go any lower than forty a pop." Chuck reached out and tried to grab the bag of pills from Angela.

Angela held onto the bag with all her might. She wasn't going to let these babies get away. "All right. I know you're ripping me off, but I guess I have no choice," Angela dug into her Louis Vuitton bag and produced five crisp one hundred dollar bills. "Here," she angrily threw the money in Chuck's face.

"You don't gotta be a bitch about it," Chuck complained as he knelt to pick up the fallen bills.

"Don't think I'm not gonna tell Lenny about this when he gets back," Angela warned.

"'Bout what?" Chuck asked.

"That you ripped me off," she barked.

"Look, you got yer shit lady," Chuck snickered, grabbing Angela's elbow to usher her to the front door. "I don't fucking rip people off."

"Do not touch me!" Angela snapped.

"Hey. Hey. Ease up. I was just seeing you out," Chuck quickly let go of Angela's arm and held up both of his hands appearing to surrender.

Angela left the apartment infuriated. *Who did that fucking idiot think he was touching me?* Once she got into her Mercedes, her mood quickly changed to excitement and elation. She opened the plastic baggy, and retrieved four oblong-shaped blue pills that had the number "160" imprinted on them. She had never seen pills like these before. Maybe they were some Mexican generic brand. Every once in a while Lenny would sell her strange looking generic pills from Mexico. Shrugging it off, she popped the four pills into her mouth and chased them down with a bottle of Evian water. Fifteen minutes later, she still felt the pangs of withdrawal and decided to ingest two more.

That was the last thing she remembered.

"Huh? Wa happened?" Angela mumbled, groggy and half awake. She tried to lift her head up, but it was too heavy. She sat, slumped over the steering wheel of her car, wondering why she felt so lethargic.

"Angela. It's me, Lindsey. I got here as fast as I could. They're going to take you to the hospital," Angela's publicist, Lindsey said, leaning in through the driver's side window.

Angela muttered, "What happened? My head feels like it's full of lead."

"You hit that car, dumbass," she said wildly, pointing to a red sedan parked in front of Angela's car. The front end of the sedan's hood was crushed under the front end of Angela's bumper.

"You're being charged with a DUI Miss Moore," a police officer chimed in.

"That's not possible. Where am I?" Angela groggily wondered through a drug-filled haze.

Lindsey leaned forward to whisper in Angela's ear so the cop couldn't hear, "You really did it this time. You're in a goddamn grocery store parking lot. You're all fucked up and for some reason felt the need to waltz into the store and walk out with a bottle of wine, which you didn't pay for. Then, you got into your car and to put the final nail in your celebrity coffin, you put your car into drive and flattened the car in front of you." Lindsey was furious.

Angela gazed into Lindsey's eyes, which appeared to be bulging out of their sockets behind black- rimmed glasses. "No. I don't remember doing that. I wouldn't do something like that." Angela rested her head on the steering wheel. She felt overwhelmingly drowsy, fighting to keep her eyes open.

Clearly enraged, Lindsey said, "Well, *you* did it, no one else. This is it Angela. You are going into rehab. We can get away with a tabloid finding out about rehab, but not this shit! The paramedics will bring you to the hospital for an evaluation, then you'll detox. As soon as you're cleared, you're going to rehab. Got it?" Lindsey was such a bitch sometimes.

Angela couldn't think about anything right now. All she could muster was, "I'll take care of it later." Then she fell asleep.

The next thing she remembered was waking up in a hospital room with Lindsey and her sister Mary holding vigil by her bedside.

"Thank God you finally woke up. Did you know you overdosed, Angela?" Mary inquired.

Angela wanted to talk but her mouth felt too heavy to open.

"They had to pump your stomach for Christ sake," Lindsey said, annoyed.

Angela just stared.

"Why'd you take so many pills? You weren't trying to kill yourself, were you?" Mary asked, shedding a tear.

"Those pills you took are nothing to mess with. I didn't know you were in to *that* stuff," Lindsey said.

Angela regained her strength and asked, "What stuff are you talking about?"

"Those oxy-something pills. You know, they're like heroin in a pill," Lindsey said.

"What? I thought they were percodans. I like percs," Angela managed.

"Well, you shouldn't take something you got off the street," Lindsey said. "I know for a fact you didn't have a prescription so don't try to tell me different."

"Why, Angela? Why?" Mary demanded, sobbing.

"Look, I definitely wasn't trying to kill myself, ok? I ran out of my usual shit and was in pain," Angela wondered how taking a few pills could go so terribly wrong.

"Well, you may have killed your career. You're in big legal trouble, Angela—drug possession, DUI and shoplifting," Lindsey reminded her.

"Oh, fuck," Angela muttered.

Angela suffered through withdrawals at detox, but once the worse was over, the chills, sweats, vomiting, and overall malaise, she settled into a rehab in Pasadena. All of the tabloids covered Angela's ordeal. Angela didn't care. She was looking forward to starting a new way of life, free from active addiction. It was like being reborn.

To sustain her recovery, Angela attended twelve step meetings as often as possible. On the evening Angela celebrated having one year clean and sober, she met Kristan, a recovering cocaine user. Kristan was in L.A. for the launch of her new lesbian genre novel and thought she'd hit a meeting before returning to New York the next day. Meeting Kristan was lust at first sight for Angela. She had read most of Kristan's books, but the photo of her on the book jacket didn't do her justice. She was much more attractive in person. Angela was smitten.

After the meeting, Angela invited Kristan to join her, her sister Mary, and a few other people from the meeting to a local restaurant for a celebratory meal. Angela was thrilled when Kristan agreed to join them. At the restaurant, Mary noticed something was different about Angela. She was acting nervous and even stuttered while giving the waitress her order. She had a feeling Angela was interested in Kristan.

When Kristan got up to go to the Ladies room, Mary asked, "Is there something you want to tell me?"

"Oh my God, yes. Kristan is so hot. She's so creative and intelligent, too. I think I'm in love!" Angela gushed.

"Well don't break her heart. We talked about this. You said so yourself you can't be in a relationship with a woman until you are ready to come out. It's not right," Mary lectured her.

Angela's mood suddenly plummeted as reality set in. She recalled having confided that dilemma to her sister. Angela grew angry thinking about what she has had to sacrifice for her career. She had everything: money, a beautiful mansion, an amazing career and all the luxuries, except love.

After dinner, everyone said their good-byes as they waited for the valet to bring their cars to the entrance. Kristan and

Angela were the last of the group to have their cars pulled around. *This is my only chance*, Angela thought. Kristan mentioned she was going back to New York tomorrow. *It's now or never.* Angela was drawn to Kristan and wasn't ready to go home unless Kristan came with her.

"Kristan, I'd really like it if you came back to my house. We could watch a movie or something," she said, nervously.

"Well, I guess so. But only for a couple hours. I have an early morning flight back to New York. I'll follow you?" Kristan said, taking the keys to her rental car from the valet.

"Great. I'll make sure you're behind me at all times," Angela said, opening the driver's side door of her silver, convertible Mercedes.

They arrived at Angela's sprawling Beverly Hills estate moments later. Kristan stood in awe as she entered the foyer of the magnificent mansion. The chandelier itself had to be worth $50,000, she thought.

"Wow, this house is incredible!" Kristan said, obviously impressed.

"Yeah, it's nice. Sometimes I feel like I'm living in a museum," Angela uttered, feeling nervous. "I can give you the grand tour if you want?" Angela suggested.

"Sure."

"This way first." Angela lightly grasped Kristan's wrist, and led her up the stairs. "I can show you the upstairs first. Then we can work our way down."

Angela led Kristan through the four bedroom, six bath, 4,000 sq. ft. home and was now in the last room on the tour—the media room. This room housed a giant screen tv, a state-of-the art stereo system that included an elaborate surround system, puffy sofas and chairs, and a pinball machine.

"Do you want something to drink?" Angela asked as she picked up the intercom phone.

"Just water, please."

"Hi Lucinda. I hate to bother you, but could you bring some ice water with lemons for two to the media room?" she asked her maid, Lucinda. Angela hated asking Lucinda for anything outside of her normal chores. However, she was her maid, after all.

A few minutes later, Lucinda appeared with two crystal glasses, a plate of fresh cut lemons, and a glass pitcher of ice water. Lucinda was from El Salvador, in her 50's, and around 4'10". Angela inherited her from Ted. Lucinda was his devoted maid for fifteen years and insisted Angela continue to employ her.

"Is that all you require, Meez Angela?" Lucinda asked in her thick accent.

"Yes, that's all. Thank you Lucinda."

Angela poured the water into the glasses and dropped the lemons in. "Do you want to listen to music or watch a movie?" she asked Kristan as she handed her a glass.

"I guess some music would be fine."

"How about some Diane Krall?"

"That's great."

After inserting the cd and adjusting the volume so that it wouldn't be too loud, Angela sat next to Kristan on one of the puffy couches.

They talked about their lives, how they were "discovered" in each of their professions, bad dating stories, and their busy careers. Over an hour had passed when Kristan looked at her watch and exclaimed, "Oh my God, it's 11:00. I still have to pack. I should get back to the hotel. I have to be at LAX by 6:00 tomorrow morning."

Angela knew this might be her only chance. She had to at

least take the risk of making a move. If worse came to worse, Kristan would say she wasn't interested and leave.

Angela reached forward and laid her hand on Kristan's knee. "Kristan, I think you are so beautiful. I'd like to be with you." She couldn't believe she blurted it out. *I'd like to be with you? How corny*, she thought. Angela's face turned deep red, her heart was pounding like a snare drum, and she felt sweat developing under her arms.

"Oh," Kristan hesitated, trying to digest what Angela just said. "Ok," hesitating again. "I didn't expect that. I guess I'm in a bit of shock right now. I would have never guessed. I usually have good gaydar, too." Kristan laughed.

"I'm serious. I want you, Kristan," Angela said, genuinely.

Kristan wanted to rip Angela's clothes off, but played it cool. She couldn't believe what was happening. *Is Angela Moore saying she wants me? Am I dreaming?* Flustered, she said, "I guess I feel the same way. I just don't want to be your bisexual experiment. I don't do that sort of thing."

"I'm gay, Kristan," Angela couldn't believe she was coming out to someone she barely knew. "It's not something I broadcast. Only a few people know."

"That's definitely reassuring. I've had my share of straight women come on to me who want to fulfill their bisexual fantasy. I…"

Angela interrupted Kristan by leaning forward and softly kissing her lips. Angela was relieved to notice that Kristan was kissing her back. Kristan felt a rush of arousal as Angela's plump, pouty lips suckled hers and their tongues delicately met, darting and teasing each other. Angela's body felt hot as their kisses grew harder and more forceful.

"Mmm. That was good," Angela moaned as she pulled away to take a deep breath and stare into Kristan's dark brown eyes.

"Don't stop. I love kissing you." Kristan nudged Angela's back onto the couch so that she could straddle her on top. Kristan lowered her head to kiss Angela. Their kisses grew stronger and more passionate. Kristan's mouth ventured down to Angela's perfume-scented neck, and alternated between kissing and rubbing her tongue into the crevices of her neck. Angela felt herself panties get moist. She hadn't been this horny since Julia.

Kristan slowly unbuttoned Angela's blouse, kissing her chest and stomach. Angela arose to remove her fully unbuttoned blouse and quickly unhook and remove her bra. Angela moaned as Kristan delicately swirled her tongue around her erect nipples. While she sucked on one of Angela's nipples, Kristan lowered her hand, searching under Angela's skirt for her wet mound. Once there, she gently began rubbing and toying with the outside of her panties. Kristan pulled Angela's panties to the side and inserted her index and middle fingers, causing Angela to arch her back in pleasure. Kristan continued to gently thrust her fingers in and out of Angela as she traced her tongue down to Angela's pelvic area.

"I'm gonna make you cum so hard," Kristan purred, quickly removing Angela's panties. She was now licking Angela's moist, sweet pussy. Angela moaned louder. Kristan teased Angela's clit with the tip of her tongue. Kristan took her time exploring Angela, inserting her tongue inside of her, stretching it upwards to locate that magic spot. Kristan had an extraordinarily long tongue and knew how to use it.

Angela had never felt anything like this. Not only was she finally getting laid. She was getting fucked by a long, skillful tongue.

Kristan concentrated on Angela's clit again, rubbing her tongue hard, circling Angela's exposed clit, while fucking her with her fingers. Angela couldn't take it anymore.

"Oh my God, I'm gonna cum so hard," Angela screamed.

"Oh my God! Oh my fucking God!" she screamed. Angela's entire body tingled and burned with passion. The orgasmic waves overcame her. They seemed to last forever. She panted heavily as Kristan made her way up Angela's body to kiss her mouth, while stroking her clit, bringing her to another intense orgasm.

Angela lied on the couch, holding Kristan, recovering from this incredible experience. After a few minutes, Angela said, "Let me take care of you now. Let's go up to my bedroom," Angela stood up and led Kristan upstairs.

Once they were in her bedroom, Angela firmly kissed Kristan, and then dove her hand into Kristan's shirt, seizing her breast and squeezing her nipple. "Come with me," Angela said, holding Kristan's hand, leading her to the four-poster canopy bed.

Kristan's entire body was on fire. Her crotch was throbbing, aching to be touched. Angela slowly undressed Kristan and made love to her with her tongue and fingers until she couldn't orgasm anymore. The women lay in bed together, spent and exhilarated.

"Please don't go, Kristan. Stay with me," Angela whispered through Kristan's soft brown hair.

Kristan intentionally missed her flight and rescheduled a week's worth of book signings to stay with Angela. Kristan's agent was pissed. Kristan didn't care. She was in love.

She sublet her New York City apartment to a friend and moved in with Angela a month later. Surprisingly, not too many people caught on to their relationship. They were discreet, but not exactly perfect about keeping their relationship confidential. Everyone just assumed they were very close friends. Tabloids spread rumors, but in the end, the public didn't seem to buy the allegations that Angela was gay.

Angela was happy, as happy as she had been when she lived with Julia. Kristan was the perfect partner. She didn't complain about Angela's busy schedule or complain about L.A. Life was absolutely wonderful. Angela was madly and truly in love with Kristan and content with their hidden relationship.

Unfortunately, love wasn't enough to keep Angela and Kristan together. Although Angela was completely and madly in love with Kristan, she was at the height of her career and refused to ruffle that by coming out publicly. After a year together, Kristan no longer agreed to their secret relationship and gave Angela an ultimatum: either Angela came out publicly or they were done. Angela resented the fact that Kristan wasn't sympathetic to her situation. Impulsively, Angela chose her career; and Kristan moved back to New York City permanently. Angela regretted her decision every day and, two months later, married Jason.

Angela sat in the back of the limo and dialed Kristan's number again. She still didn't know what she would say, but figured it didn't matter. Kristan would be so happy to hear her voice.

Kristan answered the phone, "Hello?"

"Hi Kristan. It's me, Angela," Angela said, elated to her Kristan's voice.

"Hi Angela. Is there something wrong?" Kristan asked, in a concerned tone.

"Well, yeah. I just lost the Oscar. Didn't you watch?"

"No. I didn't watch it. I'm sorry to hear you lost. I know how much awards mean to you," Kristan said in a sarcastic tone.

"Yeah. I'm not doing so well." Kristan's sarcasm didn't register with Angela.

"I'm sorry Angela, but is that the only reason you called?"

"No. I miss you Kristan. Do you ever miss me?"

"Angela, I'd rather not get into this now. You hurt me terribly. I was a mess for months after we broke up. I'm with someone else now and very happy."

"I'm sorry Kristan. I was stupid. I may have made a huge mistake."

"You *may* have made a huge mistake? You aren't even sure? You are still as confused as ever. Like I said, I'm with someone else. We live together. I'd appreciate it if you didn't call me again."

"I can't stand hearing that you resent me, that you hate me. We never had closure."

"Are you kidding me? Closure? The world doesn't revolve around you, Angela. I've wanted closure for a year and a half now. You never returned my phone calls, emails, or letters. I've finally moved on and now you call and expect me to drop everything and help you work on closure? Give you my shoulder to cry on?"

"I'm sorry Kristan. I really am. What can I do? I still love you." Angela felt like she had been punched in the stomach.

"Don't call me or contact me anymore. Please." Kristan hung the phone up.

Angela sat in the limo and began to sob uncontrollably. *What had she become?* She thought to herself. Winning a statue made of metal meant more to her than the woman she loved. *I should've just come out.*

CHAPTER 7

KATE PULLED UP to the iron gate leading to Angela Moore's estate. A guard exited his booth and approached Kate's truck. "I need to see identification, please," he said. Kate fumbled through her leather hobo bag and retrieved her driver's license. She took off her sunglasses so that the guard could identify her with the photo on her license.

"Thank you Ms. Ashford. Ms. Moore is expecting you." The guard returned Kate's driver license to her. He pointed to the winding road beyond the gate. "Follow the road straight up and park in the car port area on the right. Jonathan, the other guard, will be there to greet you and help you with your stuff."

"Thanks," Kate said.

The gate opened and Kate proceeded up the palm tree-lined cobblestone driveway. Not too far up the hill was Angela's house, a white, French style mansion. It was enormous. She wondered how people could call such a huge structure "home". Kate estimated that she could fit at least ten of her rented cottages in just one Angela Moore estate. Angela pulled into an ivy-covered carport to the right of the mansion.

A man in a security guard uniform, wearing a name

badge that said "Jonathan—Security," greeted her as she parked her truck. "Are you Ms. Ashford?" he asked.

"Yes I am," she said as she took the keys from the ignition and opened her door. "Could you help me bring some of my equipment in?" She pointed to the equipment in the rear of her truck. Kate pulled at her jean pant legs. She hated the jeans she was wearing. They were too tight and rode up her crotch whenever she sat. Kate overslept that morning and in a rush threw on whatever she grabbed first. Although the jeans were at times uncomfortable, they did accentuate her curvy hips and shapely ass.

"Yeah, I better go get a dolly for all that stuff you got back there," he said as Kate opened the rear door to her SUV and began unloading her equipment.

Jonathan returned with a dolly. Once all of the equipment was loaded onto the dolly, Jonathan led Kate around the side of the estate to a rear entrance where a short, Hispanic woman greeted them at the door, "Meez Moore said set up in the East Wing."

Kate followed Jonathan through an enormous restaurant-style kitchen, with wall-to-wall stainless steel appliances, to the East Wing. They entered a great room with high ceilings, floor to ceiling windows, and mahogany hardwood floors. The room was furnished with beautiful antique mahogany furniture and puffy sofas and chairs. The ceiling boasted fancy crown moldings and a medallion anchoring a magnificent chandelier. Kate had been in many celebrity mansions. Each one seemed more incredible than the next. This estate was the most incredible by far. The style was exactly in line with Kate's taste. She would decorate her home in this style if she had the money and the spaciousness of her very own estate.

Kate began setting up the lights, tripods, and other equipment for the shoot. She didn't rely on an assistant for this assignment. It was difficult convincing celebrities to open their homes to a photographer, let alone a photographer and her staff. For photo shoots of movie or television cast or celebrity weddings, she hired Elizabeth, a UCLA photography student who Kate mentored.

While Kate was adjusting the height of a softbox light, Angela entered the room in a long white terry cloth robe, her hair wet from a recent shower and face free of makeup. Her makeup artist and hairdresser followed close behind and settled their belongings into a corner of the room where Jonathan had delivered a vanity with large mirrors and a director's chair. Angela gave a fast side-to-side wave with her right hand directed toward Kate and, with a huge smile, said, "Good morning. Are you the photographer?"

Kate felt a rush of excitement run through her body. Angela was gorgeous, even without makeup. Angela seemed very pleasant. Kate was shocked of how cordial Angela was. Celebrities almost never spoke with her prior to the shoot. Some didn't speak to her at all, even throughout the shoot. Kate managed a slight wave and said, "Hi. Yes, I am."

"They've gotta fix me up and then I'm all yours," Angela said, pointing in the direction of the makeup artist and hairdresser. Then she asked, "Are you hungry? Or thirsty? I can have Lucinda get you anything you want."

Kate realized her mouth was gaping open, in awe of being in Angela's presence. She felt embarrassed, wondering if Angela and her entourage noticed. Kate was completely enthralled with the fact Angela was not only gorgeous and talented, but seemed to be a nice, gracious hostess as well. The only thing Kate ingested that morning was a nutrition shake. She knew her stomach would start growling soon, which it often did if she didn't eat a hearty morning meal. "Sure, I'd love some juice and a muffin or bagel," she said.

"Great, it'll only take a minute." Angela retrieved a very

small walkie-talkie from her robe's pocket, punched a few buttons, and spoke into it, "Hi Lucinda, could you please bring the photographer and me a tray of food and some juice? Some bagels, muffins and fruit would be great. Thanks." As soon as she returned the walkie-talkie to her pocket the hairdresser, a tall, thin black man, moved in to blow dry her hair. Kate turned her back to them and continued setting up her equipment.

Moments later, Lucinda entered the room with a tray of fruit, bagels, muffins, and orange juice. She delivered the food and beverages onto an antique sideboard adjacent to where Angela was seated. The hairdresser had just finished blowing out her long hair and was applying a spray-on shine serum. "Lucinda, please pull that chair over here for her," Angela requested, pointing to an antique leather upholstered chair. Angela cocked her head to get in eyeshot of Kate and asked, "I'm sorry, what is your name again? I feel so bad, I know someone told me."

Kate walked over to Angela, extended her hand and said, "It's Kate Ashford."

Angela grasped Kate's extended hand and responded, "It's a pleasure to meet you Kate." Lucinda delivered the chair next to Angela, who said, "Thanks Lucinda. I don't think we'll need anything again until lunchtime."

"You're welcome Meez Moore," Lucinda responded.

Suddenly, three dogs came running into the room. "Oh shit, who let the dogs out of their room?" Angela squealed as a little Jack Russell terrier jumped onto her lap. "Lucinda! Hurry, get the dogs," she gasped.

All three dogs were now vying for Angela's attention, wagging their tales and pawing at her from every direction.

Lucinda reentered the room, yelling "Bad doggies! Very bad doggies! Go to your room bad doggies," Lucinda waived her short, fat index finger at them. Angela was too busy petting the dogs to realize that seconds ago she demanded they be removed, which is exactly what Lucinda was trying to accomplish.

"I love my dogs. This is Buddy. He's a Jack Russell. Max and Princess are both mutts. I think Max is part Lab and God only knows what Princess is. She's some sort of terrier. At least, that's the veterinarian's opinion. Aren't they great?" Angela kissed her dogs, and then motioned for them to go with Lucinda, "Go with Lucinda. Go."

"Come doggies," Lucinda ordered. All three dogs left Angela's side and followed Lucinda out of the room.

Angela shouted toward the dogs and Lucinda, "Actually, Lucinda, hook them up to their leads in the back. They've been in their room for over two hours."

"I'll do Meez Moore," Lucinda shouted in return.

"You like animals I take it?" Kate asked, placing food from the tray onto a small plate.

"Oh my God yes. My two cats are the loves of my life. I adore them. They're probably outside catching field mouse right now. They leave me dead mousey presents on the doormat all the time. It's pretty gross, but it's their way of letting me know they love me," Angela said as the makeup assistant, a woman with very long black hair and short bangs that curled under in a Betty Page style, applied eyeliner to her upper eyelids. Maxwell, her usual makeup artist, couldn't make it. He was in Milan for a fashion show.

"I have two cats too. I like dogs but I'm hardly ever home. It wouldn't be fair to them. At least with cats I can leave them for a whole day without any worries."

"I know what you mean. I'm lucky I have help around here. Jason's hardly ever here either because of work."

"Will he be here today?" Kate was afraid she was prying, so added, "For the photo shoot. Should we plan on him for any photos today?"

"No. This is my thing. Plus, he's on set today."

The makeup artist lightly scolded Angela for moving her head around, "Please keep your face directed at me. You don't want me to have to start this process all over again."

"Sorry. I have a hard time sitting still. I hate having to go through all this primping," Angela apologized. "What do you think we should do today?" Angela inquired of Kate.

Kate sat down in the seat next to Angela and replied, "Vanity Fair mentioned they'd like a few shots in the house, which, of course would be here in this room. A few shots outside would be great too." Kate began nibbling on a blueberry muffin.

"That sounds easy enough. I had my stylist stop by last night to pick out a few outfits." Angela turned her head quickly to browse the area of the room. "Shit. Where are those outfits? I don't see them. I told her to leave them on the couch over there." She pointed to a puffy gold toned sofa upholstered with a soft microfiber fabric.

The makeup artist scolded her again for moving so suddenly, "Angela, you can't just fling your head around when I'm applying your eye makeup. I could've poked you in the eye." In a teasing tone, she added, "You're *so* difficult."

"I'll show you difficult," Angela joked. "But seriously, where the hell are those clothes? I hope she left them with Lucinda. I'll have to check."

"Thank you for the food. I was running late and skipped breakfast," Kate mentioned, taking a bite of a huge deep red strawberry.

"I'm so cranky if I don't eat breakfast. I know you're not here to wait on me, but can you get me a bagel and some fruit?" Angela asked Kate as the makeup artist dusted powder over her face.

Kate stood up and filled a plate for Angela. "What do you want on your bagel?"

"A little butter. Oh, and some melon and strawberries."

Kate prepared the bagel, and added a few pieces of the fruit to the small plate. She handed the plate of food to Angela, saying, "Here you go."

"Thanks. I'm starving." Angela took the plate and immediately stuffed a piece of melon into her mouth. She crossed her legs. The robe fell to the side and exposed her right leg. Kate couldn't resist staring at Angela's smooth, silky, tanned leg.

Kate realized that Angela caught her peering at her leg. Catching herself, she quickly looked away to her equipment, and said, "Well, everything is all set. Whenever you're ready, we can begin the shoot. Can I use your bathroom?"

"Of course. It's out this door and to the right. I bet you I'll be done eating by the time you come back. I eat very fast," Angela said as she bit into the bagel.

Kate exited the room and located the bathroom. It was a half bath that was twice the size of her home's small full bath. After relieving herself, Kate washed her hands in the exquisite marble sink, picked up a tube of L'Occitane hand cream located to the right of the sink and squeezed a dollop into the palm of her hand. The scent was a divine blend of lavender and rose.

When Kate returned to the great room, she saw that Angela's makeup session was complete and her plate of food was empty. Angela dismissed the makeup artist and hairdresser. Angela informed Kate that she'd be right back. She had to find the outfits her stylist had picked out. Kate finished her fruit and muffin and poured herself a large glass of orange juice. Kate was alone in the great room. She instructed herself to not get carried away with this crush. She had to remain professional. *This was a job, not a date. Plus, this woman is married for God's sake.* She told herself.

Several minutes later Angela returned with an overflowing armful of clothes, shoes and a small drawstring bag.

"Here, let me help you." Kate ran over to scoop some of the items from out of Angela's grip. It was too late, though, Angela began dropping pieces of clothing.

"I'll get it," Kate and Angela said simultaneously. As they squatted to pick up the fallen items, their heads banged into each other and they both sat on the floor holding their hands to their heads. Each said, "Sorry," simultaneously. They sat there on the floor for a minute, smiling at each other and giggling.

"I am the world's biggest clutz. I knew I should've asked for help bringing all these down here," Angela said, still rubbing her head. "This is the second time today I've banged my head. I just banged it in my closet on one of the shelves."

"I'll remember to steer clear of you the next time I see you coming my way," Kate joked.

"I'm not *that* bad," Angela laughed.

They both sat up to a squatting position and began gathering the fallen items. As they were grabbing for the same shoe, a black, sequined strappy high heel sandal, their eyes met. Kate gazed into Angela's ice blue eyes. Angela returned her gaze, staring into Kate's deep green eyes. Unbeknownst to the other, each woman felt butterflies in her stomach. It was a brief, yet intense moment until Kate broke her gaze by standing up quickly, letting go of the shoe.

CHAPTER 8

A NGELA HAD SPENT the two days following the Academy Awards assessing her life. She knew getting back together with Kristan was a lost cause, but realized she needed a woman, a lover, even if it was just an affair. Of course it would have to be a very discreet affair. Angela hadn't been with a woman since Kristan. She thought it was too risky for her career. Plus, she never had time.

She worked nonstop since breaking it off with Kristan. She couldn't say "no" to her agent. Each role seemed better than the one before. She realized about halfway through filming her last movie she was feeling burned out. She informed her agent, Larry that she needed at least a few months off. In true Larry fashion, he ignored her request and sent scripts to Angela with handwritten post it note messages like, "This is you. You'll be sorry if you don't read it," or "James Cameron said you have to read this. He's pretty much guaranteed you a role." Finally, per Angela's insistence, Larry caught on and stopped inundating her with scripts and messages.

After the awards show, Angela went home and took a long bubble bath. She sat in the tub, feeling sad and depressed. *Maybe I should take six months off from working*, she thought. She contemplated over whether she was depressed over not winning the Oscar or was it something else? Angela thought about all of the material possessions she owned, the enormous amount of money she had, the staff she employed and the entourage who traveled with her everywhere. *Why do I feel so lonely and empty inside when I have everything?* She woefully pondered.

Deep down, Angela knew the answer to this question. For so long she had been depriving herself of love and intimacy. It was then that she realized the key to her future happiness: to stop living this lie.

"Why does everything in my life have to be so complicated?" she mumbled to herself, positioning her back so that a jacuzzi jet pummeled her right shoulder.

As she got out of the tub and wrapped her hair in a turban-style towel, she said aloud, "That's it. Things are going to change around here." She decided she would do as Jason had been doing—get a lover or two. She'd take the risk. The pain of loneliness was too great to ignore anymore. She made a promise to herself that she'd open her mind to having an affair, maybe a relationship if she could just find a woman who didn't care about keeping it secret. She was tired of sacrificing love and sex for her career. She had needs that certainly weren't being met by the vibrator in her dresser drawer. She needed to feel the touch of another human being, and not have to resort to Jason's stockpile of pornos and dirty magazines. Jason had sex all the time, why shouldn't she?

Jason never made it home after the awards party. He went home with the Best Supporting Actress winner, who he fucked for two hours straight. If the public ever knew what really went on in the entertainment industry, they'd never believe it. As Jason told Angela about his conquest, she grew envious. *Why am I not out fucking someone for two hours?* She thought. She was tired of this charade. She decided that she would keep her eyes and heart open to the possibility of love, or at the very least some hot sex.

It was lust at first sight for Angela. Only two times in her life, prior to this, did she get the feeling she had the minute she saw Kate. Those two times were when she met Julia and then with Kristan. Kate's presence left Angela weak. Her stomach fluttered and she felt nervous and awkward, like a teenager with a crush. As Angela sat with Kate, sharing breakfast, she developed a gut feeling that Kate was either bisexual or a lesbian, or at least that's what she was hoping. It was hard to discern, but when she caught Kate eyeing her bare leg, Angela was convinced her suspicions may be true. Kate was definitely Angela's type. She was beautiful, had great breasts, and a fine ass. Kate was soft spoken too. Angela hated loud mouthed obnoxious types.

During their conversations, Angela felt anxious, like she was on speed. Angela wondered if Kate noticed her nervousness. She hoped it wasn't obvious. Angela felt as though there was so much she wanted to talk about with this woman; yet she hardly knew this person. It was as though they were lovers in a previous life or somehow the universe delivered her there at that very moment to make Angela happy and lift her spirits. Feeling vulnerable, Angela kept the focus of their conversation to work and breakfast, trying to keep the photo shoot professional. All along, she wanted to say, "Hey, let's blow this whole thing off and go upstairs to my bedroom."

After their momentary collision, Kate and Angela scrambled to pick up the fallen clothes and other items. With half of the pile now on one of the puffy couches and the other still on the floor, Kate said, "We've already lost quite a bit of time. Do you mind if I go finish a few things with setting up?"

"Go ahead. I'll pick up the rest of this mess. Go do what you need to do," Angela said, holding a bag of jewelry and other accessories.

"I just have to get my camera set and then we can begin," Kate said.

Angela continued picking up the rest of the clothes and draping them over the couch. Once she was done with the clothes, she emptied the jewelry bag onto an end table and selected an understated, yet elegant diamond and platinum necklace, fashioned like a tennis bracelet with small, round diamonds in bezel settings. Her next choice was matching earrings. She had bought this set for herself after it was loaned to her by a local jeweler for the Golden Globes. She fell in love with them and couldn't bring herself to have to return them. She loved jewelry, but hated the huge, gaudy pieces she was often given to wear at awards shows. This set was modest and simple.

"I think this gown would be great for the photos in this room. What do you think?" Angela held up a floor-length black and white form-fitting gown.

"I'd actually recommend the red gown," Kate said while pointing to a different gown on the couch. "The tones in this room are rich and dark. Red would be perfect. Trust me." Kate wasn't a stylist but certainly knew which colors and hues accentuated a celebrity with the photo shoot's background.

"If you say so," Angela returned the black and white gown and grabbed the red one. "I'll be right back." Angela left to change in the bathroom.

Angela returned looking magnificent in the red Dolce & Gabbana gown Kate recommended. "Please zip me up. I couldn't reach," Angela asked of Kate.

Kate walked over to Angela and hurriedly raised the zipper on Angela's dress. Touching Angela made her nervous. "There you go," Kate announced.

"Thanks," Angela proceeded to sit on the sofa and put on a pair of red Jimmy Choo shoes.

"I'd like to get a few shots of you standing by that antique mirror. I'll take a photo of you and your reflection," Kate, camera in hand, suggested. The mirror was a very large antique dressing mirror, about 8feet tall, with a very fancy, thick, ornate gold frame.

"You're the expert," Angela said, approaching the mirror. "How do you want me to stand?" she asked.

Kate approached Angela and made a pose in front of the mirror. "Like this, but with more hip."

Angela made a pouty, seductive pose, attempting to tease the camera—and Kate. Acting sexy in the movies was never difficult for Angela. Posing in front of Kate made Angela feel corny.

"You seem tense. It will show in the photos. Try to shake it off, ok?" Kate instructed.

"I'm sorry, this morning has been so hectic and busy." Angela took a deep, loud breath, and exhaled. Then she shook her arms and legs as if she were trying to throw the tension out of her body. *She's just a woman. Relax Angela. Visualize.* She said to herself to calm down. Angela visualized a glowing ball of light, something she learned at a new age meditation class.

Angela resumed her pose, trying to visualize the light and, for the moment, block out her desire for Kate.

"Much better." Kate clicked away. "Wow. You're doing much better."

Angela, now relaxed, flirted with the camera. It turned Kate on. Every celebrity posed in a seductive and alluring way, but this was Angela, her crush. Kate thought about how she hoped these pictures came out good. If they somehow weren't up to Angela's approval, Kate would be devastated. She certainly didn't want Angela to think she wasn't a good photographer.

CHAPTER 9

AFTER AN HOUR of photographing, and several hair and makeup retouches, Kate informed Angela they were finished with the indoor shots and that she was ready to begin photographing Angela outside. Kate was pleased that it would be just the two of them involved in the outdoor shoot. Angela instructed her hairdresser and makeup artist to wrap up. This type of situation didn't usually occur. Most celebrities insisted on having their hairdresser and makeup person as well as an entire entourage, around for the shoot.

"Let's take a break and have lunch," Angela said. She looked at her watch and said, "It's a little after noon. It's so beautiful out today, do you mind eating outside?"

"That sounds like a great idea. Don't forget to bring those bikinis with you," Kate said, pointing to the three bathing suits strewn on the sofa.

Angela, who had changed into her robe, walked over to the sofa and held up the three bathing suits.

"Which one do you think will look best?" Angela asked.

"I'm sure any one of them would be flattering," Kate said.

"Ok, I'll try them on after lunch and get your opinion," Angela said.

Kate liked that idea.

"Come with me." Angela gently grabbed Kate's wrist and led her to the kitchen. Once in the kitchen, Angela released her grasp and paused to give the cook their lunch order.

Angela greeted the chef, a tall blonde with freckles, and introduced him to Kate, "Hi Evan. This is Kate Ashford, a photographer for Vanity Fair." He waved a hello to Kate, which she returned. "We'll both have a spinach and walnut salad with balsalmic vinaigrette, sliced eggs, and mushrooms. Can you make me some of that awesome warm potato salad too?" Angela paused and turned to face Kate. "I'm sorry, Kate, is that ok with you? I'm so used to ordering for people like my publicist or agent who don't even have the time to make a lunch decision. What do you want?"

"That's fine Angela. I'm a vegetarian," Kate said, softly.

"So am I!" Angela exclaimed. "Evan, can you have Lucinda bring some ice water with lemons? We'll be out on the patio by the pool." Angela lightly grabbed Kate's wrist again and led her out the rear door. "There's a huge umbrella, so you don't have to worry about the sun beating down on you."

Angela led her to a frosted glass top table with legs of cobalt blue mosaic tiles. Angela pulled a chair out, designed of the same mosaic, and motioned for Kate to take this seat. Kate thanked Angela for seating her and took a minute to view the surroundings. To their left was the pool, which was kidney shaped and tiled with turquoise mosaics. A breathtaking, cascading stone waterfall rose above the far end of the pool, emptying into the crystal clear water. On the opposite side of the patio, to their right, was a beautiful garden, filled with purple, yellow, red, and white flowers. Kate took a deep breath, inhaling the serenity of the landscape. The garden was in full bloom, filling the air with a sweet fragrance.

Kate's tranquil feeling was soon interrupted when Jason

Saunders approached the pool area. "Hey Angie. Who's your friend?" he asked.

"Jay, this is Kate Ashford. She's photographing me for a Vanity Fair piece. And don't think about cutting in on it. It's my spread," she teased. Then she turned to Kate and said, "He's such a press hound. I don't think he ever gets sick of having his picture taken."

"Don't you worry your pretty little head. I've got my own photo shoot for GQ tomorrow," he said as he pulled his shirt over his head.

"I don't think Kate needs to see your bare chest hanging out," Angela scolded him.

"Geez, I was gonna swim a few laps. Do you mind?"

"I thought you were at the studio all day?" Angela asked.

"We had to wrap up early cuz a bunch of people got sick from yesterday's catered lunch."

"That sucks."

Jason turned to Kate and asked, "Hey, you look familiar. I know you?" He threw his shirt onto a padded lawn chair by the pool. Jason winked at Kate, who didn't quite know what to make of this gesture. Could he be flirting with her?

"I photographed you for your show's publicity stills," Kate responded, admiring his perfect physique. *No wonder Angela's married to him. He is definitely a beautiful man.* She thought. Jason was tan and muscular with six pack abs.

Jason stood there for a second, looking at Kate. "That must be it," Jason said.

"I must say that you weren't in the best of sorts that day. In fact, you were downright nasty." Though he was beautiful, Kate couldn't help but use this as an opportunity to point out his bad behavior. After all, she was interested in Angela, not him. Plus, it's always nice to knock a celebrity's ego down a notch.

Angela immediately apologized for him, "I'm sorry. He can get that way at times."

"Was I really that bad?" Jason asked.

"Yes, you were," Kate answered.

"Sorry about that. Maybe I can make it up to you some time," Jason said in a flirtatious tone.

"Don't you have to swim or something?" Angela chimed in. She knew when Jason was flirting and suddenly felt a possessive need to protect Kate.

"Woa. Guess that's my cue to go." Jason turned and dove into the pool.

"Sorry about that. He can be an annoyance," Angela turned to Kate from watching Jason swim the breaststroke and said, "He'll only do ten laps at the most. He went out last night and has a hangover."

Kate sensed that Angela and Jason weren't exactly couple of the year. Angela seemed quite annoyed by his presence. They didn't even greet each other with a kiss.

"Does that bother you that he drinks? I've read you're in recovery," Kate regretted asking that, but it seemed to have escaped her lips before she could even think about what she was saying. "I'm sorry, that's none of my business," Kate quickly added.

"No worries. It's a legitimate question. The answer is no. I don't care what he does. I don't own him. He doesn't own me. We have a different sort of relationship." Angela felt she could trust Kate. "Here comes our water. I'm dying of thirst." Angela clapped her hands once signaling her enthusiasm.

"Do you enjoy photographing celebrities?" Angela asked as she squeezed a lemon into a goblet made of etched crystal.

"No, actually, I don't," Kate said matter-of-factly.

Angela raised her eyebrows and responded, "Then why do you do it?"

"Money."

"So what would you rather be doing instead of taking pictures?" Angela asked.

"Oh, I didn't mean that I didn't like photography. I love photography. I just prefer to photograph things more meaningful than celebrities; like endangered animals, conservation and environmental projects, or a human rights story. I consider myself a photojournalist first and foremost and a celebrity photographer by default."

Angela knew this wasn't a jab at her, but used this as an opportunity to tease Kate. "So what you're saying is that my existence here on earth as an actress is meaningless."

Kate quickly defended her statement. "Absolutely not! I'm sure you bring joy to many lives through your films. I just think there are more important things going on in the world that need addressing."

Angela let Kate off the hook. "I understand. Believe me. The amount of money made each year by tabloids could help sustain an entire third world country and then some. I never understood the fascination people have with celebrities. The whole Princess Diana thing upset me greatly since it could have been easily avoided if photographers just gave her a break once in a while."

Lucinda brought their salads and placed them in front of each woman. "Thanks Lucinda. Can you bring out two slices of that fudge silk pie in a few minutes?" Angela asked. Chocolate was definitely an addiction for her. Since she got clean and sober, she ate chocolate any chance she could get. Fortunately she had an incredible metabolism that dissolved all of that fat. Plus, Angela exercised five times per week, sometimes with the help of Jason's personal trainer.

Angela was enjoying her conversation with Kate. By now she had developed a full blown crush on her. She still wasn't entirely sure about Kate's sexual orientation, though. Angela couldn't nail this one down to a definite. For the first time since Kristan, Angela had feelings for another woman. It was exciting, but at the same time, disappointing. She didn't know this woman, who technically, she reminded herself, was a member of the paparazzi.

Kate was different from the other celebrity photographers she encountered. Kate was gorgeous, with long blonde hair, a nice golden tan, a natural beauty who certainly didn't appear to be making mental notes on Angela's life to sell at a later time to a tabloid.

"So how do you deal with it all? You know, being famous?" Kate asked, cutting a large leaf of spinach.

"It's not easy having your privacy invaded on a regular basis. On the other hand, the benefits are great," she said as she swept her hand out referencing the house and pool.

"I would hate having no privacy. It must be so frustrating," Kate said sympathetically.

Angela motioned to signal that her mouth was full of food. Once she swallowed she said, "Believe me, it sucks. It's like standing naked in public everywhere I go. That's exactly what it's like," Angela made an expression as though she were in deep thought, perplexed. "Well, maybe not that bare. Maybe it's more like standing in my underwear, not completely naked. Or, maybe it's like walking out in public wearing only a bath towel. Or…"

Kate interrupted, "I think I get the point."

The two women laughed.

Jason finished swimming laps and was making his way back over to the two women. "See, I told you he wouldn't last," Angela said, loud enough so Jason could hear her comment.

Kate admired Jason's fit physique. He was definitely a fine looking man, but certainly not fine enough to fuck. Kate hadn't been with a man since high school. After her experience with Eve in Madagascar, she tried dating boys, even slept with a few. Even when she was with the most gorgeous, popular boy in school, she thought about the girls she'd rather be sleeping with.

"Angela, I can always count on you to bust my ass," Jason said as he whipped her leg with his pool towel. "What's Evan got cooking today?" He tried to poke at her potato salad.

Nudging his hand away, Angela replied, "Don't look at me like I'm gonna share my plate with you. Go get your own lunch." Although Angela was not being very nice to her husband, it was done in a joking and affectionate way.

Kate found it interesting watching the two interact with each other. They sure were chummy in a brother-sister sort of way. "Don't you have somewhere you've got to be?" Angela asked him.

Jason didn't respond. Instead, he made a funny face at her.

The dessert arrived, which please Angela very much. "I'm a chocolate addict. This is the best French silk pie you can get. It's like fudge but better!"

Realizing Angela was preoccupied, Jason decided to leave. "Well, it was nice meeting you. Sorry I was a jerk last time you saw me." Jason wiped off his wet hand and reached out to shake Kate's hand.

Kate responded by shaking his hand. "No problem. Everyone has bad days. No big deal. It was a pleasure meeting you as well."

"I'm going over to Reggie's house if you need me later," he said as he opened the patio door. Angela managed a slight wave good-bye, showing her indifference to the fact he was leaving.

Angela swallowed a piece of the pie and said, "He is like a kid. Jason thinks it's cool to hang out with Reggie because he's a rapper. They're like children. They spend all of their time playing video games," Angela explained as she opened her mouth to devour a large piece of pie.

"Boys will be boys," Kate said.

"Mmm. This stuff is orgasmic," Angela closed her eyes and moaned as she delivered another piece of pie into her mouth.

"You really do like chocolate," Kate said, trying her first piece of pie. "Oh my, it *is* awesome," she said.

"You know, I've really enjoyed your company. Wanna do lunch again? Or dinner? Off the clock?" Angela asked.

Kate's immediate thought was to say "no". She wasn't interested in lusting over someone who may not be interested in anything beyond a platonic friendship. Over time, it would become torture for her. Why bother? She thought. Then she thought about what she was thinking. How could she pass this up? Kate said, "Sure."

"Great. What are you doing tonight?" Angela asked excitedly.

"Actually, tonight wouldn't work for me. I promised a friend I'd meet her for dinner. Her girlfriend moved out and she's devastated. I'm definitely free tomorrow night," Kate said, referring to her friend, Marisol. Marisol wasn't just devastated over her partner of two years, Victoria, breaking up with her; Kate was concerned she was suicidal. She couldn't cancel on Marisol, not even for Angela Moore.

That's interesting, Angela thought, *Kate will be consoling her friend—a lesbian?* "Great. Tomorrow night it is."

Angela didn't want Kate to think she had ulterior motives for dinner, at least not yet. She still needed to feel her out to see if she could be trusted. Being a celebrity as visible as she was meant being extra careful, and in some cases downright paranoid. "I'd like to pick your brain about organizations I could donate to. I haven't been involved in many charities and would like to give something back to the world. Plus my accountant says I need a tax write-off."

"Oh sure, I have a couple of organizations in mind already. I'll bring their brochures along." Kate hoped this wasn't the only reason Angela wanted to join her for dinner.

"Do you mind picking me up? That way I'll have a better chance of sneaking out of here." The paparazzi knew Angela's cars. She hated using a limo service unless it was for a special event.

"It's a date. Let's wrap up the rest of this shoot, eh?" Kate arose from her chair. "While you're changing into the bikinis, I'll go get my equipment."

"No. I said Jonathan would take care of that. I need your help in deciding which bikini to wear," Angela insisted.

Kate wasn't going to argue with Angela. "Ok, but I don't need all of the lights. They can go back in my truck. Here are my keys." Kate reached into her jean pockets and produced her car keys.

Angela called Jonathan on her little walkie-talkie and repeated Kate's instructions to him. After Jonathan retrieved Kate's keys, the two women headed for a small pool house by the garden.

"You wait out here and I'll come out and model for you. Be honest and let me know which suit looks best." She entered the pool house while Kate stood and waited like a patient parent waiting for her child to try on school clothes.

Angela reappeared in a white halter bikini with turquoise bead and suede trim. "Well, what d'ya think?" she asked.

Kate gave a thumbs-up signal and remarked, "That looks very nice, a definite keeper." What Kate really wanted to say was how incredibly hot she looked and could she please jump her body right there.

The two remaining bikinis, a black bra top and Burberry plaid triangle top bikini looked incredible on Angela, but the white suit was the winner. Kate thoroughly enjoyed photographing Angela in her bikini. She took shots of her in the pool, next to the pool, by the waterfall, and by the patio.

After the photo session, Angela and Kate said their good-byes and told each other they looked forward to their dinner together.

As she pulled out of the gated home, Kate noticed she had a message from Marisol on her cell phone. She dialed Marisol's house. "How are you?" Kate asked, concerned for her friend.

Marisol answered on the first ring thinking it could be her departed lover, Victoria. "Oh, it's you," she said with disappointment in her voice. "I'm ok. I just can't believe this is happening to me. I miss her so much." Marisol started to cry.

"It's gonna be ok, Marisol. I'll pick you up at 7:00." What Kate really wanted to tell Marisol was how great her day was. Marisol was her best friend, but too fragile at this moment to talk about her day with Angela. She didn't want to seem as though she was rubbing it in. Kate was a good listener and would spend the evening listening and consoling.

That evening, Angela sat in her bedroom, thinking about Kate. "I definitely have a major crush, you guys!" she announced to her dogs, lying on the bed next to her. "You guys are the only ones I can trust to tell. Well, that's not true. I can tell Jason," Angela felt compelled to share her feelings with someone. She called Jason on his cell phone.

"Hey, what's up, Angie?" Jason yelled over some very loud background music. "Let me go in the other room. I can't hear you." Jason left the music-filled recording studio and settled in his friend Reggie's living room on an enormous black leather sectional.

"I'm in big trouble. I have a major crush on that photographer that was here. We're having dinner tomorrow night. I can't wait," she exclaimed.

"Be careful Angela. I don't think this is a good idea. She's a member of the paparazzi," he warned.

"Not really. She's definitely not what I'd call a paparazzi photographer. She doesn't even like taking pictures of celebrities. She just does it for the money. She'd prefer photographing wildlife or something."

"Just be careful, if you know what I mean. Actually, Angela, I don't think this is a good idea. Can't you cancel?" Jason warned.

"Screw you Jason. Don't lecture me about being careful when your dick has been in every twat in Hollywood." Angela was furious over Jason's sudden concern for protecting their relationship and reputations.

"Whatever Angela. You know the only women I fuck are celebrities who have as much to lose as me. I'm warning you. Don't do this. You're not thinking straight. You're just still upset over Oscars," Jason pleaded.

Angela hung up the phone. "So much for being my best friend," she said to the dogs.

CHAPTER 10

JASON SAUNDERS WANTED to have sex with Angela Moore the moment he laid eyes on her. It was at a movie premiere in which Jason played a supporting role. When he wasn't working on the set of his television show, he dedicated his time to building his movie career.

Angela's publicist, Lindsey, introduced the two stars. Lindsey attended every event with her and made it a point to flaunt Angela to every important person in attendance. Jason had seen many photos of Angela and movies in which she acted. Until this evening, he had never met her in person.

Jason found himself instantly attracted to Angela. After exchanging "hellos", he insisted that Angela and Lindsey sit with him.

"You should come and sit with me," he told her, as his date, a tall, buxom redhead named Chloe, poked her elbow into his ribs and let out an "ahem", which meant, "Remember me. I'm here too."

Jason quickly corrected himself, "I mean. You should sit with *us*."

"Sure. We'd love to," Angela said in a friendly tone.

However, as soon as Angela accepted the invitation, Lindsey tugged at her arm, pulled her to the side and firmly whispered, "Remember, we're going to try to make an effort to sit next to Bob Vogel? He's producing that movie. The one I told you has your name written all over it." Lindsey was just like any other typical Hollywood publicist—all business. She was one of the best in the business.

Angela whispered an "oh, yeah." Then she turned to face Jason and said, "Actually, it turns out we have prior seating commitments, but thanks."

"That's ok. I'll catch up with you another time," Jason said, disappointed.

"Jason, there's Steven what's-his-name—the director. He's my favorite. I want to meet him. Maybe he can get me a movie role," Chloe said, pulling Jason in the direction of the director.

Damn publicists, Jason thought. It reminded him that his own publicist, Marcy, was lurking somewhere trying to find him. Jason promised Marcy he'd meet her at the premiere. When he came upon her by the entrance to the event, he quickly steered Chloe in the other direction.

Jason wished he'd never brought Chloe. Earlier, while getting ready, he had thoughts of not bringing a date. He had a feeling he'd regret it. Now he realized he should've paid attention to his instinct. If he hadn't brought Chloe with him, he could have maneuvered his way into sitting next to Angela.

Plus, Chloe was embarrassing him with her star struck behavior. Jason wanted to tell her the truth—that she was a terrible actress and the only acting she was capable of doing would be for the Playboy channel. He wanted to tell her she didn't have a chance in hell of landing a reputable movie role. Chloe was nice and all, even intelligent—she was a sophomore at Stanford, majoring in engineering, when she was "discovered" by Playboy. However, he witnessed firsthand how horrible of an actress she was after accompanying her to an audition he had lined up. As hard as she tried, she couldn't shake the bimbo persona. One look at her, even on a bad day, made you think, "This chick should be in Playboy." She was too tall and voluptuous, not to mention drop-dead gorgeous.

While Chloe gushed over the famous director, Jason kept his eye on Angela, who was giving an interview. He was captivated by Angela's beauty. She was ten times more beautiful in person than in photos or on screen. In person, she resembled Vivian Leigh, the actress who portrayed Scarlett O'Hara in *Gone with the Wind*. There was something addictive about her. Jason had to have her.

Jason pulled Chloe's arm and said, "Time to go in."

"Just a minute," she said, still enthralled by being in the presence of the director, who didn't seem to mind Chloe's attention at all. His wife, though, didn't seem as approving.

"*Now*, Chloe," he said firmly, squeezing her arm a bit harder and pulling her towards the theater's entrance. He could see Angela ahead of them entering the theater and didn't want to lose sight of her.

"Ow. That was rude, Jason. I was in the middle of a conversation with him. You probably blew it for me," Chloe whined as she obediently followed Jason into the theater.

Yeah, I blew it for you. You were doing a fine job of that on your own. He thought.

"I want to get a decent seat. It's *my* movie, after all. The reason we are here in the first place." Little did Chloe know that seats had already been reserved for them. In order to stay close to Angela, Jason played it off as though they were to fend for themselves in finding a seat. He hurried, pushing through people to ensure he eyed where Angela was seated. At least if he were close enough to see where she was seated, he could follow her to the bathroom and put the charm on her.

Marcy approached him from behind, laying her hand

on his shoulder. "There you are. I've been looking all over for you. Do you know how many photo and interview opps you blew by taking off on your own? I hate when you do that. All of our seats are over there. What are you doing way over here?" she asked, pointing to the center aisle. Jason swore Marcy's lot in life was to drive him crazy.

Jason spotted Angela. She was wearing a lemon yellow vintage tea length dress, which aided in the visual distinction. He watched her take a seat in the left side of the theater, where he was currently standing. Content that he knew where she was sitting, he obeyed Marcy. "I'll follow you." he would have to turn his head frequently, but was ready to excuse himself to the bathroom if Angela left her seat.

About three-quarters of the way through the action-packed, blow up everything in sight film, Jason noticed Angela had left her seat. He quickly excused himself from his publicist and Chloe, who were on either side of him, telling them he had to go to the bathroom. He stood in the hallway, outside of the restrooms, pretending to be engaged in a conversation on his cell phone. Within seconds, he saw Angela exit the ladies room. Watching her from behind a large potted plant, he made his way toward her as she reached to open the door to the theater.

"Hey, Angela. You enjoying the movie?" he asked, suddenly appearing behind her.

Angela, startled, let go of the door handle, spun around, and said, "Oh my. You scared me. I didn't know you were behind me."

"I'm sorry. I hope you don't remember me as some scary guy," he said with a chuckle.

Angela laughed. "No, I was deep in thought, I guess. I get like that when I'm alone—unaware of my surroundings. I tend to zone out," she said. "Your movie's great. In fact, I want to get back in there so I don't miss the ending."

"Well, why don't we do something after the movie? Maybe my place?" He made it obvious that he was coming on to her. He stared deeply into her eyes, and produced a devilish smirk.

"No. But thanks for asking. I already have plans to attend one of the after parties," she replied, turning her body halfway and extending her hand to reach for the door handle again.

He put his hand over hers to stop her from leaving. "Come on," he tried to persuade her. "I'll bring my so-called date home. I promise you'll have a great time." Jason lifted his brows in a way that emphasized his request.

Angela, annoyed, responded, "I don't think so."

Jason was relentless. "Look. I think you are the most beautiful and sexiest woman I've ever laid eyes on. Please meet me later."

"Believe me, I'm flattered. But, no." Angela pushed Jason's arm aside and pushed open the door, leaving Jason behind, clearly dumbfounded by his inability to woo her, something he certainly wasn't used to.

He decided to let her go for now, returning to his seat, in the hopes of catching up with her after the movie.

After the movie, Jason informed Chloe he had someone important to talk to and told her to meet him at the limo with Marcy. He knew he'd get a tongue lashing from Marcy for taking off. Chloe expressed her displeasure, asking where he was going that was so important and why couldn't he bring her along. As she began to whine, Jason assured her he wouldn't be long and to just do as he asked.

Jason pushed through the exodus of satisfied movie-goers to Angela's exit aisle. "Changed your mind?" Jason asked, suddenly appearing on her right side, startling her again.

Angela, more annoyed than before, said, "You have got to stop doing that. I feel like you're stalking me."

Jason, defensively said, "Wow, you sure are a bitch. I just wanted to get to know you. You don't have to be so fucking rude."

Angela tersely responded, "Do you think I'm stupid? I know what you're trying to do. I've heard all about you and believe me, I have no interest in becoming a member of the Jason Saunders fuck 'em and leave 'em club. So get it through your head. I'm not going anywhere with you. Stick with your date."

Although her resistance pissed him off, it also, strangely, turned Jason on. "Well excuse me Miss goody two shoes. You know, don't believe everything you hear. It's your loss. See ya." Jason waved a sarcastic good-bye and walked off to catch his limo.

Jason saw Chloe waving her arm from the limo, trying to get his attention. He jogged over to her and quickly entered the limo to avoid the paparazzi.

"Where's my publicist?" Jason asked her as he entered the limo.

"She left with some movie producer woman. She told me to tell you to call her first thing tomorrow morning," Chloe responded.

"So we're all alone?" Jason locked the doors and informed the driver he would be locking the partition window for privacy.

"What are you up to?" Chloe asked in a cute, seductive way.

"Come here baby let me show you," Jason said, pulling her closer to him. Jason was horny, as usual. Though he recently turned thirty-two, he felt like an eighteen year old in his prime. He met Chloe at a Playboy Mansion party. She was Miss September. He'd been seeing her, well, having sex with her every night for the last three weeks. Although she gave dynamite blowjobs, he was tired of her. He already decided earlier that day he'd break it off. It was just a matter of days. He would stop returning her calls. She would insist on seeing him again. He would ignore her. She would eventually get the picture. That was his routine. Once in a while, though, he'd get an obsessed ex-girlfriend. Then he'd have his handlers deal with getting rid of her. He wasn't sure exactly what his management team did, but he knew threats and money went hand in hand to send them on their way.

"Ooh. I can't wait to get you in my mouth, baby," Chloe cooed. While Chloe bobbed her head up and down on him, he thought about Angela. *Why on earth would she pass up an evening with me?* He asked himself as Chloe took care of business. *She must like playing hard-to-get or something. Or, maybe she was PMS-ing.*

Jason had every right to be conceited. On the Hollywood hunk scale, he was right up there with Brad Pitt and George Clooney. He had it all—a sense of humor, great face, great hair, great body, and talent. He was definitely a catch. He had thick dark hair, green eyes and the perfectly white Hollywood smile. He wasn't too tall and not too short. The tabloids referred to him as Hollywood's Bad Boy for his partying and womanizing reputation.

Jason certainly wasn't one to pine over a woman. Women were a fleeting thought in his mind. They came and went. Angela was different. The next day, Jason dumped Chloe, like he had planned, and continued to muse over Angela, something he hadn't planned. He fantasized about making love to her and hoped he'd get another chance to seduce her.

A few months later, Jason, on hiatus from his television series, was delighted to accept a role in a film opposite Angela. It was a love story set in Mexico. Jason vowed to himself he would have his way with her by the end of the filming.

He decided he wouldn't be as obvious as he had been at the movie premiere. He would go slow with her, gain her trust. She was obviously one of those women who needed a long, "getting-to-know you" stage.

Jason couldn't wait to begin working with Angela. He felt like a schoolboy with a crush. Angela, on the other hand, wasn't exactly overjoyed to see him the first day of production.

"Just for the record, I won't put up with your come-ons. I am a professional and don't want to be bothered with your stupid games," Angela told Jason, arms crossed, nose turned upward.

Jason got an instant hard-on the minute Angela began her lecture. He laughed, not because he thought she was funny, but because Jason was actually nervous, feeling intimidated by her demeanor.

"You think this is funny? I'm serious. I'll withdraw from the movie due to harassment. So back off. This is your only warning. No second chances." Angela unfolded her arms and sat down as the director called the meeting to begin.

"Do we have a problem?" the director asked, annoyed.

"No. Just something between Jason and me, that's all. It's fine," Angela said very nicely, putting on an act for the director.

"Yeah, everything's o.k," Jason said.

"Good. We've got a movie to make, which I may remind the two of you is a love story. I can't have my two main actors acting like they hate each other when it's a goddamn love story," the director snapped. "Kapeesh?"

Jason and Angela nodded simultaneously in agreement.

As the production team discussed locations and which type of film they'd use, Jason began writing on a notepad. When he finished, he put the pen down, and slid the pad of paper in front of Angela.

She read the note, which said, "I agree to never act like an asshole toward you ever again. I hereby state that I will honor and respect you. If I don't abide by this contract, I give you permission to punish me accordingly. I'm sorry. Please forgive me." Angela managed a smirk, fighting back laughter. *Maybe I am being full of myself. We do have to get along for the sake of this movie.* She thought.

She wrote back, "I hereby acknowledge this contract and will punish you if the need arises." She pushed the note in front of him and crossed her arms.

After the meeting, Jason approached Angela to apologize again. "Look, Angela, I'm really sorry for my behavior at the premiere. It won't happen again. Let's start fresh. O.k.?" Jason pleaded in a childlike manner. *I'll be patient. Soon you won't be able to resist me.*

Angela hesitated with her response and said, "O.k. But I'll be watching you, mister. No funny stuff. We have a movie to make."

When there were breaks in filming, Angela and Jason spent much of their time in Angela's trailer, becoming the unlikeliest friends. They'd play cards, watch tv, talk. Sometimes, Angela would play Playstation video games with Jason. Jason was addicted to video games. He never had a video game system growing up, so it thrilled him to have every type of gaming system and game available.

As a child, the only time he was able to play video games was when his mother brought him along to the local bar, where there was a PacMan and space invaders-type game. His mom was a fall-down drunken alcoholic, who gave her son quarters to play video games so she could sit at the bar without any interruptions. Jason would occasionally glance at his mother out of the corner of his eye. Once she was good and drunk, she'd let men stick their hands down her shirt and up her skirt.

When Jason was twelve, he discovered first-hand that his mother was not only the bar drunk, but also the bar slut. Jason was sitting by the pool table, waiting patiently for his mother to appear from the ladies' restroom. He was tired, thirsty, and out of quarters. It was midnight and he had school the next day.

Figuring she must've passed out in the bathroom, he gently pushed the restroom door open, and peered in to see his mother getting groped by a large biker dude with a ponytail. After seeing the young boy, the biker dude barked, "Get lost, kid."

"Get outta here Jason," his mother screamed. "That's it. Yer grounded ya dumb fuck."

After that, Jason hated going to the bar with his mother, even though he could play video games. It wasn't the same, now that he knew what his mother was doing when she'd disappear for a time from her barstool.

Angela and Jason were quite compatible, spending most of their free time together. The days were long, hot, and grueling. When there were breaks in filming, they'd escape to Angela's air-conditioned trailer. Jason made Angela laugh, while Angela played a nurturing role for Jason, helping him with his lines and listening to him open up about his dysfunctional upbringing. Jason contemplated making a move on Angela. She had turned out to be a great friend, like the sister he never had, and in some ways the nurturing mother his mother had never been. He loved being near her. It was a strange feeling for him. The only time he'd enjoyed female companionship was when sex was involved. Even then, he preferred to not have his dates sleep over or hang around.

Angela was different. She listened to him and never

whined. God, how he hated the whiners he fucked. Angela and Jason became very close. Jason even cried in front of Angela as he told her how horrible and neglectful his mother was.

Every time Jason thought it would be the right moment to kiss Angela, something would happen to interrupt the mood—someone would knock on the door, or Angela would get a phone call, or Angela had to suddenly go to the bathroom.

One day, a couple months into shooting of the film, Jason decided he would make his move on Angela once and for all. He had been a good boy long enough, he decided. It was time to take their little friendship to the next level. That day, while in her trailer, Jason and Angela were sitting, facing each other, gossiping about the film's director, who they both had come to despise. Jason interrupted Angela mid-sentence by quickly moving forward to kiss her. Their lips met for a second. Then, Angela pushed Jason back and retreated to an opposite side of the trailer. As she jumped back, she quickly blurted, "I'm a lesbian, Jason."

Jason was silent for a second, and then asked, "What did you just say?"

"I can't believe I told you that. I meant to slap you, but I guess I felt sorry for you." Angela regretted having told him she was a lesbian. She only shared her secret with a select few and never thought Jason would be one of them.

Jason didn't believe her at first. He figured she was the type of woman who made up the story that she was a lesbian because she was some freak who didn't like sex or just hated men. "If you really don't like me, just say so. You don't have to say you're a lesbian. I mean, I just don't get it. I thought you were attracted to me," he said.

"No, that's not it. I do like you. I've enjoyed getting to know you. I hope this won't ruin our friendship." She hesitated, looked down at the floor, and continued her confession, "I wasn't lying. I really am a lesbian. All those tabloid stories—they were true. Angela Moore is a lesbian. I just broke up with my girlfriend, Kristan." She suddenly felt panic and worry. She sat next to Jason again, put his hands in hers and said, "Please don't say anything. No one can know. I need to know I can trust you."

Jason felt crushed. His fantasy wasn't going to come true. No sex with Angela. What a let down this was. "I-I don't know what to say. I'm a bit shocked I guess," he sat there, holding Angela's hands in his.

This definitely wasn't what Jason had planned for, but decided to support his new friend by telling her, "Of course you can trust me." He paused, looked into Angela's eyes and asked, "You really don't like men at all?"

Angela laughed. "Of course I like men. I just prefer to have sex with women. I know it's hard to believe there is actually a woman on this planet who doesn't want to have sex with you, Jason. So get over yourself. Please tell me we can still be friends. I'd be so sad if we couldn't," she said, cocking her head to the side, smiling, awaiting a positive response.

"Angela, this is definitely the weirdest relationship I've ever had with a woman. Let's see how it goes," Jason agreed, but disappointed.

"Thanks, Jason." Angela leaned forward and wrapped her arms around him, giving him a hug. She held on for what seemed like an eternity.

After that day, their friendship continued—and grew stronger. They continued to meet in Angela's trailer, talking, laughing, and playing. Everyone on the set assumed they were having an affair. After the filming ended, they continued to spend time together. They were often photographed leaving one another's homes, having lunch together, frolicking on the beach, shopping. Wherever they were spending time together, the paparazzi were right there with them.

The press couldn't get enough of the couple. Both of their agents knew they weren't dating, that they were "just friends". That didn't stop them from trying to sell their two clients on the marriage idea. Both agents gave well-rehearsed presentations. They reasoned that although both Jason and Angela's careers were skyrocketing, a union of this magnitude could bring even better opportunities their way. They'd be the Hollywood Power Couple. It worked for Brad and Jennifer, Brad and Angelina, years ago with Bruce and Demi. Why not for them?

Jason and Angela discussed the proposition at length. At the very least, each agreed this would be a wonderful way to honor their friendship. Angela thought it would be a great way to prove the tabloids wrong, though they were right on, that Angela Moore wasn't a lesbian. Jason also offered brotherly love and support. He helped her get through her break up with Kristan.

Jason had his own motives for accepting this proposition. For the first time in Jason's life, he had a woman in his life he loved. He had no sisters, and was estranged from his mother, who was an unemployed barfly his entire life. She loved him unconditionally, like a mother or sister would. He loved sharing his life with her. She understood him. She didn't care that he was a gigolo. Jason could tell Angela anything and she would still love him.

Jason's life with Angela was perfect; at least it was before Kate Ashford came along. When Jason informed Angela he didn't think it was a good idea for her to get involved with Kate, he meant it. Immediately after Angela's confession of lust for this woman, Jason felt an intense wave of jealousy and anger. At that very moment he knew the dynamics of their relationship had changed. Not for the reason he relayed to her—that a lesbian affair would ruin their image and careers. If the tabloids got a hold of Angela's sexual preference, Jason's fans would pity him and love him even more. Women everywhere would rejoice over the prospect of Jason Saunders being single again. For these and many other reasons, he didn't worry for a minute that his career would flounder if he and Angela were to break up. What he really feared was actually losing Angela, something he never thought could happen until now.

He realized that not only did he love Angela. He was madly *in love* with her too. He felt threatened. At first, he had no clue why he felt so enraged over this other woman. When he thought about it later, he realized he had never actually met a woman Angela was attracted to. As he thought back to their lunch on the patio, he remembered seeing the attraction in Angela's eyes for this woman. It infuriated him. The whole situation was unsettling and strange. Jason had never met a possible love interest of Angela's. She had been celibate, not wanting a relationship since marrying Jason. In Jason's mind, Angela was just Angela, not a lesbian, not a woman for any other man. Angela was Jason's and that was it.

After spending the afternoon at Reggie's house that day, he went to a famous model's house and had sex with her. While he was fucking the leggy model, he imagined the model was Angela. Fantasizing about Angela turned him on so much that he finished prematurely, something he hadn't done since he was a teenager. He was so enmeshed in the fantasy of having sex with Angela; he almost moaned her name. He quickly dressed and left the model's home, embarrassed by his weak sexual performance.

As he drove home that night, he thought, *"Maybe Angela secretly feels the same about me. Maybe the lesbian thing was just a stage or a moment of confusion. What the fuck am I going to do? I'm screwed. I better stop this right now. Maybe it'll go away. I hope.*

CHAPTER 11

KATE FULFILLED HER duty as Marisol's best friend by listening to her sob throughout their entire dinner together at the new "in" spot in Santa Monica, Silk. Silk was a Thai restaurant that took your breath away the moment you opened the door. The aroma of Thai cooking spices was so strong; Kate could taste them as she breathed in the heavy, warm air. Kate loved trying new restaurants and found her pad thai dish to be the best she'd ever had. Marisol, however, didn't care for spicy ethnic food and opted for a simple salad.

It was, indeed, a most difficult time for Marisol. She had just learned that her partner of two years, Victoria, had been seeing someone else for the past month. Marisol was devastated. Kate, not knowing what to say, could only sit there and listen as Marisol recounted her despair over and over again.

"What am I going to do, Kate?" Marisol sobbed, toying at her cabbage salad with her fork. "I loved her. We were supposed to spend the rest of our lives together. I was going to have our baby. We had already picked out a sperm donor." She dropped the fork and blew her nose into the soft cotton dinner napkin.

It hurt Kate terribly to see her friend in so much pain.

That damn Victoria, Kate thought. Kate never did like her, but always made an effort to be pleasant for Marisol's sake. Victoria had never been faithful to Marisol. Kate warned Marisol of rumors that Victoria was unfaithful, but she would never accept the truth. She was in love with her and refused to believe Victoria would do such a thing as cheat on her. Marisol even went so far as to accuse Kate of being jealous of her relationship with Victoria. It was one of those "kill the messenger" situations. Kate knew the time would come when Marisol would see things for what they really were. Instead of relishing in an "I told you so" moment, Kate was concerned for her friend and wanted to do anything to make her feel better. She wished she could do something to take all of the pain away for her.

"Marisol, you need to eat. You'll get through this. This will pass. It just takes time." Kate paused. She decided she didn't want Marisol to be alone while going through this difficult transition. "That's it. You're staying at my house until you start feeling better. I don't want you to be alone," Kate instructed. It had only been a few days since Victoria moved out of Marisol's home in Bel Air, but it was apparent to Kate that Marisol hadn't been eating or taking care of herself. When Marisol opened the door to greet Kate earlier that evening, Kate noticed that Marisol appeared thinner and her hair was matted from not being washed in a few days. When Kate hugged her friend, she detected the stench of body odor and stale cigarette smoke. Marisol hadn't smoked in five years, but it appeared she had taken up the nasty habit again.

"Thanks Kate, b-b-but I think I just want to be alone. I don't need a babysitter. You have too much stuff going on." Marisol said, tears welling up in her swollen, red eyes. On a normal day, Marisol was very attractive. Her mother, who passed away when Marisol was ten, was Chinese. Her father was Irish and German. She kept her straight, black hair all one length to her shoulders. Like Kate, she wore little makeup, except lip gloss occasionally. Marisol was naturally gorgeous and thin, even though she never exercised and, on less depressing days, ate everything in sight.

"You're staying with me and that's it. You can stay with me as long as you need to. It'll be fun, like old times," Kate said, referring to when they were roommates. Kate had just begun a career photographing celebrities and Marisol was soon becoming *the* Hollywood event planner. Mutual friends set them up on a blind date. They went on several dates, kissed on a few occasions, but realized they were meant to be good friends and not lovers. They just didn't click on a romantic level, but did connect as friends. They lived together as roommates for five years until Victoria came into the picture. Marisol, who had become the most sought after event planner in Hollywood, had money to burn and bought a beautiful house in Bel Air. Victoria, a very butch self-described "artist", basically freeloaded off of Marisol's success, never having to worry about paying bills or working. Victoria was a kept woman. The only thing Victoria did contribute to the household was her abstract, cubist genre paintings, which hung in every room.

Marisol was happy. She had found the woman of her dreams. Victoria was artistic, great in bed, and exactly her type, with hardened features, super short spiky hair and athletic build—a butch through and through. Whatever Victoria wanted, she got. Kate, on the other hand, couldn't understand what Marisol saw in her. Although Victoria was an attractive butch-type, she was lazy and not a very nice person. When Marisol had friends over for dinner or a small gathering, Victoria was rude to her guests. Sometimes she wouldn't join Marisol's friends and colleagues, opting to isolate herself in a room upstairs, painting.

The first time Kate found out Victoria was cheating on Marisol, she stumbled upon her kissing another woman at a popular lesbian bar in Los Angeles. Kate contemplated telling Marisol, but feared hurting her dear friend. Finally, she couldn't keep the secret any longer.

"Marisol, this is so hard for me. I ran into Victoria the other night and she was with another woman." Kate felt instantly relieved after getting this off her chest.

"Yeah, so?" Marisol obviously didn't get the point.

"So. They were kissing. Making out," Kate declared.

"Kate, you obviously mistook her for someone else. Victoria and I have never been better. I can't believe you of all people would do this to me," Marisol responded.

Dumbfounded by Marisol's naivety, Kate insisted it was Victoria she had seen. "It was her, Marisol. I'm not blind and I know it was her. Believe me. Why on earth would I tell you this if I wasn't 100% positive it was her?" Kate insisted.

"Kate, I really don't want to talk about this anymore. Especially if you're going to insist it was her." Marisol picked up her cell phone. "Actually, let me ask her myself." Marisol dialed Victoria's number and asked her if she was at the club making out with someone. A few minutes later, she seemed satisfied, hung up the phone and turned to Kate. "I told you it wasn't her. She said she's never even been to that club."

Kate never brought the topic up again to Marisol, though she heard stories of Victoria's affairs from friends and acquaintances. It pained her terribly, but Kate chose to mind her own business and stay out of Marisol's love life. She knew Marisol would find out the horrible truth one day.

That day came and all of Marisol's hopes and dreams went out the window when she arrived home from a full day of meetings to find Victoria's belongings and paintings gone. Victoria left a good-bye note that read, "Dear Marisol, I realized that I couldn't stay in this relationship any longer. I don't love you anymore. I fell in love with someone else. I am sorry, but I need to move on. Good-bye, Victoria." For Marisol, it was like a death and was grieving the loss. Immediately after she read the note, she phoned Kate.

"Ok, I guess I don't want to be alone. I'd love to take a long bubble bath in your Jacuzzi. Mine's broke. Victoria was supposed to call to get it fixed." Marisol's eyes filled with tears as she mentioned her ex-lover's name.

"That sounds like a great way to take care of yourself," Kate felt like saying, *Yeah, and a bath would be great since you're starting to reek.* She continued very politely, "Listen Marisol, you'll get through this. I promise you these terrible feelings will pass. Let your assistant handle your appointments and if you have to reschedule, so be it. I don't have anything pressing going on until next week. Next Thursday I have a photo shoot with some big wig rap star. I forgot his name. I think it's Z or E-something." Kate purposely avoided mentioning her dinner plans with Angela the following evening. Kate decided she wasn't going to tell any of her friends about Angela. Kate didn't want them making a big deal out of it. Plus, she wanted to respect Angela's privacy.

"I don't expect you to devote all of your time to me. I'll be ok," Marisol said.

Kate decided to make something up about her plans with Angela. "Oh, I forgot. I have one thing I have to do tomorrow evening. It's no big deal, just a minor production meeting. It may run longer than I'd like, knowing the players involved." Kate immediately felt terrible for lying. Marisol was already in such a vulnerable state. If she ever found out that Kate was lying to her, she'd be crushed.

CHAPTER 12

JASON KNOCKED ON Angela's bedroom door. "Do you want breakfast Angela?" he asked through the closed door.

His knocks woke her up. "Open the door and come in. I don't feel like getting up yet," Angela said as loudly as she could in her weak morning voice.

Jason walked in and for the first time felt shaky over entering her bedroom. *Maybe she'll notice my love and desire for her. What am I going to do then? Did I remember to put deodorant on?* He thought, nervously. Jason didn't have to report for filming that morning as half the cast had food poisoning. Regardless, he was ready for the day and it was only 7:00.

"What's the matter with you? What are you doing up this early? Didn't you go out last night?" Angela asked, her voice still in a weakened, just-awoken state. She sat up and stretched her arms to the ceiling.

"Naw. I was home early last night, 'round 11:00. What do you want for breakfast? It looks like a nice day. We could eat on the patio," Jason suggested, nervously. He told himself to stop this nonsense and calm down. It was just Angela. He never got nervous, not even when he met the President of the United States or the Queen of England.

"It's so early. I don't even know if I'm hungry yet," she answered, then thought for a second and decided she'd be hungry soon enough. "I don't care, whatever we got. Eggs. Cheese. No bread. I'm feeling bloated, so definitely no bread. Are you o.k.?" she asked. "Come and sit down for a minute. Let's talk," Angela said as she patted her hand on her thick, down comforter.

"Yeah. I'm fine. I'm just hungry. I have a lot of stuff to do today," Jason said, turning around to exit the room. "We can talk at breakfast. I'll see you in ten or fifteen minutes?" Jason admired how gorgeous Angela looked, even in the morning. Jason had always noticed her beauty, but never really appreciated how beautiful she truly was. His feelings felt wrong to him, icky in a way, as though he was lusting over his sister. He quickly left the bedroom and made his way toward the kitchen to order their breakfast.

At breakfast, Angela confided in Jason that she was meeting Kate that evening. She contemplated not telling him, for fear he'd give her the same lecture he'd given her yesterday. Ultimately, she decided that although Jason was acting like a jerk and being unfair, she wasn't going to lie to him or keep anything from him. She was so sick and tired of lying to people about her sexual preference. She didn't want to start lying to Jason about her intentions. Keeping track of lies is hard work. While changing into a long waffle textured white robe, she prayed that his mood had changed from last night.

"I'm meeting Kate tonight," Angela said, starting the breakfast conversation.

Jason felt like he just got punched in the gut. "You're *what?*" he asked, furious.

"Don't you start with me, Jason. What the hell is wrong with you anyway? You have no right to say anything. You're a man slut for crying out loud," Angela said, pointing her index finger at him.

"That's going to change. I think I want to settle down. I mean, I'm going to be careful for our careers. Since I'm willing to make the sacrifice, I was hoping you'd do the same." Jason hoped she'd see it his way and maybe even agree to not see Kate.

"Are you out of your mind? I've sacrificed the last year and a half for us. I'm certainly not gonna start doing it now. Plus, do you actually expect me to remain celibate or play with myself for the rest of my life?" Angela asked, her face turning red with anger.

Jason knew he wasn't going to win this argument. He would have to convince her some other way. "Fine. Do what you want," he said, throwing down his fork and pushing his plate of eggs toward the middle of the table.

"I will," Angela said, adamantly, while taking her last bite of scrambled eggbeaters. "Now, I need to make some phone calls. And, yes, one of those happens to be to Kate to confirm our date," she said as she stood up.

Jason followed her lead and stood up, responding, "Look, I'm really sorry Angela. I really did mean it when I said I wasn't going to run around anymore."

Angela stood still, crossing her arms.

Jason held his arms out to offer Angela a hug. She stood still and quiet for a minute, but then relented into his arms to receive a hug. Jason held her and whispered into her ear, "You know I love you and worry about you, that's all. Be careful." Jason meant what he said. He felt an exciting feeling he had never felt before while holding her in his arms. It was like he had butterflies all over his body. *This must be what love feels like. He* thought.

"Just lay off, o.k.? I'm not stupid. If I think for one minute that Kate is meeting with me as a blabber-mouth tabloid reporter, I promise you I will end the date and never talk to her again. I really need to return my mother's phone messages. I'm sure she's freaking out because I haven't called her back in two days. You know how she is. Wish me luck," Angela said. After Angela left, Jason sat down and realized he had a raging hard-on. He went up to his bedroom and relieved himself, the entire time thinking about making love to Angela. As he lay in bed, he thought, *I can get any woman in Hollywood. Why did I have to fall in love with my wife?*

"You know, Angela, it wouldn't hurt to call your family back. Mary and Joe said they've left messages for you since you lost the Oscar," Angela's mother, Teresa, said. Teresa was great for nagging and being dramatic. But why did she have to say, "*Since you lost the Oscar*"? Angela knew she didn't win. She certainly didn't need good ole mom reminding her of this fact. Teresa was right about Angela's brother Joe and sister Mary. They had left several messages of condolences over her loss, pleading for her to return their calls. Angela didn't feel like talking to anyone. She didn't want to burden her sister or brother with her situational depression.

"All right mom. I'll call as soon as I get off the phone with you," Angela assured her mother. Then she remembered her mom mentioning something a week ago about coming to visit for Memorial Day weekend. Her parents always made a big deal out of holidays. Whether it was for July 4th, Labor Day weekend, Thanksgiving, or Christmas, her parents insisted on the family getting together. They loved coordinating holiday get-togethers.

"Were you and dad still planning on coming out to visit?" Her parents stayed with her two or three weeks out of the year, regardless if it was a holiday or not. Her father would golf, while her mother would hang around the house, annoying Angela, reminding her of what she does wrong. Her mother always pointed out Angela's faults. In high school, she'd ask, "Why'd you get a B. Why didn't you get an A?" She'd be quick to point out her shortcomings rather than console her. One time, Angela didn't get the lead in the school, so Teresa pointed out, "You didn't get the lead for the school play because your voice is too squeaky. You need to work on that" Or, when Angela decided to move to New York to pursue her dream of acting, her mother said, "Be prepared to fail. You're just one of thousands of actresses. You really need to finish college first so you'll have something to fall back on when the acting thing doesn't work out." When Angela got her first movie role and moved to the west coast, Teresa said, "Angela, I just can't see you making it in Hollywood. Why don't you find a nice guy to marry and settle down like your sister Mary."

Angela's former psychologist advised her to work on setting boundaries with her parents. After all, she was a grown up now and was capable of making choices of what she would and would not tolerate.

However, as annoying and judgmental as her mother was, that didn't keep Angela from loving her and wanting to spend some amount of time with her. She loved her family. They kept her grounded. Angela's family was the only semblance of normalcy left in her life. Hollywood was filled with so much drama and chaos. It was like living on another planet. Sometimes she liked the lifestyle of being a famous actress and other times hated it.

"Yes. The last week of May. Memorial Day week. I found a great deal on airfare on the Internet. Two roundtrip tickets for only $275.00 a person. Isn't that a great deal?" Teresa was very proud of the discount she uncovered, something Angela found quite amusing. Her mother and father still acted as though money were tight, though Angela deposited two million dollars into their bank account two years ago. Teresa and

Fred tried to return the money, but Angela wouldn't have it. Although her parents never mentioned the transaction again, they continued to spend their money frugally. It drove Angela crazy. She wanted them to travel and live it up.

"That's great mom. I can't wait. Email your itinerary. I'm gonna have to let you go now. I'll see if Mary's home," Angela said. She was glad she had an excuse to get off the phone. Angela wasn't in the mood to listen to her mother. It was that time in the conversation when she'd start going into great detail about her and her father's ailments. Her parents always had some health problem going on to complain about that was usually not life-threatening. Angela's mom always had a stomach problem, while her father always had some sort of cold or flu.

"Ok. Say hello to Jason for us."

"Ok. Bye mom. Love you."

"Love you, too, dear."

She was grateful that her mother didn't try to get in the "when are you and Jason going to give me some grandkids" speech. Angela was the only sibling left to provide her with a grandchild. Her sister Mary had two kids. Her mother had given up hope of a grandchild from her brother, Joe, since he was gay and wasn't planning on adopting a child with his gay lover, Enriquo, anytime soon.

Angela would love to have kids. She even thought of adopting, but Jason freaked out during that conversation. Angela assured Jason she fully intended on being a single parent. It had nothing to do with him. However, since Jason lived in the same house, he put his foot down and refused to continue the conversation. She compromised that as long as she had this marriage deal with Jason, she would put off adopting a child. It wouldn't be fair to the child to have this fake marriage thing going on and a fake dad who resented him or her. Till then, she often fantasized of the day they'd divorce, which they both agreed would happen in two or three years. "Angela Moore and Jason Saunders Divorce!" would be plastered on every tabloid cover. Their power couple union would come to an end and both would be as powerful as ever before, with all of their fans' sympathy and encouragement.

Angela dialed her sister Mary's house. After the call went to voice mail, Angela said, "Hey Mary. I'm sorry I didn't call you back. I've been a bit depressed. I've been keeping to myself, isolating…" Angela was notorious for leaving long, detailed voice messages. This time, Mary picked up before she could continue on with her message.

"Sorry. I was trying to find a pencil sharpener that works. We're doing homework and not one of the three pencil sharpeners I have actually sharpen a pencil. Anyhow, I'm so glad you called. I was worried about you. Why didn't you call me back?" Mary was the most genuine person Angela knew. She was a great mother, daughter, sister, and, up until the demise of her husband, a great wife. Mary and Angela looked nothing alike. Mary was blonde and very tall, almost six feet tall without heels on.

Mary was drop-dead gorgeous. She was a very successful model when she met her late husband, Robert, an investment banker. After marrying Robert, she stopped modeling to raise her family. Tragically, Robert died in a small aircraft accident when his company's private jet crashed on a routine run from New York City to Boston. It had been three years, but for Mary it was like it happened yesterday. She tried to date, but it never felt right for her. Angela convinced Mary to move out to California from New York six months after the accident. Mary chose a nice suburb in Orange County to raise her children so they would be close to Aunt Angela.

Angela adored her niece and nephew. Her favorite was Brian, her sister Mary's 8 year old son. Brian had been diagnosed with Asperger's Syndrome, a high functioning form of autism, when he was four.

"I know. I wanted to be alone. I'm sorry," Angela said in a soft, guilt-ridden voice.

"Well, I just want to make sure everything's ok with you. Do you want to come over? Or, maybe have us over to your place?" Mary asked. Angela could hear the kids in the background, vying for Mary's attention. Mary also had a six year old daughter, Vanessa.

"Sure, let's get together this weekend. I'll come over to your place. By the way, Mom and dad are coming out the end of May. Have you talked to Joe recently?" Angela asked.

"I know, mom already told me about it. Joe's freaking out over you not calling him back. He's such a drama queen. Please call him after we hang up. Okay?"

"Yes I promise. I miss the kids. I can't wait to see Vanessa and Brian this weekend," Angela said. Angela agreed to baby sit for her niece and nephew so her sister could go on a date. Angela planned a blind date for her sister with a really nice screenwriter she knew.

"Brian's been talking about you non-stop. He said he was going to beat up those Academy Award idiots for not giving you the award." Mary cupped the phone with her hand and said to the kids, "Yes it's Aunt Angela. Ok. Ok." She uncupped her hand and said into the receiver, "The kids want to say hi."

"Sure, put them on." Angela felt happiness she hadn't felt in a very long time. Her family was coming to visit and she had a date with Kate that evening.

Mary's voice was angelic. Her esses made a slight shrilling sound, like a Christmas bell, when she said them. Hearing Mary's voice on the other end of the phone was like an instant Valium for Angela. Why hadn't she called her earlier? It would have made her feel so much better. Angela missed her sister. Mary and her brother Joe were the only people in her family who knew she was a lesbian and that Jason wasn't exactly her husband.

Mary completely disagreed with Angela and Jason's union. She believed that marriage was something special for two people who are in love. Plus, Mary wanted her little sister to be happy, not living the lie she had created out of her fear of being exposed.

"Aunt Angela. I read all of the Tin Tin books you sent me. They're cool." It was Brian. Angela sent him the complete volume of books about Tin Tin the reporter and Snowy the dog, which was a popular comic strip in Europe.

"I knew you'd like them. Hey, I'm coming over to visit on Saturday. What do you think of that?"

"Awesome. Can you bring the dogs?"

"Maybe another time. You can see them when you come to visit me. How come you haven't sent me any emails lately?" Angela asked. Brian occasionally sent Angela emails with pictures he'd taken with the digital camera she gave him for his birthday last year. Some of the pictures he sent were of his dog yawning, his unsuspecting babysitter sitting on the toilet, and pictures of himself that he'd take by holding the camera at arm's length.

"Mom said I can't go on the computer till next week. I'm grounded," Brian said in a sad tone. "My room was a mess and I forgot to clean it." Brian went on to tell Angela about his teacher, Tin Tin's adventures, and about how he was going to be in a school play.

It was amazing how well Brian was doing. Just last year, Angela offered to pay to send him to a private school. The other students were teasing him at public school and the teachers complained that he was uncontrollable, due to his social disability. Mary tried to work with the school's special education department so that Brian could receive services for his disability and still be included with his peers. When the school refused to provide the services Mary requested, Angela made an appearance at a special education committee meeting to advocate for Brian. Angela threatened to sue the school for educational neglect. Since then, Brian has been receiving the special education services he deserved, which include a full-time classroom aide.

"Brian, let me say hello to your sister. I'll see you soon. I love you honey." Angela would love to listen to him all day, but wanted to say hello to her niece and then start getting ready for her date with Kate.

After she spoke with Vanessa, she called to reserve a private table at her favorite Italian restaurant on Melrose Avenue in Hollywood. Angela had been obsessing over whether this "date" was actually going to happen. Her tendency to think catastrophically had her convinced she was going to be stood up by Kate. To ease her mind, she called Kate to confirm they were still meeting.

CHAPTER 13

"HI KATE," ANGELA said, cradling the phone between her shoulder and ear as she painted her toenails.

It was three hours until they were to meet and Kate was praying that Angela wasn't backing out. "We're still on, right?" Kate asked.

"Oh, yeah, of course. I just wanted to let you know where we're going. It's an Italian restaurant on Melrose Avenue. They have a private dining room in the back for celebs. We can get away with dressing casual—jeans, t-shirt, or something."

Thank God, Kate thought. *She wasn't canceling.* "Sounds great. I might leave early because of traffic, so I could on time or a little early. Is that o.k.?"

"Sure. That's fine." Angela had been ready for two hours, primping and revisiting the bathroom vanity mirror several times. She couldn't believe how nervous she felt. She was frightened by the way she felt. She hadn't been this excited over someone since Kristan. Perhaps Kate felt the same way? Or was their meeting simply an excuse for Kate to delve into Angela's life? Angela hated the thought that Kate may be meeting with her for the sole purpose of extracting fodder for a gossip column.

"I still have to take a shower, but it doesn't take me long to get ready. Depending upon traffic, I should be able to get there in about two and a half hours." Kate would primp in the car. She didn't want Marisol to know she was going out on a date. Marisol's depression seemed to be lifting, but to be on the safe side, Kate asked her friend Jamie to drop by and sit with Marisol while she was gone.

"Ok. See ya then. Bye."

"Bye."

"Who was that?" Marisol said as she reached into the refrigerator for a bottle of water, surprising Kate.

"Oh, just one of the producers I'm meeting with tonight." Kate hated lying to her, but it was for her own good.

"That's right. You'll be leaving for that soon, huh? I was thinking about going back home. I've been feeling better," Marisol said, prior to sipping from a bottle of Evian.

"No. I like having you here. It's been really good for me, too. Please don't go." Kate walked over to the kitchen counter to set the phone in its cradle. She definitely didn't want Marisol going home yet. She was still concerned about her mental state. Marisol had just finished an hour long crying session ten minutes earlier. "Just stay tonight and then we'll talk tomorrow morning. You'll have me all to yourself the rest of the week. Ok?"

"Well." Marisol looked up at the ceiling, noticing a tiny spider. "I suppose. I don't really feel like going anywhere." Marisol pointed to the spider scurrying across the ceiling. "I hate spiders, you know. Could you get that spider before you hop in the shower? It's freakin' me out."

"It's just a tiny spider."

"Look, I can't stay here knowing there's a spider running around. I don't mean to be a primadonna, but it's my only phobia."

"O.k. Hand me a paper towel," Kate requested.

Marisol ripped a section of paper towel from its roll and

handed it to Kate, who was now standing on a kitchen stool. "Here. Be careful," Marisol said as she handed the paper towel to Kate.

Kate reached up and, using the paper towel, pinched the spider between her fingers, careful not to kill it. Kate stepped off the stool, opened the back door, and threw the spider outside.

"Happy? Now, I've got to get ready," Kate said as she walked passed Marisol, into the bathroom. *I need to get ready for my secret dinner date. Someday, Marisol, I'll tell you all about it.*

A half-hour later, the doorbell rang. "Can you get the door Marisol?" Kate shouted from the bathroom.

"Yeah. Yeah. I'm coming," Marisol muttered, clashing in a purple terry cloth bathrobe and leopard print slippers.

It was Kate's friend, Jamie. Kate and Jamie, a fellow photographer, met on an assignment in Chile ten years prior. They kept in touch and occasionally met for lunch to compare notes on their latest photojournalist assignments. Jamie had many more interesting stories to tell than Kate. Jamie traveled the world on a full-time basis covering human rights stories. A week ago she was in Sudan photograph-ing victims of torture. Two months before that she was in Algeria photographing refugees. Kate often worried about her friend's involvement in these volatile countries. Jamie's assignments were risky, in some cases, life-threatening. Kate was relieved when Jamie called to tell her she was taking six months off from fieldwork to rest and regroup, maybe even write a book about her experiences.

Kate could hear the two women talking and came out of the bathroom. She almost didn't recognize Jamie. She had cut her thick, dark brown, down-to-her-ass hair. She looked like an entirely different person with short hair. Sure enough, it was indeed Jamie, smiling her big beautiful, bright white smile. Kate had always thought Jamie should do one of those Got Milk? commercials. She had perfect, white teeth. They were all hers-no veneers. Jamie was the type of person who made you smile the minute you saw her smile. She had a sweet demeanor and exuded a happy aura.

"Oh, shit. I forgot you were stopping by Jamie," Kate fibbed.

Jamie promised Kate she would play along and stay with Marisol until Kate came back from her "meeting". Like Marisol, Jamie thought Kate was going to a production meeting. Although Jamie and Marisol had never met, Kate thought Jamie could offer some advice and moral support to Marisol, since Jamie's girlfriend of eight years ran off with a stripper a year ago.

"Where are you off to?" Jamie asked, pretending to be surprised that Kate was leaving.

"Oh, I have this ridiculous meeting about this big job coming up. It's a huge production thing. Why don't you stay and hang out with Marisol? If that's ok with you Marisol?" Kate knew Marisol wouldn't be rude and say "no".

"Of course. Why would I mind?" Marisol didn't seem to care. Kate's plan was working. *I'm a genius*, she thought. *Jamie will occupy Marisol and keep her mind off Victoria while I spend the evening with Angela.*

"I'd love to get to know you better, Marisol. I've known you from listening to Kate for years now and can't believe we never met in person before," Jamie said.

"It *is* amazing we haven't met before. I've heard so much about you too," Marisol added.

"Good. You two can get to know each other. I have to run. I wish I could stay. I'll see you later." Kate grabbed a sweater from the hallway closet and as she was running out the door, yelled back, "Love your hair Jamie. You finally look like the bull dyke you truly are. It's about time."

She could hear Jamie yelling back, "I'll take that as a complement."

Kate felt relieved. She was glad *that* part of the evening was settled.

CHAPTER 14

SHIT. I FORGOT *to call Joe.* Angela remembered as she grabbed an apple from the fruit basket in the kitchen. She had to call him. Mary was right. He *was* a drama queen, literally.

Joseph Moore was the oldest child of Fred and Teresa Moore. He had been the stereotypical football and basketball hero in high school and vied for the Heissman trophy while at Penn State. He was the son every mother and father dreamed of having. Angela adored growing up with her big brother. She thought he was the best person in the whole world.

Angela and Joe were very close. She knew a side of Joe no one else knew about. Joe loved to play dress-up in girl's clothes. Angela was the only person Joe entrusted with his secret. So it was odd for Angela to sit there at a football game, rooting for her rugged, defensive back brother, when the night before he was asking her to buy him queen size pantyhose the next time she was at the mall.

Joe met his wife, Melissa, while they were students at Penn State and married after graduation. While sharing a dance at Joe's wedding reception, Angela asked him if Melissa knew about his dress-up games.

"Don't ever bring that up again, Angela. I've put that life behind me," Joe said, tersely.

"So Melissa has no clue?" Angela asked.

"Of course not, Angela. She would never understand."

"But that's you, Joe. How can you change just like that?" Angela asked.

"I'm married now. I have to do things differently."

Joe got a job in New York City as a sales rep for a large medical supply company. Everything seemed picture-perfect. Joe was quickly promoted to Vice President of Sales, netting over $300,000 a year plus bonuses. After three years of living in Manhattan, Joe and Melissa purchased a beautiful home in suburban Connecticut. Joe didn't want to leave the city, but Melissa convinced him it'd be best for raising children.

A month after Joe and Melissa moved into their dream home, Joe showed up unexpectedly at the little studio apartment Angela shared with Julia.

"I can't do it anymore Angela. I'm living a lie. All I can think about is dressing up in drag and being with men. I thought I could do it. I went to church and prayed. I'm trying so hard for mom and dad's sake." Joe was clearly tortured by his dilemma.

"Then don't live a lie. Be the person you want to be, Joe." Angela thought back to that day as she picked up the phone to call Joe.

"I know. I have to leave Melissa. I've been leading a double life with other men, hanging out in drag and gay bars. I hate my job, too. I feel like such a phony." Joe was crying.

"That's because you *are* a phony," Angela said matter-of-factly, rubbing her hand across Joe's back to comfort him. "You need to be true to yourself. Forget about mom and dad. Of course they would never understand you being gay, dressing up in gowns and stiletto heels. Now's as good a time as any Joe. Follow your heart. Melissa deserves to know the truth so she can get on with her life."

"Can you imagine both of us coming out at the same time to mom and dad? It would kill them both."

"Yeah. Well, what they don't know won't hurt them."

Joe followed her advice. He divorced Melissa and used a substantial amount of money he'd secretly been setting aside to open a drag-themed restaurant in Greenwich Village. He had been very wise about hiding money from Melissa. Over the years, he deposited all of his bonuses with a friend who was president of a bank in the Cayman Islands. This secret behavior paid off. Melissa was very spiteful during the divorce proceedings. She took control of every asset and fought him tooth and nail for every last penny. To get on with his life, he signed over their dream home to her.

Joe had no choice but to tell his parents the truth about the reason for his divorce from Melissa. If he didn't tell them, Melissa promised she would. His parents expressed their disappointment to Joe when he told them the truth about his lifestyle. They reminded him that God didn't approve of homosexuality and that he would be going to hell. They refused to talk to him for a year. Only after Angela intervened, did they gradually come around. Today they tolerate Joe's life and his partner, but don't approve of it.

Seeing her parent's reaction to Joe's coming out admission scared the shit out of Angela. She lived her entire life seeking the approval of her parents. She couldn't imagine telling them, "Mom, Dad, I'm gay."

At least Joe was happy being out and living with his partner.

Angela dialed her brother's restaurant.

"Lena's. Can I help you?" the host answered.

"Is Joe Moore there? This is his sister Angela."

"Angie baby. It's me, Scott. I mean, Flo. 'Member me? I

can't believe you didn't get that Oscar, darling. Such a travesty. You definitely should've won over that douche bag bitch."

"That's nice, Flo. Is he there? I'm kind of in a hurry," Angela lied.

"Sure. You take care honey."

"Candy.....Oh, Candy," Angela could hear Flo yelling. Candy Cane was Joe's drag name.

"My baby girl Angela. Where have you been? I've been sick to death," Joe picked up another line as Flo hung up.

"I'm sorry Joe. I've been depressed and feeling sorry for myself. Forgive me?"

"I can't stay mad at you. You're the reason for my happiness," Joe said.

"You are so dramatic. How is it that *I* became the actor in the family?"

"*I'm* a performer too. It's just like acting. So I haven't been nominated for an award. *Some* people think I should be, you know."

"I know." Angela decided to tell Joe about Kate. "I have to tell you a secret, Joe."

"Please. Please. Do tell," Joe said with excitement.

"I've got a huge crush on this woman. We're going out to eat in an hour."

"'Bout time sunshine. Who is she?"

"She's a photographer. I'm crazy about her. She doesn't know, though. At least, I don't think she suspects. Actually, I'm not entirely positive she's into women," Angela gushed.

"Well, you better get moving. Life's too short. When 'er you going to dump that beefcake husband of yours and stop the charades?"

"You know, that's exactly why I didn't tell Mary. She'd say something like that, but now you?"

"To thine own self be true, baby. To thine own self be

true." Angela could practically see him shaking his head in disgust on the other end.

"All right, Joe. It's just a dinner date. Let's do one thing at a time."

"I've said enough. I just want you to be happy—as happy as I am."

"I do too."

CHAPTER 15

KATE FELT A sense of relief once she got behind the wheel of her truck and began her journey to Angela's house. Finally, she was able to do something for herself, something enjoyable. Taking care of Marisol was beginning to wear on her. There was also the matter of her ex, Tami. Kate was highly annoyed by Tami's inability to let go of their relationship.

That morning, Kate decided she had to do something about Tami's incessant phone calls and emails. She snuck away from Marisol to the back patio, phone in hand. She couldn't continue to ignore Tami's creepy, stalker-like behavior any longer. Things definitely weren't working out the way Kate had planned or hoped. She knew breaking up with Tami would be difficult and expected some resistance from her. Kate figured it would be uncomfortable for both of them at first, but eventually Tami would move on and get over it. Kate had assumed this is how it would go, a little drama and crying in the beginning, and then she'd never see or hear from Tami again. Boy, was she wrong.

For a brief moment, Kate thought about Tami's good side and that maybe things weren't *that* bad after all. Tami obviously loved her. Was it so bad to be madly, insanely, in love with someone? Holding her phone, readying to push the "send" button, Kate paused for a moment to reflect on why she broke up with Tami. *Did I do the right thing by breaking up with Tami? I was head over heels crazy about her in the beginning.*

Tami was gorgeous. She had beautiful, stick-straight long highlighted blonde hair, a kick-ass body, nice tan, and a beautiful, girlish face with deep aqua-blue eyes. Tami was intelligent, had a great sense of humor and possessed a boatload of money. Tami treated Kate to last-minute trips to Mexico, the Caribbean and Hawaii.

Sex was incredible. There wasn't anything Tami wouldn't do to ensure that Kate was satisfied. She was an incredibly giving and ambitious lover. Tami helped Kate with her career and bought her a four-carat diamond encrusted eternity band as a symbol of her commitment and devotion. Tami also gave up drinking and drugs for Kate. Tami was a party animal when they first started dating. Eventually, Kate told her that if she didn't get a handle on her addictions, it would be over. Tami, to the surprise of Kate, swiftly quit everything, including smoking, cold turkey.

Kate suddenly realized where her mind had drifted and couldn't believe she was second-guessing herself. She quickly reminded herself that Tami was, well, a fucking nutcase. Kate didn't like her, let alone love her anymore. Tami came from enormous wealth and was a spoiled rotten brat. Though she was incredibly beautiful, funny, and all of those other wonderful things, she was horribly insecure and needy.

Kate pressed the send button and waited for Tami to answer.

"Kate. Finally," Tami said as she read Kate's name and phone number on her cell phone's caller id. "Where have you been? Didn't you get my messages?" Tami asked.

"Uh, yeah," Kate responded sarcastically. "Of course I did. That's why I'm calling you. We need to have a conversation about your phone calls and emails. You need to stop calling and emailing me. It's over, Tami," Kate firmly ordered. Kate felt a huge weight being lifted from her chest.

"Kate, I'm sorry I've called so much. I can't help it. I love you. How can you just turn your feelings off like that?" Tami asked with desperation in her voice.

"We went out for five months, not five years. It's not like we were married. You obviously wanted more than I could give you. And, yes, I did have strong feelings for you. But you have a lot of issues you need to work on. I just can't be in a relationship with someone who's as jealous as you are and doesn't trust or believe me," Kate said.

Tami began to cry. "I'm sorry. I swear to you I'll change. I'll go see a therapist like you suggested. I just can't lose you Kate."

Kate felt the weight return to her chest. This wasn't going as well as she'd hoped. "Tami, it's over. How many times do I have to tell you? Don't contact me anymore. I hate to do this, but I'm telling you right now that if you continue to contact me, I will have to get a restraining order against you. It isn't normal to call someone twenty times within a thirty-six hour period or to email them over a dozen times. We are not a couple anymore. Do you understand how out of line it is to be acting this way?" Kate wanted to hang up the phone, as she was now furious, but allowed Tami a response.

"Fine. I'll leave you alone if that's what you really want. But you will regret this Kate. No one will love you like I do." Tami's tone frightened Kate.

"Don't you dare threaten me. Let it go. O.k.?" Kate demanded.

"O.k.," Tami muttered.

"Bye, Tami."

"Bye."

Kate had a feeling this wouldn't be the end of this discussion. The Tami she knew was an unstable, unpredictable woman.

Tami Montgomery felt a ball of fire burning in her stomach after their conversation ended. *How dare she break up with me and refuse to see me. She is obviously out of her mind. We belong together. After all I did for her. I got her photo gigs she would've only dreamed of if it wasn't for me. And, the vacations I brought her on.* She went to the bathroom to relieve her full bladder. *That ungrateful bitch! Why doesn't she love me? Why?* Sobbing uncontrollably, she arose from the toilet and threw the phone as hard as she could at the bathroom mirror, shattering it.

Tami hated not getting her way. Her father, Barry, was one of the richest, most powerful and successful television producers in Hollywood. Though he despised his daughter's lifestyle, the parties and, of course, the women, she was still daddy's little girl. Tami was Barry's only daughter. Whatever Tami wanted Tami got. Life for the Montgomery family was lavish and easy. They owned homes in Beverly Hills, New York, Miami, and Colorado. Their family was considered by most to be Hollywood royalty. Tami never worked a day in her life and basically partied for a living. Her father provided her with anything and everything she wanted. Thanks to daddy's money, Tami had the best body, face, and hair money could buy. It drove men crazy when Tami rejected their advances.

She promised to remain in the closet—for daddy. Regardless, everyone who was anyone in Hollywood knew she was a lesbian. Being beautiful and rich definitely had its advantages. Tami always got the women she wanted and would swiftly dump them as soon as she grew tired of them. She definitely wore the pants in her relationships.

Kate was different. For the first time in her life, Tami had no control over someone. There was nothing daddy's money could buy to keep Kate. Tami used her father's connections to get Kate incredible photo assignments, most recently the Angela Moore spread for Vanity Fair. She hadn't liked the fact that Kate worried so much about money. Tami would do anything to make sure Kate was happy.

Tami left the bathroom in disarray. She'd have her housekeeper clean it up. She paced, contemplating what to do next. She refused to accept Kate's decision to break up. Tami wanted Kate back and would do anything to make it happen. *I know what I'll do. I'll call Paul.* She thought. She arose from the couch to locate the cordless phone, which she needed to find because her cell phone was destroyed.

"Where is that fucking phone?" she screamed aloud after an unsuccessful search of the living room and kitchen. She pressed the pager button on the phone's base and found it next to the hot tub in her master suite.

She dialed Paul, her driver and master of Tami's evil deeds.

"Hi Paul. I need you to get off your ass and do something for me. And, you gotta keep this between you and me. Got it?" Tami firmly requested.

"Whatever Tami. What's up?" Paul replied, still half-asleep in one of the Montgomery's guest cottages. He had been Tami's driver for two years now and nothing surprised him when it came to Tami. She was a party girl when he first started working for her. He'd drive her to and from all of the L.A. lesbian hot spots. She'd pick up different women all the time. He loved getting paid to watch her make out and in some cases have full-blown sex with her one-night stands in the back of the limo. In all this time, she never knew he could see through the limo's partition glass, which had been tinted incorrectly so he could watch her having sex. He'd secretly pleasure himself while he drove her around, peeking into the partition.

Tami drank like a fish, smoked tons of pot, and cocaine was her preferred nightcap. Paul had an endless supply of drugs. He'd score drugs for Tami and skim some for himself.

All that changed the night she met Kate Ashford. Paul knew this woman was different. Tami stopped going out, preferring to hang in at either Kate's house or hers. It was a very boring time for Paul. No excitement and, worst of all, no drugs. Maybe this phone call would change that.

"I need you to follow someone," Tami said.

"Follow *who?*" Paul asked.

"Kate," Tami said.

"What *for?*" Paul asked, in a hostile tone.

Tami wasn't in the mood for his surliness. "It doesn't matter. Just go to her house today and let me know if she goes anywhere. Call me as soon as you know anything."

"Know *what? What* am I supposed to know?" Paul had no clue what Tami was up to.

"Just let me know who comes and goes, where she goes. It's not that difficult, Paul." Tami raised her voice, angry and losing her patience. She wondered why she kept him around. He could be such an idiot at times. "You've been overpaid too long for too little work in return. Now's your turn to actually work for all that money my father pays you. If you can't handle it, I'll certainly find someone who can," Tami ordered.

"All right. All right. Jeezuz, don't flip out. You want me to call you every hour or something?" Paul didn't want to lose this gravy train. Tami was right. He *was* overpaid. He'd never get another gig as good as this one.

"Call me on my cell when shit happens. Otherwise, don't bother me," Tami said before hanging the phone up without saying "good-bye".

Paul got up out of bed and grabbed a pair of jeans draped

over a nightstand. After buttoning his jeans, he sat back onto the bed and thought about whether Tami had finally lost her mind. She was so desperate that she was now resorting to stalking. He would be her stalker by proxy. He didn't feel right about doing this. It was illegal. That's all he needed was to get arrested for stalking. He'd never get another job in Hollywood again. It would actually be more accepting to get arrested for buying drugs, than to get caught stalking someone. Paul knew he had to do whatever Tami requested of him. He couldn't afford to lose this job. He had the perfect set-up with the Montgomery's.

He contemplated calling Tami back to try and reason with her. However, he knew her stubborn personality wouldn't budge. Instead, he grabbed his keys off the dresser and made his way out the door to Kate's house.

CHAPTER 16

ANGELA WAS GETTING more excited and nervous by the minute. Kate would be arriving in an hour and they'd be spending the evening together. Angela wasn't sure how she would proceed with the evening, whether she would open up to Kate with confidence or not. Would she reveal her attraction to Kate? Would she try to kiss her? Or would the entire evening be a front for a platonic friendship? Angela didn't want to settle for the latter. She wished she could be "normal", not having to worry about being dishonest and putting on a front. After playing out the different scenarios in her mind that morning, Angela decided she'd play it by ear, feel the situation out, no sense dwelling on it.

While she waited for Kate to arrive, Angela resolved to make peace with Jason. She strolled into the media room where he was watching a violent war movie on their enormous flat screen television.

"Hey Jason. How do I look?" Angela had to practically scream over the huge bombs and machine guns emanating from the media room's elaborate surround sound system. Angela painstakingly chose a Roberto Cavalli jeans, Prada t-shirt, and Chanel suede jacket ensemble. After a dozen clothing changes, she finally settled on the outfit she was now wearing. She chose to wear very little makeup, since there was no sign of acne left from her horrible breakout a few days prior. Her dermatologist's team of aestheticians worked miracles on her skin after just one visit.

Angela didn't feel like dealing with her long hair, so she tied it back in a ponytail. She wanted to look attractive, but not as though she was going to a special event or on an official date.

"You look fine," Jason responded, barely managing a glimpse of her, continuing to fixate on the television. He knew if he turned his attention to her he'd feel that jealous pang and would be caught in her spell.

"What? I can't hear you," Angela shouted. "Turn that down."

Jason turned the movie's volume down a few notches. "I said you look fine." Jason continued to avoid looking at her.

"You didn't even look at me, dummy," Angela protested.

"Well I'm into this movie," he snapped.

"Well I'll leave you to your precious movie then," Angela said, clearly showing her annoyance with him. Angela was growing concerned for Jason. She'd never witnessed him so moody in all the time she'd known him. *Maybe he was on drugs.* She thought. *Or having a mid-life crisis already?*

She left the room and made her way to the front sitting area by the foyer to wait for Kate's arrival and begin reading a trashy novel she ordered from a lesbian book club she belonged to under the name "Ruth Miller".

"She's heading towards your house Tami." Paul called to inform Tami of Kate's whereabouts.

Maybe she's coming to see me. Maybe she had second thoughts. I knew she'd come to her senses. Tami thought.

"Keep following her and call me back." Tami felt optimistic. Kate never had a reason to go to Beverly Hills in the evening other than to visit her.

Jason hated the way he felt. He was depressed and lovesick like a little teenage boy. It was awful. He fell in love with his wife. He was in love with a woman who was at that very moment waiting for her date with another woman. He thought he'd try one more time to get her to not go out with Kate. He paused the movie he was watching, and entered the room where Angela was, reading a book and waiting for her date, in the front room by the foyer.

"Hi Angie. You sure you don't want to stay in with me and watch a movie, eat popcorn and chocolate?" Jason asked.

"Of course I'm not going to." Angela lowered the book she was reading and gave Jason an "are you out of your mind" look. "Sorry Jason. You know I'm looking forward to this. Plus, you *must* have some hot babe you could fuck tonight? Right?" Angela insinuated, raising her eyebrows.

"As a matter of fact I don't," Jason said sternly, obviously irritated by Angela's suggestion. "I told you I'm not doing that anymore. I'm going to be a faithful husband from now on."

"Faithful? What are you talking about? Did you hit your head or something? You've been acting so weird these past couple of days," Angela said, with a giggle.

Jason didn't find it amusing. He decided he had to tell her the truth about his feelings towards her. It was the only way she could understand his behavior and possibly cancel this ridiculous date she had planned. He decided right then and there that he would tell her he was in love with her. The huge weight of this secret he'd been carrying around would be lifted from him.

"Angela, I've gotta tell you something." Jason felt himself beginning to perspire. He was nervous. His mind began telling him things like, *"Don't tell her. She'll laugh at you."* or *"Don't tell her. She'll leave you."*

Angela was annoyed. She was at a great part in her book and Jason was interrupting her. "Just spit it out," she demanded.

All Jason could muster was, "Um, Uh."

"Are you on drugs or something? Is that it?" Angela asked, accusingly.

This angered Jason. "What! Of course not. I can't believe you'd think that. This has nothing to do with drugs. I'm..." Just as he felt the words about to empty from his mouth, Jason was interrupted by the intercom.

"Miss Moore. Your guest has arrived," the guard said.

"She's here!" Angela leapt from the chair. "Now tell me what you needed to tell me. She'll be here any second," Angela said excitedly. She placed a bookmark in her book and threw it onto the chair she'd been sitting in.

"I'm in...I'm in..." Jason didn't feel like the moment was right. Quickly, he thought of any possibly relevant words to replace his intended sentence completion, "love with you." Instead, he finished the sentence with, "A movie opposite Catherine Erickson. I know you despise her. I'm sorry."

"God, Jason. She threatened me in front of a dead person. I thought we both agreed we wouldn't work with her." Angela crinkled her nose, creating a look of disgust.

"I know. There wasn't anything my agent could do. The producers wanted both of us."

"Just don't let her bad mouth me and get away with it. Ok?"

"Yeah."

When Angela was still a struggling actress, new to Hollywood, Catherine Erickson, went out of her way to treat her costar, Angela, horribly. Catherine openly mocked and poked fun at Angela. She was downright nasty and cutthroat, a true diva. She treated her like crap and even went so far as to sabotage Angela from getting several great movie roles. Catherine was an aging star, rumored to be approaching fifty (nobody knew her real age), who saw Angela as a major threat.

Angela never forgot how cruel Catherine had been to her and took revenge by doing exactly what Catherine had done to her—refuse to work on the same set as her. As Angela grew to become a bigger star than Catherine, Angela's agents sideswiped Catherine out of four award-winning movies. When Catherine found out that Angela was secretly spearheading a campaign against her, her hate and jealousy grew even more.

Six months ago, Catherine displayed her worst behavior yet at the wake of a movie star who had overdosed on heroin. As Angela knelt, saying a prayer at the altar of the dead actor's coffin, Catherine slid in next to Angela.

How rude. She can't even wait until I get up before kneeling down. Angela was thinking.

Catherine leaned into Angela, and said, "If you ever try to blacklist me from a movie again, I promise you will be *very* sorry. I'm warning you. Don't ever cross me again."

"Shh," Angela uttered, placing her index finger to her mouth. "Do you have any respect for the dead, Catherine?" Angela could feel Catherine's negativity. It was a bit scary. Catherine clearly would go to any length to threaten her.

"I'm warning you Angela. Don't fuck with me." Catherine made her final threat, then quickly got up and stormed out of the funeral home.

"What the hell did *she* want?" Jason asked, as Angela arose, leaving the altar.

"Let's just say that if I fuck with her anymore, I'll be sorry," Angela said.

"She's such a loser. Don't listen to her. No, in fact, go ahead and fuck with her. What's she gonna do? Sick her plastic surgeon on you?" Jason laughed. Catherine was rumored to have had multiple plastic surgery operations and claimed to be 42, yet birth records claimed otherwise.

"Yeah, I *will* fuck with her," Angela held true to her word and kept Catherine out of her most recent movie, "Battleday", an upcoming summer release about an Iraqi war hero who returns home to work detail for the Secret Service and ends up risking his and his family's life to save the President from a terrorist plot. Angela plays the war hero's wife, who becomes a hero in her own right when she helps her husband unravel the terrorists' plot.

Catherine was livid when she found out she'd been forced out of the movie. She personally called Angela screaming, "This time you've gone too far, bitch. I promise you will regret this!"

"Of course I won't let her bad mouth you. It just feels strange since she threatened you and all," Jason said sincerely.

"Just because I can't work with her, doesn't mean you have to give up opportunities. Plus, if both of us forced her out of movies, I think she may actually go through with her threat and kill me once and for all. That's a place I don't think I want to go with her," Angela joked.

"I'm glad you're so understanding. I was worried you'd be mad. It's not like I'm a huge movie star like you. If it were my television show, I would get away with it, but not this movie. I think they'd can me first if I suggested they get rid of Catherine," Jason said.

"Yeah, they would. But why on earth should I be mad? There are plenty of actors and actresses I despise who I have to work with. Why would it be any different for you?" Angela wondered.

Jason felt defeated. He wished he had told her what he really wanted to say—that he was madly in love with her. Then the doorbell rang and Angela quickly ran to the door. She yelled, "Bye" to Jason. Before he could say anything, she slipped out the front door, quickly closing it behind her.

CHAPTER 17

RECOGNIZING HER FROM the day of the photo shoot, the guard waved Kate through the gates to Angela's house without asking for id. Kate's heart was beating fast as she pulled into the carport. Before exiting her truck, she reapplied her Burt's Bees Lip Therapy. It left her lips feeling tingly from the peppermint ingredients. She ran her fingers through her hair and adjusted the tube top she was wearing under her peasant blouse.

Immediately after Kate rang the doorbell, Angela opened the door and walked out, closing the door behind her. "Hi Kate," Angela said, while extending herself to give Kate a slight hug. Angela felt butterflies in her stomach. Kate looked beautiful and smelled even better, like rose petals and peppermint. Angela wanted to bring her up to her room and kiss her from head to toe. Angela was getting wet thinking about it.

"Hi," Kate said, stunned by Angela's sudden exit from the front door. Kate felt like she was a teenager on her first date. She felt so young and full of lust. It was like she was sixteen and with Eve all over again.

"I'd ask you in but Jason's got some of his perverted buddies in there who'll just leer at you and make obscene comments. Is it ok if we just go?" The truth was that none of

151

Jason's buddies were in the house. Angela didn't want Jason and Kate in the same room together, especially since he's been acting weird. She also feared he'd start offering up his opinions again about "being careful". Plus, she didn't want the object of her affection interacting with fake husband, anyway. Sometimes he really complicated her life way too much for her to want to continue with this charade.

"I'm a big girl. I can handle perverts. But, if you're ready, that's fine." *Angela seems awfully anxious about leaving so quickly. Maybe there was something else going on that Angela wasn't telling her?* Kate thought.

"Yes. Let's go," Angela said, hurriedly.

"You'll have to direct me to where we're going," Kate said as she approached her SUV.

"The restaurant isn't that far. Once you get to the end of the driveway, head toward Santa Monica Boulevard." Angela pulled the seat belt over her shoulder, locking it, and then shut the car door.

"Are you hungry? You really seem in a hurry." Kate turned the ignition of her car and reversed out of the carport.

"Yeah, I'm pretty hungry." The truth was that Angela wasn't very hungry. She was nervous and it scared the crap out of her. She felt like she had no control over her feelings, like a little girl with an out-of-control crush. "I've also been holed up in that house all week. It feels great to be out of there," Angela said.

"I know what you mean. I couldn't wait to get out of my house. I'm having Marisol stay with me. She is so depressed. I love her, but she really is a downer to be around right now," Kate said, in a melancholy tone.

"That's so nice of you to look after your friend. What exactly happened?"

"Her girlfriend, live-in lover, whatever you call her, left her for another woman."

"Yeah, that's what you said the other day. Didn't she have a clue it was coming to this?"

"Nothing she would acknowledge or believe. Friends tried to warn Marisol about Victoria and her cheating ways, but she just wouldn't listen. It's a blessing in disguise. She deserves much better. Marisol's a wonderful gal."

"How did you meet?"

"We were set up on a blind date and..."

Angela interrupted in obvious astonishment; "*You* were set up on a blind date with *her?*"

"Yeah, but it wasn't right. I mean, it didn't work out that way. We were meant to be friends." Kate hesitated, assessing Angela's facial expression. "What's the matter, you seem surprised?" Kate inquired.

Angela felt a tinge of envy towards this Marisol woman. "No. I kind of had a feeling you might be, well, you know."

"Gay? Is it that je ne sais quoi I have?" Kate laughed. It felt great to have her preference for women out in the open.

"It's just a vibe, nothing else." Angela didn't exactly feel ready to talk about this.

"Like gaydar?" Kate asked.

"I guess. You know, I'm very open-minded." Angela had no clue why she said that. It made no sense. The words came gushing out of her mouth.

"*Are* you?" Kate asked in a jokingly, seductive voice.

"I mean. Stuff like that doesn't matter."

"Well why would it?" Kate grew serious.

"Just that some people are so close minded is all. And I'm not."

"I suppose you're right.

"So you don't like Marisol in *that* way?"

"No, not in *that* way I don't."

"Are you dating anyone right now?" Angela asked.

"No. I was dating a woman for about five months. We

broke up a few weeks ago." Kate made a twirling gesture with her finger on the side of her head as to mean "crazy" or "cuckoo". "Let's just say she has a whole slew of issues she needs to work on and isn't exactly playing with a full deck of cards."

"I'm sorry." Angela didn't know how to respond. Kate was able to be open and honest, something Angela hoped she could be some day. Angela went from feeling hopeful to being concerned and cautious. *Maybe she's trying to entrap me into revealing that part of myself. Maybe she thinks if she is upfront and honest, then I will be too.* She thought. Though she was suspicious, a part of her ached to want to tell Kate that she too was a lesbian. She was attracted to Kate and it was torture not being able to express who she really was to her.

"Not me. I should've broken up with her two months ago when she started showing her true colors. She's obsessive, jealous and crazy. She won't stop calling me and I can't take much more of it," Kate said.

"I'll kick her ass for you. How's that sound? If she saw "The Eye of the Samurai", she'd think I have a black belt in karate. That'd scare her," Angela said. "Truth is a stunt double did almost all of the martial arts tricks. I don't have a fighting bone in my body."

Kate laughed, "Actually, you probably could kick her ass. She's only around 5'2" and 95 pounds." Kate came to a dead end three-way traffic light and turned west onto Santa Monica Boulevard. "Ok, now I need you to point me to where we're going."

Angela instructed Kate on which direction to drive. *So far so good. No paparazzi in sight.* Kate thought as she pulled into the restaurant's parking lot. For a minute there, she had the feeling someone was following them, but no camera flashes appeared as Angela and she walked from her car into a side entrance to the restaurant. Kate definitely didn't want to be on the receiving end of the camera. She lied to Marisol and Jamie about where she was that evening. They'd find out where she really was that evening and who she really was with if her picture was taken and splashed all over the tabloids.

Tami was devastated when Paul informed her that Kate's final destination in Beverly Hills wasn't Tami's house. Tami recognized the address Paul provided. It was Angela Moore's home. *Why was Kate visiting Angela Moore?* She wondered. Then it dawned on Tami that Kate must have been photographing her for an assignment. *Or maybe Angela is having an affair with my Kate!* Immediately, Tami was insanely jealous of the notion. *That stuck-up phony bitch. Everyone knows she's a closet lesbian and her husband is a huge perv. So help me God, if they are seeing each other, I'll see to it that it won't last.*

Tami and Angela had their own history together. They screwed around right before Angela got clean and sober. They met at a rave show catered to the gay community and quickly began sleeping together. They'd stay up all night snorting cocaine, popping ecstasy, and fucking every orifice of each other for hours. The intense and adventurous sex they shared was addicting and mind-blowing while they were drugged up, but both women had very sore pussies the following morning.

Tami thought about that period in her life. It was brief, but was some of the best, most intense sex she'd ever had. That was until Angela left for England to shoot a movie. When Angela returned from filming, she had that public incident where she was arrested and had to go to rehab. Angela cleaned up and got sober, something Tami wasn't ready to do. The next time their paths crossed was at a Hollywood party. Angela arrived with Jason and ignored Tami, acting as though they'd never met. Tami didn't give a shit. It wasn't like Angela was ever a great love of hers. Not like Kate. Tami was convinced Kate was her soul mate. Kate was the woman she was meant to spend the rest of her life with.

"Stay and see how long she visits. If she leaves, follow her," Tami ordered. She wished she were there with Paul, close to Kate, watching her every move.

"Gotcha Tami," Paul said. He felt like saying, "Tami, you've lost your mind. Move on. There's other fish in the sea. Get a fucking life." Instead, he dutifully followed Kate as she exited Angela's gated home.

CHAPTER 18

"ANGELA BELLA! I have not seen you in so long. You don't like my food no more?" Franco Valero, the owner of the popular Hollywood Italian restaurant, Franco's, greeted Angela. He extended his fat, stubby hands to welcome Angela with a hug.

Angela leaned in to hug Franco, but recoiled quickly, not giving the short middle-aged restaurateur ample time to fully embrace his body with hers. Franco was the type of man who took advantage of a simple hug and manipulated it into a vise grip. "Oh, please. I was here a month ago. You know I love your cooking." Angela winked. Franco previously confided to her that he couldn't cook for shit. His restaurant was a huge success due to his entrepreneurial talents, but the real cook was his cousin Ricardo, his master chef. Ricardo was a stellar chef, but lacked the social skills and business know-how to make it on his own as a restaurateur. Franco and Ricardo split the restaurant's profit 50/50, which made both men content.

"Who is your beautiful friend?" Franco asked.

"This is Kate Ashford. Kate's a photographer."

"Piacere." Franco gently took Kate's hand and placed a delicate kiss upon her knuckle.

"It is a pleasure to meet you as well." Kate withdrew her hand very slowly, as to not appear rude.

"Did you set up the usual room?" Angela asked anxiously. She wasn't in the mood for idle chitchat with Franco. She knew he wouldn't be such a kiss-ass if she were a regular, ordinary person instead of a movie star. If Kate had walked in off the street looking for a table, she'd have been turned away. Franco was a phony friend, like all the others in her Hollywood life.

Speaking of phony friends, Angela's agent, Larry, called her that morning. Although Angela didn't want to speak to him, Larry was persistent in mentioning a blockbuster movie role. He claimed it was the role of a lifetime—an opportunity she had better not pass up. Angela, angry that Larry didn't heed her warning to give her a break from working, told Larry not to bother, that she wasn't interested in any movie roles right now. She was firm in telling him not to call her for a couple of months. If he didn't respect this request, she'd start looking for new representation. Larry pleaded his case, which only incensed Angela more. She came very close to firing him at that moment, but decided not to act too hastily. In the end, Angela always won. After all, Larry worked for her, something Angela had to remind him of quite often.

"Of course. Only the best for Signora Angela. Right this way," Franco gushed.

Angela turned around to face Kate and rolled her eyes, revealing her annoyance with Franco. Kate placed her index finger to her lips and whispered, "Be nice."

"I'll try," she responded in a delicate whisper.

The two women followed Franco to a back room. As they walked through the rear part of the restaurant, patrons pointed and whispered, "Was that Angela Moore?" It felt like the longest walk through a restaurant Kate had ever taken. All the attention Angela attracted left Kate feeling exposed.

Franco unlocked the door to the private room and motioned for the two women to enter. The private room was bigger than Kate anticipated. The walls were decorated with oil paintings of Tuscany and lattice and real ivy. Fresh flower arrangements were situated throughout the room and candles provided a romantic atmosphere.

"Artero will be your waiter. Allow me to tell you the specials first." As Franco recited the specials, he politely pulled the chairs out for Angela and Kate.

Once Franco was finished, Angela dismissed him. "All of it sounds great. Can you have Artero bring some Pellegrino? I'll have a ginger ale, too. What about you Kate?"

"Pellegrino's fine."

"Anything you want. If Artero isn't treating you to your satisfaction, you come get me right away." Franco was very eager to please Angela.

"Thanks Franco." Franco left the room. Minutes later Artero, a tall handsome young Italian, brought their drinks with a basket of warm bread and butter pads.

"Would you like a few more minutes to look at the menu?" Artero asked.

"I know what I want," Angela responded.

"What do you recommend?" Kate inquired.

"The spinach fettucine dish with mushrooms is outstanding."

"How's the eggplant parmigiana?" Kate asked, ignoring Angela's suggestion.

"Oh, that's really good too. It's layered really thin like lasagna with lots of mozzarella," Angela said.

"I'll have that with the bleu cheese crumble house salad." Kate closed her menu and handed it to Artero.

"I'll have my usual, the spinach fettucine and mushroom

dish and a Caesar salad." Angela handed her menu to Artero and picked up the basket of bread, offering some to Kate.

Kate took a slice of bread and a pad of butter.

Angela, buttering her bread, said, "So tell me about the organizations you support." She felt a nervous high just being there with Kate. It was a struggle putting on the platonic façade.

"Well, there are so many worthwhile organizations out there. I brought information I printed off the Internet on two organizations in particular that I think are great." Kate reached into her oversized handmade raffia tote and retrieved several sheets of paper. She handed one of the pieces of paper to Angela. "This is one of my favorite organizations. It's the Africa Rainforest and River Conservation. Their mission is to put an end to the rampant animal poaching occurring in the Western and Central regions of Africa. Their other conservation issues are logging, mining, and political instability." Angela sat across from Kate, mesmerized by Kate's passion for this charity.

Kate continued, "All of these issues are interrelated. Logging is destroying the African rainforest. The logging crews hire poaching teams to kill the forest animals for meat. Tropical Africa is rich with mineral resources, but with political instability, the mining projects contribute to watershed degradation, road building, and eventually, poaching." Kate pointed to the contact information portion of the page and then handed more sheets of paper to Angela, adding, "All of their information is printed on there."

"Have you done any work for them?" Angela inquired, peering at the papers in her hand.

"Actually, I took those photographs," Kate said, with a wide smile. She pointed to the photos on the sheet of paper Angela was holding. The first photo was of an African tribe forced to abandon their tribal home by a logging company. The second photo showed several beautiful and exotic animals slaughtered and gutted. Both were heart-wrenching photographs. "I've actually done more pro-bono work for this next organization."

Kate held up the next organization's printed material for Angela to see. "This organization is the Wildlife Conservation Society. They are based at the Bronx Zoo, but oversee field projects to save wildlife and wetlands across the globe. I'd love to work for them some day. They're my mother's favorite organization. She donates her veterinary services to them when she can." Kate handed the set of stapled sheets to Angela, who was enjoying listening to Kate's enthusiasm.

"So that's where you get your love of animals? Your mom?" Angela asked.

"Yes. She's a great woman. We went through some rough times when my parents got divorced. I was very angry with her. But, we've gotten through it and are now very close."

"Where is she now?"

"Australia, saving koala bears. She's done so much in her life. She's even conducted field studies with Jane Goodall."

"She sounds like an amazing person," Angela remarked.

"She is," Kate said, handing the last set of papers to Angela. "This is a great organization, too. It's The African Conservation Foundation." Kate sighed.

"What's the matter? One minute you're all excited about these organizations, now you seem down about something," Angela pointed out, showing concern.

"Here I am showing you these organizations to contribute money to and what they really need is people's time—like my time. Instead, I am here, doing what I'm doing," Kate said, taking a sip of water.

"Well, you know there could be worse things you could be doing than having dinner with moi," Angela quipped.

"Actually, this dinner and spending time with you is probably the best thing I've done in a while. I just wish I devoted more time to doing good deeds." Angela knew then that Kate wasn't a spy for the tabloids. She was a real person who wanted to help the world.

"Well, for what it's worth. You're sort of saving me. I've been so bummed lately," Angela said.

"Since the Oscars?" Kate asked, showing concern.

"Well, that's when the depression hit me. But that isn't when it started. I've just realized a lot lately. I can totally understand what you meant when you said you'd rather be doing this type of work rather than the celebrity photographing bullshit. That's all I've been doing is making one movie after another. The good news is that I decided to take a two month hiatus from work. I might even extend it to six months if I have to."

"I think I'm due for a hiatus myself. Unfortunately, I can only afford to take a couple weeks off every six months."

"You know, I have to admit something to you. I wasn't completely sure of your intentions in meeting me tonight. You know, like if you were affiliated with a tabloid or something," Angela said.

"Did you actually think I made up that story about my true love being photojournalism?" Kate asked, appearing offended.

Angela felt the need to explain her suspicions. "Well, it seems everyone I know or meet in this town tells me what they think I want to hear or what will benefit them, instead of what is actually the God's honest truth. I didn't mean to offend you or anything. I just wasn't sure if you were one of those paparazzi jerks. Deep down, I now know you aren't like them." Angela hoped she hadn't insulted Kate.

"I guess I forgive you for thinking that of me," Kate said jokingly. "After all, you just met me. I completely understand why you'd be suspicious. But this is the last time I'm going to tell you this: I am not a member of the paparazzi. Besides, they're so slimy. I work alongside them and can't stand it! I feel like a dolphin in a sea of sharks." Kate and Angela were interrupted by Artero, who delivered their salads.

"I do too. I feel like almost everyone I associate myself with wants to bite off a piece of me. I just don't understand why you absolutely can not devote yourself to the photojournalism thing full time," Angela said.

"Money. I guess I've got a thing about money. I don't feel safe not having a certain amount to fall back on. In return, I'm suffering by working in a field I hate. I've promised myself I'll quit photographing celebrities entirely in two years. I'll have the nest egg I can survive on. I can't wait." Kate broke a piece of bread and handed it to Angela.

"I know what you mean about the money thing. I have millions and it never seems enough to quit and leave Hollywood. Well, it's not just the money. I enjoy acting and am so grateful I have a career that I love that also pays me an insane amount of money." Angela was happy the dinner was going so well.

"You are lucky. Plus you have a husband that makes a lot of money, too. I think because it's only me I can rely on, I'm even more obsessive about financial security."

Angela quickly responded, waving her finger and shaking her head back and forth. "Oh no. It's not what it appears, Jason and me. I mean, my money is completely mine and his is his." Angela so badly wanted to reveal the entire truth about her marriage.

"Why's that?" Kate wondered.

"That's just what we decided to do." Angela wanted to end this conversation. Luckily, Artero appeared with their main entrees.

"Anything else for you ladies?" Artero asked.

In unison, both women said "no" and proceeded to eat their meals.

As she twirled a piece of fettucine around her fork, Angela felt the sudden urge to blurt out that she too didn't date men, including her own husband. Instead, she asked, "So, have you always dated women?"

"Yes, actually, I have. Except when I experimented with boys when I was a teenager," Kate said matter-of-factly.

"Are you always so candid and honest about being a lesbian?"

"Yes. I came out to my family when I was seventeen and since then have had absolutely no reason to be anything but honest about my sexuality. It's just not an issue."

"You're lucky." Angela decided to play naïve. "Someone like me could never come out and be honest—if I were a lesbian," Angela said with an innocent smile.

"I don't believe that."

"What do you mean you don't believe it?"

"I mean I don't get that. Why go through life not being true to yourself."

This statement frustrated Angela. How could a celebrity photographer not understand her need to appear straight? "Of course you don't get it. You're not in the public eye like I am."

"You're right, I don't know what that's like. It must be hard having your life be an open book."

There was an uncomfortable moment of silence as the two women finished their dinners.

After she swallowed her last bite of fettucine, Angela broke the silence by saying, "My life is so complicated. You have no idea. I'm sick of it. I envy you so much. You know what you want and have a plan. You don't care what people think."

"No. You're right. I *don't* know what it's like to be you. It makes me grateful that I'm not in your position. I'm sorry for appearing insensitive." Kate wanted to console Angela with a hug. She was obviously frustrated with her very public life.

"You weren't being insensitive. I know it's hard for people to imagine rules we celebrities have to abide by. Most of them we make up ourselves. Being a celebrity can be a very paranoid existence."

"Hey, why don't we get out of here?" Kate suggested.

"Good idea," Angela agreed. "Artero!" Angela said loudly.

Artero appeared immediately. "Some coffee or dessert?"

"Not tonight. We're going to head out. Put this on my tab and say good-bye to Franco for me," Angela instructed as she stood up and motioned for Kate to stand up.

After Artero left, Angela grabbed Kate's hand to lead her out of the private room of the restaurant. "Come on, let's make a mad dash." Angela led Kate out of the restaurant, walking very fast, managing to pass the restaurant patrons unnoticed.

CHAPTER 19

PAUL PULLED INTO a parking lot across the street from Franco's. As he watched Kate enter the restaurant with Angela Moore, it dawned on him that this may be the perfect opportunity to make some serious cash. It could very well be that the reason Tami was having him follow Kate around was because Kate and Angela are an item. He salivated at the prospect of catching Angela Moore in such a liaison on camera. He could make a killing off of the photos. And why not? He deserved it. The Montgomery family never gave him extra money. There were never bonuses or raises. The only extra money he received was a hundred-dollar bill they'd give him in a card for Christmas. His other buddies who worked for celebrities got at least a thousand dollars for Christmas.

Sure, he'd be the first to admit that he didn't do a heck of a lot to deserve a bonus or raise. His job was easy. He could smoke pot all day and drink all night. On the other hand, he *was* on call for Tami 24 hours a day, seven days a week. Didn't that account for anything?

Figuring Kate and Angela would be in the restaurant for a while; Paul decided to find a drugstore to buy a disposable camera. He paused and remembered Tami had him buy a new Canon digital camera with an enormous telephoto lens attachment three weeks ago. Tami's intention was to give the camera to Kate as a surprise present for no particular occasion. Tami must've forgotten about it, with the break-up and all. Paul realized the camera was still in its box at the guesthouse. He'd have to go all the way across town. He decided it was worth a shot.

If he didn't make it back in time for when Kate and Angela exited the restaurant, he'd just have to make something up to tell Tami. He wouldn't dare share with her that Kate and Angela shared dinner, at least not until he had some moneyshots. He'd tell her nothing out of the ordinary happened, that Kate was at Angela's for a brief moment, then went to some restaurant by herself. Tami would have to believe him. After all, he was the only one following them.

Paul did a u-turn in front of Franco's and almost hit a parked Ferrari. An onlooker shouted, "Learn how to drive asshole."

"Fuck you!" Paul shouted out the window. He proceeded back to Tami's to retrieve the camera.

Kate and Angela ran to Kate's car and quickly got inside. "Now, if I could manage to do that everywhere I went, life would be grand. Sometimes it takes me hours to make an exit. I get suckered into signing autographs or allowing someone to take a souvenir photo. Some days I like it. I feel like I've put a smile on someone's face. But most of the time I would just like to be unnoticed—normal, like everyone else," Angela said.

"What exactly constitutes as normal in this town?" Kate snickered.

"Ok, here's normal for you: at least we haven't been bombarded by any annoying flashbulbs this evening. Sometimes, it's just as simple as that. Those flashes you photographers use at night are so bright and blinding. You don't realize how painful they are to the eye," Angela said.

"Angela, for the millionth time, I'm not one of *those*

photographers. I don't sneak up on celebrities, blinding them with my bulbs. I've never ever done that in my life," Kate said

"I'm sorry. I didn't mean it to sound the way it did, honestly," Angela said apologetically.

"I know. But from here on out, you have to believe me. I'm not one of them. Trust me."

"I do trust you. I enjoy talking to you, Kate," Angela said, admiring Kate.

Kate inserted the key into the ignition and asked, "So where to now?"

"I really don't feel like going home yet. Jason and his buddies will be there, which will annoy me. It sounds like your house is off limits with your friend Marisol staying there."

"Well, we really can't go to my house anyway, seeing that I lied to my friends about who I was meeting." Kate hesitated and said, "How 'bout we drive around the hills, check out the pretty lights of L.A. from above? I know the perfect, secluded place. I did a shoot there last week. There's a gorgeous view of the city. It won't take long to get there, either."

"Sounds like a good idea. Let's go. I could use the company."

"I find that hard to believe. You must have a whole slew of friends and admirers," Kate remarked, pulling out of the restaurant parking lot.

"Absolutely not!" Angela exclaimed. "I've been working non-stop for seven years. Until last week, my agent and publicist were up my ass 24-7. My social life has become one Hollywood event after the other. My publicist instructs me where to go, who to schmooze. I'm telling you, this is the most ordinary night I've had in a long time."

"You must have other actresses for friends?"

"You'd think. Unfortunately, they're as busy as I am.

Plus, I never really have anything in common with them. It's complicated."

"Well, sorry to hear that. What about your sister? Tell me about her."

"She's beautiful. A great mom. A wonderful sister. Basically, she's perfect. I love her so much that I convinced her to move out here with her two kids after her husband died in a plane crash."

"That's awful. When did that happen?"

"It's been about three years. She's great, though, very resilient. I'm so blessed to have her in my life. I'd trust her with anything. She's so honest and will call me on my shit every time."

"I'd love to meet her someday. She sounds very special."

"She is." *I hope you do meet her someday, Kate.*

The hill region Kate drove to was deserted. Kate hadn't exaggerated; the view of the night skyline and glimmering city below was beautiful. It was completely silent, except for the sound of crickets' chirping in the distance. For a brief moment after leaving the restaurant, Kate thought someone had been following them, but for the last few miles there wasn't another car in sight. She parked at a ledge where there was a wide guardrail. Kate turned the truck off. She thought about unbuckling her seatbelt, but decided to leave it buckled as she gazed at the flickering lights of the city below.

She looked at Angela and ached to kiss her. She thought all night about touching Angela, caressing her, making love to her. It was torture. Angela looked so beautiful and sexy in her jeans and tight t-shirt. She couldn't remember ever feeling this strongly for another woman. The mere sight of Angela turned her on. If she were a man she'd have had a raging hard-on all night.

While Kate was gazing at the city below, Angela gazed

at Kate and said, "This reminds me of those make-out places you see in movies."

Kate turned her head to meet Angela's eyes. "Well, then I guess I brought you to the wrong place, huh?" Kate teased.

In an overtly seductive tone, Angela said, "I wouldn't say *that*."

Kate got a very strong feeling that Angela just came on to her. *Could it be? Or maybe she's teasing me because she knows I'm a lesbian.*

Angela and Kate sat in silence for a few minutes, admiring the view of the city.

"Do you like Dido?" Kate asked, holding up a cd.

"I don't like her newer stuff. I liked her first cd."

"Me too. This is it," Kate said as she inserted the cd.

The song, "Here with me" started to play.

Kate asked, "What is it about you and Jason?" She wondered immediately after asking this if she would be told, "It's none of your business".

"Why? What is your impression of our marriage?" Angela asked, inquisitively.

"You both appear to have a brother-sister type of relationship. I just don't see you two together at all," Kate responded.

"Well, aren't you Miss Intuitive?"

"So I'm right?"

Without hesitation, Angela blurted out. "Yes. You are absolutely right." There was no turning back now. She would take this leap of faith. It felt right.

"I'm not sure I understand," Kate said, perplexed.

"O.k. Here goes nothing." Angela lost all desire to continue with her façade. Her heart told her to trust Kate, so she decided to do just that. "I can't believe I'm telling you this. I hardly know you, but, I feel I've known you for a very long time."

"What is it Angela?" Kate hoped Angela wanted the same thing as Kate.

"I can't believe I'm going to do this." Angela was terrified. She was shaking and her palms were sweaty. Deep down, Angela knew this was what she wanted. For once, she would act like the woman she really was, not the manufactured Hollywood doll she wasn't.

"What is it?" Kate asked, anticipating what would happen next.

Angela hesitated, looked away from Kate toward the city below. She turned to look into Kate's beautiful green eyes.

"My marriage to Jason is a sham and I'm a lesbian. There I said it. I can't believe I just said that." Angela let out a sigh of relief. "It felt good to get that off my chest. You have no idea how badly I wanted to tell you over dinner and on the drive up here." Angela's heart was racing and her skin felt red hot. She couldn't believe those words actually came out of her mouth. She wondered if she had done the right thing. Life was too short and if she ever hoped to have any kind of romance with Kate, she had to get the truth out.

"I kind of figured something like that," Kate said.

"You did not. Did you?" Angela asked.

Although Kate had predicted this, she was still shocked that Angela actually trusted her enough to share this information with her. "Yes, I did. I'm still a little shocked, though. That's some heavy stuff you just laid on me. I feel honored you trust me with this information. It must have been eating away at you all evening."

Angela took Kate's hand in hers and said, "I hope this changes the way you see me now. I mean, in theory I'm not really married and I'm definitely not straight." Angela stared into Kate's eyes. It was pitch black outside; except for the glowing light of a half moon that shown through the windshield, illuminating their faces. It was incredibly romantic.

There was a brief moment of silence. Kate's hand began to tremble. She felt hot and moist between her thighs and her clitoris began to pulsate. She wanted to say so much. She wanted to confess her feelings to Angela.

"Wow," was all she could muster.

Kate didn't have to say anything, though. Angela wasn't going to let this opportunity of them being alone together pass her by. She lifted Kate's hand to her lips, slowly and delicately placing a kiss on each knuckle, one by one. Then, she opened her mouth and slid Kate's middle finger inside and began sucking on it.

She inserted two more fingers and began sliding them in and out of her mouth. Kate moaned spontaneously, enjoying what Angela was doing to her. She ran her other hand through Angela's hair and cradled her hand at the nape of Angela's neck.

Kate removed her fingers from Angela's mouth and brought Angela's face toward her to kiss her. She was kissing Angela's lips, sucking on them, just as she had fantasized.

They kissed for what seemed like an eternity, making out like teenagers, exploring each other's mouths and lips with their curious tongues.

"I want you so bad, Kate," Angela moaned.

"I want you too," Kate whispered.

Angela arose and climbed over the armrest to straddle Kate, never breaking apart from their passionate kisses. Kate adjusted the seat to go as far back as it could go while Angela fumbled to unbutton Kate's peasant blouse.

Once her blouse was unbuttoned, Angela pushed Kate's tank top down to reveal her breasts. "You are so beautiful," Angela cooed.

Angela lowered her head and, with her tongue, toyed with Kate's nipple. Angela stopped for a brief moment and asked, "Is this o.k. for you?"

"Yes. Of course. Don't stop."

Kate slid her hand down to unbutton Angela's jeans. After she unbuttoned the last button, with Angela still on top of her, she pushed the garment, along with her underwear, down below her knees. "Lift your foot out of the pant leg," Kate ordered.

"Let's keep our clothing partially on just in case a cop comes patrolling or someone else parks nearby," Angela, feeling a bit paranoid, said.

"Good idea. Just lift one foot out."

With Angela still toying with her nipple, Kate reached up from beneath her and plunged her hand except her thumb into Angela, causing her to moan in extreme pleasure. "That feels so good," Angela panted. Kate thrust her fingers in and out of Angela, occasionally kneading the balls of her fingers into Angela's g-spot area.

Angela was incredibly turned on and wet. She kissed Kate's mouth, darting her tongue in and out as Kate continued to knead Angela, fucking her with her hand.

"Let's get in the back," Kate suggested. Angela climbed into the backseat of the SUV as Kate followed. Immediately, Kate dove down to pleasure Angela with her tongue. Kate's moist, wet tongue and lips played with her clit and the opening to her vagina. Kate moistened her hand and, while her mouth continued to feed off of Angela's clit, began fucking Angela again. The intensity of Kate's hand and mouth created a burning fire of euphoria for Angela. She came as Kate's tongue stroked her clit from side to side and her hand kneaded that special area inside of her. It was one of the most intense orgasms she'd ever felt. Kate continued to pleasure Angela, rubbing her clit with one hand and fucking her with the other, bringing her to two more orgasms.

Angela sat up and helped Kate remove her jeans. Angela couldn't wait to taste Kate's pussy. While Kate finished pulling her jeans off, Angela dove her hand onto Kate's mound, kneading her clit. Angela rubbed and kneaded Kate's sopping wet pussy until she screamed in ecstasy. Angela wasn't finished pleasuring Kate. She inserted her fingers into Kate's ass and pussy simultaneously, and dove her head down to lick her clit.

Kate felt like a volcano ready to erupt. The waves of pleasure she felt throughout her entire body were unreal. She felt as though she was in another dimension—on an entirely different plane. Her orgasm was fierce. It burned throughout her entire body lifting her up and dropping her like an amusement park ride.

Unfortunately, Kate's pleasure was short-lived. "Did you hear that?" Kate asked. She thought she heard a rustling noise outside.

"There's no one around. We would've seen the lights from a car. Come here." Angela pulled Kate toward her to kiss her mouth. "Don't get paranoid on me now. Let's just lay here for a minute, and enjoy each other." The two women lay in each other's arms in the back seat of Kate's car.

Paul raced to Tami's guest house to retrieve the camera. As he pulled into the driveway, Tami called him.

"Where are you dumbass?" Tami yelled.

Paul hated when she called him names. It made him want to punch her. He'd never hit a woman before and promised he never would, but Tami was vicious. "Nowhere. Kate left Angela's and went to some restaurant alone. You're right, she must've been at Angela's for business."

"Well where the fuck are you now?" Tami insisted.

"I'm waiting outside the restaurant in case Kate leaves with someone," Paul lied. He was right down the driveway from Tami's house.

"Ok. Well, call me when she leaves." Tami hung the

phone up, something she often did. In fact, she rarely said good-bye before hanging up.

Paul hurried into the guest house and found the camera still new in the box. He grabbed the camera and scurried to the limo. He turned the headlights off so as not to be noticed driving away from the house. *I'm gonna be rich. I may even get enough money to quit working for this bitch.* Paul said to himself.

"Oh my God! It's midnight. We must've fallen asleep," Kate said, hurrying to get dressed.

"What?" Angela asked, still a bit groggy.

"Hurry up and pull your pants up. We fell asleep. My watch says it's midnight," Kate said.

Angela stretched her arms out and, half asleep, began buttoning her jeans. "It's a good thing the windows are fogged up. Otherwise, that would've been a really great photo of us half-naked in the back of your car."

"Next time we should be more careful. Anyone could've caught us up here." Kate climbed into the driver's seat and turned the key in the ignition.

"Oh. So there's going to be a next time?" Angela asked.

"Unless this is a one-night thing for you," Kate said.

"I certainly hope not. Why don't you stay at my house tonight? I'm sure Jason went out, which really doesn't make a difference anyhow," Angela suggested.

"There's nothing more I'd rather do. But I have to get back to Marisol and Jamie. They think I'm at some production meeting. I hated lying to them." Kate wished she could spend the night in Angela's arms, but couldn't think of an excuse to tell Marisol and Jamie of why she wouldn't be home.

"I understand," Angela said. For the remainder of the drive to Angela's house, they held each other's hands in satisfied silence.

Kate parked in front of Angela's front door and said, "Angela, for what it's worth, tonight was incredible. I don't usually have sex with someone on the first date, either. I don't want you to think I'm some floozy."

"Of course not and the same goes for me. The only women I've had one night stands with wound up being long-term relationships. Well, that's not true. There was one woman who I slept around with, but that was only when we were both fucked up after partying all night," Angela said, thinking about Tami.

"Really?" Kate asked in a joyful tone.

"Kate, I want to see you again. I'm crazy about you," Angela confided.

"So what are we going to do about this?" Kate asked.

"I guess we continue to see each other, but discreetly."

"Of course. By the way, does your family know? Jason must know. He's o.k. with it, right?" Kate asked.

"Yes, Jason knows. I'm probably the only woman he'd ever agree to marry. He's such a commitment-phobe man-slut." Angela laughed, and then got serious. "No one in my family knows except Mary and my brother Joe. Mom and dad are strict Catholics. They didn't talk to my brother for a year after he came out to them. I'm terrified of the day I will tell them."

"So you do plan on coming out someday?"

"I guess. I'm so scared, though. I can't imagine doing that right now."

"I understand. You would definitely be on every tabloid's front page. That's for sure."

"And then some."

"So, back to Jason. What's it between you and him? You never did anything with him, did you?"

"No way!" Angela exclaimed. "We got married to create the whole Hollywood Power Couple thing. He's actually been a great friend to me. At least until he found out I was going out with you tonight"

"*Me?* Why would he care?"

"He's afraid I'll screw up the whole mirage of a marriage thing. He's such a hypocrite. He fucks every starlet and Playboy model that looks at him. And yet for some reason he thinks I'm the one who's going to fuck things up. I'm really pissed at him right now," Angela said, clearly letting Kate know how angry she felt.

"I don't blame you."

"Look, Kate. I know my life is a fucked up thing to be a part of, but I like you a lot. Can I call you tomorrow?"

"Please call me tomorrow." Kate leaned forward and kissed Angela. "And the next day." She kissed her again. "And the day after that." She kissed her again. "And the day after that".

"I will," Angela said, and gave Kate a long, supple and tender kiss.

Kate interrupted their kiss to say, "Now, I need to get back to my horribly depressed friend. I almost feel guilty that I've had this wonderful evening, while my best-friend is at my house feeling suicidal over her lover leaving her."

Angela kissed Kate one more time and said good-bye.

CHAPTER 20

"MIZ ANGELA! MIZ Angela! I try calling you. You no answer your cell phone." Lucinda came running into the foyer yelling frantically.

"What's the matter?" Angela asked, taken by surprise as she shut the front door. She had purposely left her cell phone in her bedroom, not wanting to be disturbed during her date with Kate.

"Iz terrible." Lucinda was crying, barely able to speak. Angela never saw Lucinda this upset, except the day her mother died.

"What is it Lucinda?" Angela asked forcefully as she placed her hands on each of Lucinda's shoulders and shook her slightly.

"Meester Saunders. He's…He's…" Lucinda continued to cry, sputtering her words.

"Get a hold of yourself, Lucinda. *What's* the matter with Jason?" Angela grasped Lucinda's arms more firmly and shook her again.

"He's been in a terreeble accident. He's at the hospital."

"What? Is he ok? Where is he? What hospital?" Angela felt her heart sink. She couldn't believe what she was hearing.

"He barely alive when they find him. They air lift him to Cedars Sinai."

"What happened?" Angela asked as she walked to the kitchen to get her car keys. Lucinda followed behind.

"He drive too fast. His car flipped," Lucinda sobbed.

Angela grabbed the keys to her Range Rover off of the hook next to the kitchen light switch, turned around quickly, and sprinted to the front door.

"Everyone has been calling—your family, Meester Saunders' friends, everyone. I want to go with you to the hospital."

"No. I need you to stay here. If anyone calls, tell them I'm on my way to the hospital. They can reach me on the Rover's car phone. The number's in my desk drawer," Angela shouted to Lucinda as she exited the house.

Angela was shaking so badly that it took her several attempts to get the right key in the ignition. Her mind was racing a mile a minute. *What if he dies? I didn't even get to say good-bye because I was having sex with Kate. I was so mean to him earlier.*

As soon as she pulled out of the carport, she used her car phone and Onstar system to connect her with the hospital.

"Hello, Cedars Sinai. How can I direct your call?" The hospital operator answered in a wearisome, lethargic tone.

"Hi, I'm Jason Saunder's wife. I need to know his condition," Angela said frantically.

"I'm sorry, but we cannot give that information out over the phone."

"Are you kidding me? I'm his wife. Angela Moore. You must know me?" Angela demanded.

"If you happen to be her, which I highly doubt, you'll get here or call someone who's here. Till then, I'm sorry, but there isn't anything I can do or say over the phone."

"Then put me in touch with someone who can"

"Miss, I'm telling you there is no one in this entire hospital who can release confidential patient information. Haven't you heard of the HIPAA law?"

"Fuck you and your HIPAA. Just tell me if he's alive or dead."

"I'm sorry, but I can't divulge that information over the phone."

"Thanks for nothing bitch." Angela hung the phone up and dialed Jason's publicist's cell phone.

Marcy, Jason's hell-in-high heels publicist, answered on the first ring. "Hello?"

"Marcy, thank God I got you. This is Angela. What happened and how is he?"

"You're lucky you got me. I'm outside smoking a cigarette. They won't let me have my cell phone on in the hospital. Can you believe that shit? They say it interferes with their machines. I hate fucking hospitals."

"Jesus Marcy, who fucking cares. How's Jason?"

"Well, it's not good. He ruptured his spleen and has other internal injuries. He's in surgery right now. We just don't know," she said.

Angela couldn't believe what she was hearing. Her best friend was in the hospital and could die. It felt so surreal, as though it wasn't really happening. "What exactly happened?" she asked.

"He was driving too fast," she said. She sarcastically added, "What else is new?" She took a puff of her cigarette, exhaled, then continued, "He was going too fast around a sharp bend and flipped his car over an embankment. He's lucky to be alive. You should see the photos of the car."

Good ole Marcy. What a fucking sarcastic bitch. That's it. Jason's firing her ass—if he makes it through this. "Well, I'm on my way to the hospital. Can you arrange for me to get in with no problem?"

"There's a ton of reporters outside. The hospital already had a press conference. Everyone's been asking where Jason's wife is?" she said, in a not very nice, hostile tone.

"Well, I'm here now. When did this happen, anyways?" Angela turned onto the street where the hospital was located.

"You're five hours late. It happened around 9:00." Angela calculated that she was at the make out point with Kate when it happened.

"Yeah, I know I'm late. Shit happens. I'll be at the hospital in a minute. Tell the hospital I'm on my way and don't want a problem getting in"

"Will do," Marcy said while exhaling a plume of smoke.

Angela arrived at the hospital and, as Marcy had promised, it was swamped with paparazzi. *Where am I going to say I've been?* She thought. I know. I'll have Mary be my alibi. Angela dialed her sister.

"Mary. I need you to do me a favor," Angela said.

"Where have you been? Everyone's been trying to find you. Did you hear about Jason?"

"Yes. It's awful." Angela hesitated. "I have another problem. I'm going to tell the reporters I was with you this whole time and didn't have my cell phone on me. Ok?"

"Why? Where *have* you been?" Mary asked, angrily.

"Mary, I really can't get into it right now. I'm at the hospital now and need to go in."

"If you want me to lie for you, at least tell me where you were for the past five hours and what you were doing."

"I was on a date."

"On a date? When are you going to stop this charade? It's not right Angela."

Not in the mood for her sister's opinions, she responded, "I need to go into the hospital. Just back me up, ok?"

"Ok. But you better tell me everything later. Call me as soon as he's out of surgery."

Angela parked the car illegally next to a yellow curb that was close to the hospital's front entrance. It said "Fire Lane No Parking". She figured she would send Marcy or someone back out to park it in the parking lot. She ran into the awaiting line of paparazzi photographers.

"There's Angela," they chanted.

The camera flashes blinded Angela. She pushed her way through and grasped to open the front door. "Where have you been Angela?" was the last thing she heard from them. She ran to the front desk where a black elderly woman was sitting.

"You're Angela Moore," the woman exclaimed, recognizing the movie star.

"Yes. I need to get to where my husband is. Do you know where he is?" Angela managed as she was short of breath from running.

"Go down that hallway." The woman pointed to her left. "Take the elevator to the third floor. Follow the signs to the surgery waiting area."

"Thanks," Angela said. She made her way to the elevator.

God, please let him live. Let his surgery go well. Angela prayed for Jason to be ok while she waited for the elevator. The elevator door opened and Angela joined an elderly man with a walker who must have gotten on in the basement below the lobby. It felt as though it was the slowest elevator she'd ever been on. To her relief, the elderly man with the walker didn't recognize her. She didn't feel like dealing with the starstruck right now.

"I'm going for a walk," the man said.

"That's nice," Angela responded. *Maybe he's not supposed to be out on his own like this.* Angela suddenly realized. "What floor are you on?" she asked.

"Floor? I'm going home. I had a very nice walk," the man responded.

They arrived at the third floor. "You're coming with me," Angela instructed the man, pulling at his walker. He slowly obeyed Angela, strutting slowly behind her. Angela caught the attention of a nurse, who took a hold of the old man.

Angela darted down the hallway, following the operating room signs. At the end of the hallway, Angela caught sight of Marcy and headed towards her. "Anything change? When does he get out of surgery?" Angela asked a nurse who was talking to Marcy.

"You're his wife, right?" the nurse asked.

"Yes. How is he?" Angela asked, wiping her brow as her face was damp from sweat.

"We don't know. They're still operating. It could be quite a few hours before they're done with him."

"Just tell me he's not going to die."

"I can't do that. But chances are good he'll recover. He's in good hands. I'm sorry I don't have any more information. One of the doctors will be out to talk to you." The nurse walked back to the nurse's station.

Angela took a seat in a waiting room chair. "You don't have to stay, Marcy."

"Are you sure? I mean. I would like to get some sleep. You'll call me as soon as you know anything, right?"

"Yeah. I promise."

Marcy left in a hurry. She was a chain smoker and needed a fix.

Angela thought about how sad it was that no one else was there except Marcy and her. Jason had no family other than his estranged mother. He had millions of fans, and Reggie would probably be on his way at some point. However, the only family he really had was Angela and her family.

Kate sat in a very uncomfortable waiting room chair. She obviously wasn't going to be able to sleep. So, she selected magazines to peruse. She picked up an issue of People magazine. The cover was a photo of Jason with the heading "Sexiest Man Alive". Angela started to cry.

"Hey, what's the news Angela?" It was Reggie.

"You know as much as I do. He's still in surgery."

"Man, I'm so sorry Angela. I hope he makes it." Reggie was 300 pounds, dark skinned, and resembled the deceased rapper, Notorious B.I.G. He had a heart of gold and was a great friend to Jason. He knew their marital situation was fake, but also knew how close of friends Jason and Angela were.

"Want anything to drink or eat?" Reggie asked.

"You are a doll. I can't believe I'm saying this, but I could really go for a hamburger and a coke." Angela hadn't craved meat in years since becoming a vegetarian.

"I thought you were a vegetarian," Reggie pointed out.

"I know. What am I saying? A veggie burger, then."

"Ok. I'll order some food and have it delivered."

Thirty minutes later, Reggie returned with a veggie burger, fries, and a coke. Angela took a small bite out of the burger and felt like vomiting. She suddenly had no appetite, but forced most of the meal down as she knew she needed nourishment to help deal with the stress she was under.

A doctor dressed head to toe in scrub gear approached Angela in the waiting area. "Are you Mrs. Saunders?"

"No. I mean, yes." Angela wasn't accustomed to being called Mrs. Saunders. "Actually, it's Angela Moore"

"Your husband has multiple internal injuries. He had a ruptured spleen, his liver was bruised very badly. He broke his arm and has lacerations over much of his face and body from the windshield shattering. We've had to do a considerable amount of stitching."

"Is he going to live?"

"Chances are good. He's responding well, considering the amount of trauma he endured. He'll be in the recovery room in about another hour. He's going to have a long recovery."

"Thank you so much, doctor." Angela was relieved. He has a good chance of making it. That was all she needed to hear.

"When can we see him?" Reggie asked.

"Once he's out of the recovery room and in his own hospital bed." The doctor paused to look at his watch. "I'd say another few hours."

"Thanks man," Reggie said.

The doctor walked away and Angela sat down again, realizing all she could do was sit there and wait.

CHAPTER 21

KATE FELT LIKE she was in a dream. She never in a million years thought her crush with Angela would ever come to fruition like it had that evening. She was experiencing bliss like she had never experienced before. She wished she could share her happiness with someone, but knew she couldn't. This was a delicate situation—sleeping with a movie star. It wasn't like she could tell her closest friends, Marisol and Jamie, that she'd met the woman of her dreams—Angela Moore.

It wasn't that she didn't trust her friends. She honored her promise to Angela to keep their relationship a secret. Realizing this, Kate felt a tinge of sadness come over her. She was on cloud nine and couldn't share it with anyone.

Kate didn't like secrets or sneaking around. She never had to do that in her life, not even with Tami. Tami went everywhere with Kate. Tami even introduced Kate to her family. However, Tami's wealthy parents were downright rude to Kate. Tami and Kate didn't care, though. At the time, they were only interested in each other. Screw everyone else.

That certainly wasn't the situation for Angela. Kate would just have to deal with keeping it all a secret—for now.

***

"There you are. Where have you been? We were worried. It's almost 1:30," Jamie said after hearing Kate enter the house.

Kate entered the living room, where Jamie was lying on the couch. "Where's Marisol. In bed?" Kate asked.

"Yeah. She cried for the past hour, then passed out. So where were you?"

"Oh, that meeting I had was out of control. Sorry it took so long."

"Bunch of jerks?"

"Oh yeah. Those production people think people like me have nothing better to do till midnight." Kate hated lying. She wondered if it was obvious she wasn't being truthful.

"You must've heard the news about Jason Saunders?"

"What news?" Kate felt an unpleasant rush permeate through her body. *Oh God. Did somebody find out about Angela and me?*

"Jason was in a terrible accident. He might die," Jamie said. "You know, he's the only guy on the planet I could imagine having sex with. He's a hottie."

"No way! That's horrible. When did this happen?" Kate felt a sense of relief after discovering it had nothing to do with her and Angela's tryst. Not knowing when the accident occurred, her thoughts turned to sheer terror, wondering if Angela was o.k.

"It's been all over the news since like 9:30. They interrupted my favorite show for it."

Angela's o.k. Thank you, God. "I hope he's o.k. Poor Angela," Kate said.

"Poor Angela? Poor Jason is more like it," Jamie said, giving Kate a strange look.

"Yeah, that's what I meant. Well, she's his wife. I'm sure she's very upset."

"Who cares?"

"That's not nice."

"What's wrong with you? You hate movie stars."

"Oh nothing, never mind. I'm just tired."

"Your friend Marisol's a piece of work. I tried to cheer her up by sharing the whole story about my ex leaving me for that stripper-hobag. I think it made her feel better to know she's not alone. Remember I cried for a month and lost twenty pounds from not eating?"

"Yeah. That was pretty bad."

"Uh huh. I heard she's living in New York now."

"That's good. The farther away the better. By the way, thanks for coming over."

"No problem. I'm gonna get going. Now that I'm back, make sure you keep in touch. Let's plan on getting together, okay?" Jamie said as she inserted her arms into her hooded sweatshirt.

"Of course, Jamie." Kate gave Jamie a hug and saw her to the door.

I can't believe Jason was in an accident and might die. Angela must feel horrible. She was out with me the entire time. I wonder if she's at the hospital. Kate thought as she lied in bed, unable to sleep. I wish I could contact her or go to the hospital to comfort her. This relationship is already proving to be difficult.

CHAPTER 22

ANGELA SAT NEXT to Jason in his hospital room, holding his hand while, at the same time, thinking about Kate. She wondered if Kate knew about Jason's accident and wished she were there at the hospital supporting her.

Angela felt pangs of guilt. Here was her husband, who almost died and now couldn't wake up, and all she could think about was Kate and how much she missed her.

Reluctantly, Angela used the phone in the hospital room and dialed Kate's phone.

"Hello," Kate answered, groggy. It was 8:00 in the morning and she was still in bed.

"Hi. I'm at the hospital right now and can't really talk that long," Angela whispered.

"How is Jason?" Kate asked, concerned.

"He's got a lot of recovering to do. He'll be o.k., eventually. He's asleep right now. Well, actually he's comatose."

"Are you o.k. Angela? Do you need anything?"

"Yes. I need you."

"How do we manage that?"

"I'll let the hospital know that you are a close friend of the family and to let you through. Do you mind coming today?"

"Of course not. I want to see you Angela."

"I want to see you too. I miss you already. Last night was incredible."

"I can be there by noon."

"Thank you Kate."

Angela hung up the phone and returned to Jason's side. Seconds later, the phone rang. It was Mary.

"I'm downstairs and they won't let me up. Could you please talk to this lady?" Mary handed the phone to the receptionist.

"Sorry to bother you Ms. Moore, but could you verify that it is alright to send this woman up? Her id says she's Mary Moore Stone."

"Yes, that's my sister."

"Thank you Ms. Moore."

"One more thing," Angela quickly added. "There will be another woman coming to visit, a close friend of the family named Kate Ashford. Please make sure she gets through. Call me immediately if there are any problems."

"Yes, ma'am."

Moments later, Mary entered Jason's hospital room and was shocked by Jason's appearance. "Angela. Is he going to be o.k.?" Mary asked anxiously. She had a look of panic on her face as tears began to well in her doe-like brown eyes. Jason had cuts and stitches all over his face. He was pale, bloated, and unrecognizable.

"Eventually."

"What's *that* supposed to mean?" Mary asked in an angry tone.

"Calm down. You being tense isn't helping me any."

"I'm sorry, Angela. I'm just so upset over this."

"The doctor says he'll need more surgery, but will be o.k."

STANDING NAKED IN PUBLIC

"This is just awful, Angela." Mary started to cry and opened her arms to give Angela a hug.

"All we can do is pray. He's strong. He'll make it. I know he will." Angela started to cry as well.

Mary released her arms from Angela's embrace and walked over to Jason's bedside. She took his hand and held it in hers. Mary and Jason had always shared a close sister-in-law/brother-in-law relationship. Mary adored Jason. She often told Angela she'd wished they were a real married couple as Jason was a great brother-in-law and uncle to Mary's kids.

"I've already made arrangements with Vanessa and Brian's nanny to take care of the kids for as long as you need me. I'm here for both of you and will stay as long and often as you need me," Mary said, tears streaming down her perfectly chiseled cheekbones.

"Thank you, Mary. I don't know what I'd do without you." Angela was grateful to have a sister like Mary. "Actually, I have a friend dropping by who I may need to go over some work with," Angela added.

"How can you possibly think about work at a time like this?" Mary asked.

"It won't take long. I'm sorry that life still happens, Mary," Angela responded bitterly.

"You're right. But Jason needs you right now," Mary reminded her.

A feeling of indifference suddenly came over Angela. She felt like saying, "What about what *I* need right now?" Instead, she said, "I hear you loud and clear Mary."

Just as Angela awaited her sister's rebuttal, the hospital room's phone rang. Angela hurried over to answer it.

"Hello," Angela said

"Angela. It's Lindsey," Angela's publicist said, sounding very irritated. "Why haven't you contacted me? You know you need my help with this. I've already gotten a dozen phone calls wondering why it took you so long to arrive at the hospital."

"What difference does it make?" Angela paused, and added, "I was with my sister." Mary shot Angela a look, which Angela translated as, "When were *you* with *me?*"

"O.k. Well, there's going to be a lot more the press is going to want to know. I can be there in ten minutes."

"No. I don't need you right now, Lindsey."

"Angela, you're obviously not thinking clearly."

"Look. How 'bout this, you come down to the hospital and play gatekeeper to the paparazzi outside?" Angela compromised. This would keep Lindsey busy and away from her when Kate arrived.

"Then what?" Lindsey asked.

"What do you mean then what? Just do as I say. Inform everyone I'm distraught and have no comment at this time. Tell the public they can do what I'm doing—praying for Jason's recovery."

"Well, it's more complicated than that," Lindsey responded in a sarcastic tone.

"Whatever, Lindsey. This is the last time I'm telling you. Just do what I asked." Angela hung up the phone. *How did I get like this?* Angela wondered. People who worked for her were dictating what she should do. She hated it.

"What was that about? When were *you* with *me?*" Mary inquired.

"It's just Lindsey being the bitch that she is. Just forget about her. She's freaking out over this whole thing with Jason and the press. I really can't deal with her right now. Just please do me a favor and tell Lindsey and anyone else who asks that I was with you, at your house, last night."

"Where *were* you, *really?*" Mary asked.

Angela really didn't feel like telling her sister the truth.

Consequently, Mary was the only confidante she had. Angela decided to confide in her.

"I went on a date with a woman I'm crazy about," Angela blurted.

"Well, you know how I feel about this secret life you lead. It's so dishonest and..."

Angela interrupted. "Yes, Mary, you make that very clear every time we discuss my personal life."

"Let me finish." Mary shot Angela a stern look. "I know you know how I feel about everything. I really just want you to be happy, Angela—for both of you to be happy. I love you. I also love my brother-in-law. For now, I'll cover for you. Once Jason's better, I strongly recommend you make a decision about the secrets you are carrying around with you."

"Thanks for covering for me. Can we please change the subject? I'm feeling extremely overwhelmed and stressed out."

"O.k.," Mary agreed.

An hour later, Angela looked up from holding Jason's hand and saw Kate enter the room. Mary was on the other side of the bed, holding his other hand, sobbing. Angela had been crying, but had faith Jason would be o.k.

Kate looked beautiful in a James Perse tee and jeans. Angela's heart felt like it had skipped a beat. She forgot for a moment where she was. Kate approached Angela, who stood up and hugged her.

"Ahem." Mary cleared her throat, indicating she wanted Angela to introduce her to her friend.

Angela quickly broke from her embrace, turned to her sister and said, "This is my friend Kate. Kate, this is my sister, Mary. She and I have some work to finish on a Vanity Fair spread. Kate was the lead photographer."

Kate and Mary shook hands and exchanged "pleased

to meet you" greetings. An awkward moment of silence followed.

"Do you mind staying with Jason while I get some work done?" Angela asked Mary. Angela could tell by the look on her sister's face that she was suspicious of Kate.

However, true to form, Mary politely agreed to sit with Jason. She'd get her chance to interrogate Angela later.

"I probably won't be back for a couple of hours. I still have to shower and get changed."

"That's a good idea. You may want to have some of your things sent over here, since this is where you'll be spending most of your time until he's ready to go home," Mary said, motioning her head toward Jason.

"I guess your blind date is off, huh?" Angela asked.

"How can you even think about that? Of course it's off," Mary responded, angrily.

"Well, your life should go on despite this," Angela countered.

"Don't start with me Angela." Mary turned to Kate and said, "It was nice meeting you."

"You too," Kate said.

Angela and Kate exited the hospital room. "Come over here." Angela scanned both corridors to see if anyone was looking. When she saw that no one was in sight, Angela grasped Kate's wrist and led her to a storage closet. It was pitch black in the closet. She quickly closed the door and fumbled for a light switch. It smelled of wet mops and disinfectant.

"Shit, I can't find the light switch," Angela cursed. "Listen, I'm going to call my driver. I want you to meet me at my house. You leave first. I don't want to cause a commotion for you, which is what's bound to happen if you leave with me."

"I don't care about the paparazzi."

"Kate, you have no idea what it's like to have every move you make taped, photographed and printed."

"Angela, I don't care. I just want to be with you." Kate lifted her hand and, in the darkness, felt around for Angela's mouth. Once she knew where her lips were, she leaned in to deliver a deep, forceful kiss.

"I want to be with you too Kate," Angela muttered, pulling away from Kate's lips. "Trust me on this. Go ahead and I'll meet you at my house." Angela peeked outside of the closet. The hallway was still clear. "Go ahead. I'll see you soon." Angela nudged Kate out to the hallway.

CHAPTER 23

THE PAPARAZZI HAD basically set up camp outside of the hospital. Angela knew she needed to play the devoted wife role and give a statement to the press. After exiting the hospital's front entrance, Angela pointed to a random news reporter and motioned for him to come over to her. Lindsey hadn't arrived yet. She was going to be pissed off when she learned Angela gave a statement without her being there to authorize it.

The reporter, a young, attractive surfer-looking fellow, put the microphone in front of Angela and asked, "Did you want to make a statement, Angela?"

"Yes. I would like to take this time to thank all of Jason's concerned and devoted fans. Jason is resting and his prognosis is good. I ask that everyone continue to pray for his recovery. We must have faith during this difficult time. Thank you." She pushed the microphone to the side and made her way to her driver, who was waiting a few feet from the media circus.

"I feel like an emotional mess." Angela turned to Kate and started to cry. Kate and Angela were sitting on a couch in Angela's living room.

Kate reached her arms around Angela and held her tight.

"I'm so sorry, Angela. I know you care for Jason very deeply. He'll be o.k."

"Jason's like my brother. If anything happens to him I just don't know what I'll do." Angela continued to cry while Kate held her tightly.

"I'm here for you Angela."

Angela kissed Kate, long and hard. It felt so comfortable and secure to have Kate hold and kiss her. For the first time since she heard the horrible news about Jason, Angela felt safe and happy. She wished she could sit there in Kate's arms forever.

"I really like you a lot, Kate. Actually, I'm crazy about you," Angela said, while her head rested on Kate's shoulder. "I don't know what it is. I can't stop thinking about you. It almost seems wrong to feel this way with everything that's going on with Jason."

"I feel the same way, Angela. Last night was incredible. Maybe this is poor timing—you and me."

"Please don't say that." Angela raised her head and looked into Kate's eyes. "Last night wasn't just about sex. I want to be with you. It's more than that."

"I just want to make sure you're o.k. with us seeing each other, considering the circumstances."

"Welcome to my life. There's always some drama going on. There's never an ideal moment to have a relationship," Angela said, sarcastically.

"Then, let me know what I can do for you. I'm here as your friend, too."

"Please, just hold me," Angela said, as she stretched her body onto the length of the couch and pulled Kate in for her to do the same.

Kate held Angela, while stroking her hair and head. Angela began to doze off, thinking, *this is certainly not about sex, this is about love. I'm falling in love with this woman.*

When Angela awoke, Kate was gone. A feeling of panic came over her, wondering why she wasn't there with her. Angela realized that Kate had a life too. Maybe she had a photo assignment.

Moments later, Kate appeared. "Well, hello sleeping beauty. You sure needed that nap. How do you feel?"

Angela beamed with excitement over Kate's presence. "I feel o.k. What time is it? How long have I been asleep?"

"It's around 2:00. You've been asleep for four hours."

"Thank you for staying with me. Don't you have to work?"

"Actually, my day is free. I was supposed to spend the day with Marisol. She's feeling better now and made plans to go to some museum, or maybe it was a garden, with my friend Jamie. They invited me to go, but I'd rather see you."

"I'm glad Marisol's doing better," Angela said, still feeling hazy from her long nap. "I should probably get back to the hospital."

"I can bring you," Kate offered.

"I'd like that."

CHAPTER 24

OVER A MONTH had passed since the accident and it was time for Jason to be released from the hospital. He was still in a great deal of pain and would require some assistance. Since Mary was at Jason's bedside every day, she offered to help him once he returned home. Angela happily took her up on the offer and hired a nurse to help with baths and medication.

During Jason's recovery in the hospital, Angela and Kate's love affair blossomed. When Angela wasn't at the hospital and Kate wasn't working on an assignment, they met at Angela's home, spending nearly every night together, in each other's arms.

Ten days after the accident, Jason awoke from the coma. He was groggy from the morphine, but managed to open his eyes and mumbled something about Angela. It was a day for celebration. He recovered miraculously every day that followed.

Angela was relieved to have lost all feelings of guilt around her new relationship with Kate. Sex had been the furthest thing from her mind, until it appeared Jason was going to be fine.

Kate and Angela celebrated Jason's awakening by making love for the first time since that evening in Kate's truck.

Angela illuminated her room with candles and brought out her arsenal of sex toys.

"Since your truck wasn't exactly the most romantic setting for our first time, I thought I'd make up for it tonight," Angela told Kate as she led her up the stairs into the bedroom.

"I don't care where we do it. I'd fuck you in a back alley and love every minute of it," Kate whispered into Angela's ear, following her from behind.

"Right now we don't have to resort to that," Angela said, pulling her onto the bed. They immediately kissed, lying next each other.

Angela's kisses set Kate's belly on fire and made her clit throb. No woman had turned Kate on like this, except maybe Eve. Women came and went in her life. There'd been great sex, but nothing as emotional and loving as what she experienced with Angela.

"I'm already soaking wet down there," Angela said.

"Let's do something about that." Kate began removing Angela's clothes. Once she had removed every article of clothing, she started licking every crevice of Angela's body; her toes, the backs of her knees, the inside of her thighs, her neck and arms.

Kate ordered Angela to lie on her stomach and ran her tongue from Angela's neck, down her spine and toyed with her tailbone. Kate couldn't wait any longer to taste Angela. She ran her tongue over and around Angela's ass, down to her vulva and into her pussy. She tenderly licked the walls of her vagina and progressed lower to Angela's clit.

Angela moaned loudly with pleasure as Kate focused on caressing her clit with her tongue, delicately running her tongue slowly and strategically on and around her clit.

Angela came with such force it was as though her entire body had experienced a tidal wave of spasms.

"I'm not done with you. Can I use this on you?" Kate reached into Angela's sex toy box and pulled out a long, thick vibrating dildo.

"Please do," Angela cooed.

Kate held the purple dildo and greased it with lube.

"Turn over," she instructed Angela so she could fuck her from behind. She began with slow movements, gradually inserting the member. Once Angela felt comfortable with the dildo, Kate started to thrust faster.

Angela screamed in ecstasy.

Angela put her hand out to stop Kate. "I want to turn around. I want to kiss you and look at you while you fuck me," she said.

Kate fucked Angela while their mouths hungrily devoured each other's. Angela reached to the box and retrieved a pocket rocket vibrator and began stimulating her clit while Kate continued to fuck her.

"I'm going to come again," Angela said, her stomach rising, legs trembling.

Deciding she was spent, Angela nudged Kate off of her and laid on her back, her chest lifting and descending as she gasped for air.

"That was incredible," Angela said.

"I think I'm in love with your pussy," Kate said.

Angela sat up. "Now I want to make love to you. Lie down," Angela ordered.

Kate lay on her back, while Angela delicately ran her fingers over Kate's entire body. Her touch was so light, like a feather teasing every inch of Kate's soft, tanned skin. Angela caressed Kate's feet and very slowly ran her fingers up her legs, then plunged her fingers into Kate's silky, wet hole.

Kate's back arched as she felt the waves of pleasure throughout her entire body. Angela inserted four fingers and reached inside Kate to stimulate her g-spot. She ran her tongue over Kate's clit, flicking the pink little organ while fucking her with her hand.

Kate's orgasm came quick. Angela chose a clitoral vibrator from her box and stimulated Kate while she inserted two fingers into Kate's ass. She used her fingers to slowly caress the inside of Angela's anus, while teasing her clit with the vibrator. Angela pressed the vibrator onto Kate, allowing the vibrations to bring Kate to another orgasm.

After they made love, Kate and Angela snuggled in the bed and watched an old French film.

There was one problem with Jason's return home: privacy. Angela certainly didn't want to disrespect Jason in any way. His recovery was more important than her getting laid. However, though their house was enormous, it still wouldn't be like Kate and Angela had complete privacy.

Kate suggested they rendezvous at her house. Angela refused that option as it wasn't safely guarded from the paparazzi like Angela's house. Angela decided she needed to have an honest and open conversation with Jason about the situation. Jason still had no idea Angela was in a relationship with Kate.

After the fan fair of Jason's return home, Angela asked the nurse and Mary to leave his bedroom—that she had something important she needed to discuss with him.

"What's going on, Angie?" Jason mumbled through his pain killer haze.

"I've fallen in love with someone," Angela blurted.

"When?" Jason was shocked, in a sedated sort of way.

"Right before your accident. It just happened. Like that," Angela said, snapping her fingers.

Jason appeared sad and dumbfounded.

"She will be over here a lot. I thought you should know," she said.

"Who is she?" Jason couldn't believe his ears. He made it back from death's door. And for this? While he slept in the coma, he had a vision of a woman who looked like Angela with angel's wings. The woman told Jason to go back, that she'd be there for him on the other side. He thought it was a sign that finally he'd have Angela as his real wife.

"The photographer, Kate Ashford."

Jason could feel his heart breaking and his gut wrenching. "I see," was all he could muster. "I need to be alone. I'm tired."

"You're not happy for me? Why can't you be happy for me?" Angela began to cry.

"I'm happy for you," Jason lied. "Just be careful. She's a photographer for Christ's sake. You're playing with fire, Angela."

"She's not *that* type of photographer, Jason. We're in love. Kate's a very important part of my life now."

"And I'm not?"

"I have enough love to go around." Angela couldn't believe she had to defend herself to Jason.

"Anyhow, that's the way it is," Angela said, exiting the room.

"Jason's being so moody and weird. I think it's all the pain meds he's on," Angela told Kate about her interaction with Jason, while they dined in a private room of the newest fad restaurant in L.A.

Earlier, Angela was assured by the restaurant's owner she'd be able to sneak in through the back, avoiding any contact with fellow diners. When Angela and Kate entered through the back entrance, Catherine Erickson and her husband, Howard were waiting in the candle lit corridor for their private dining room to be readied.

"Hello, Angela," Catherine said.

"Hello, Catherine," Angela said.

Their exchange was like the famous Newman/Seinfeld interactions from the Seinfeld sitcom. It reeked of sarcasm.

"I hope Jason is doing better. We do have a movie to make," Catherine remarked.

"He's doing fine. I'll notify him of your concern," Angela responded, her brow furrowing with spite.

The maitre'd interrupted their conversation and led Angela and Kate to their private room. Kate sensed the tension between Catherine and Angela and asked, "There's obviously no love lost between the two of you. Want to share what's going on?"

Angela told Kate about Catherine's contempt for Angela. She also shared the funeral story in which Catherine threatened Angela in front of the dead body in the casket, and Angela's refusal to work with her.

"What a bitch," Kate said.

"Yeah. I'm surprised she hasn't gone as far as hiring a hit man to kill me. She hates me that much," Angela said.

"Don't say *that*. Is it that bad between you and Catherine?" Kate asked, concerned for Angela's wellbeing.

Angela laughed. "No. She's just a major asshole. I'm not going to lose sleep over her, that's for sure."

In the process of Paul racing back to get a photograph of Kate and Angela the evening of their first date, he was pulled over for speeding. Paul was nervous and fidgety when the officer asked for his driver's license, which led the officer to suspect Paul was under the influence of something. Paul agreed to a breathalyzer and passed. However, Paul was antsy and sweating, so the officer insisted he must be on drugs. While searching the vehicle, the officer found a marijuana roach Paul left in the limo's ashtray.

"Can't you do anything right?" Tami asked as she finished signing paperwork to release Paul from police custody.

"I'm sorry. It's a big mistake," Paul responded, fearing what Tami's next words.

"You are such a fuck up. I don't know why I don't fire you." Tami took her copy of the paperwork. "Let's get outta here."

Like a dog with its tail between its legs, Paul sheepishly followed Tami out of the police station.

"How hard is it to do one thing I ask of you? Huh?" Tami asked as she opened the door to her new Bentley.

"I said I was sorry. Plus, it's bullshit they busted me for marijuana possession. The shit is practically legal here."

"Well obviously the cop didn't like you from the start. You have that suspicious look to you. Maybe you should work on that."

"Where's the limo?" Paul asked

"*You* have to get it out of impound later. I'm not paying for it," Tami scowled. "So, I take it you didn't get to see if Kate left the restaurant with anyone, huh?"

"No cuz I was on my there when the fucking cop pulled me over." Paul couldn't wait to get home and away from Tami. He refused to divulge that, in fact, Kate was with Angela at the restaurant. He would continue to keep that to himself with the hope he could still get a money shot of the two women.

"You owe me for bailing your ass out. I want you to follow Kate this whole week."

"Tami, I was released to you. There wasn't any bail."

"Whatever Paul. I still had to take time out of my busy day to pick you up and sign all that shit to get you out."

"Ok. As soon as I get the limo back, I'll go to Kate's house."

"No. Change of plans. You're going to rent a car—an ordinary looking car. The limo is too easy to identify. Plus, it can be traced back to me."

"So, in other words, I'll be the one who goes down for stalking if I get caught."

"Exactly. If you don't like it, get another job."

CHAPTER 25

ANGELA'S MOTHER AND father arrived on a Saturday. As soon as they arrived at the airport, Angela was fantasizing about when they would return home. Angela was relieved that she was able to convince them to stay at Mary's house, telling them Jason needed peace and quiet. She wasn't about to let her parents keep her from sleeping with Kate for an entire week.

Mary didn't mind having them stay at her house. Her mother helped take care of the kids so Mary could grant her nanny the vacation she'd been requesting. Her dad was hardly ever around. He spent most of his time at the nearby golf course.

Angela hosted a dinner at her house their first night in town.

"Mom and dad, this is my friend, Kate." Angela introduced her parents to Kate, who was already seated at the dining room table.

Angela's parents gushed over how wonderful it was to know that Angela had a friend and how beautiful Kate was.

The dinner was awkward for Kate and Angela. Angela's mother went on and on about how Jason needed to get well again so Angela could get pregnant. Angela felt terrible that

Kate had to sit there and listen to her mother rant about Jason and Angela's relationship.

Jason excused himself after the first course. He said he was tired, but Angela knew he'd heard enough from her parents.

Kate later confided to Angela that it really didn't bother her. After meeting Angela's parents, Kate understood why it would be difficult for Angela to tell them she's gay. They were two senior citizens who were definitely set in their ways. It also didn't help that they were devout Catholics and Conservative Republicans.

"I hate lying to them. It isn't fair," Angela complained.

"I wish you didn't have to lie, either. It's just the way it is for now." Kate wrapped her arms around Angela and pulled her head into Kate's chest.

"I can't believe they talked me into going with them to Mass tomorrow morning," Angela said.

"Want me to go with you?" Kate asked.

"You'd do that?" Angela smiled, looking up at Kate.

"Sure," Kate said and kissed Angela's forehead.

"I love you so much, Kate," Angela said.

"I love you too, Angela," Kate said.

Angela was relieved the day her parents returned to Mary's house. She could act however she wanted with Kate in her own house. No pretending Kate was her friend. She couldn't wait for the day she didn't have to lie to anyone anymore.

"I'm in love with her, mom," Kate told her mother. Her mother was the only person she could trust with her secret—the only person who wouldn't intentionally or accidentally divulge that she was in a relationship with Angela Moore. Sharon Ashford barely knew who Angela Moore was. Her mother had seen a movie Angela was in years ago, but had to be reminded of which movie it was. Nevertheless, she eventually remembered the movie star. The fact that Sharon lived in the middle of nowhere in the southern region of Australia, meant she didn't have access to celebrity news. The only time she saw a tabloid was passing by an airport newsstand.

"I'm so happy for you," Sharon said excitedly. "But aren't the two of you going to want to go public about your relationship some day?" Sharon asked, with concern in her voice. "You can't hide it forever, you know."

"We haven't discussed that yet," Kate responded.

"Why not?"

"We just haven't discussed it yet." Kate didn't feel like getting into the Angela coming-out discussion with her mother. "We'll cross that bridge when it comes."

"Well, I just don't want you to get hurt. If she is as big a movie star as you say, she may never want to go public. What kind of life will that be for you? Will you be content hiding your relationship forever?"

"I really don't know, mom. We love each other. That's all that matters right now." Kate didn't expect this line of questioning from her mother. She knew her mother would be honest—and show concern. However, it felt like her mother was interrogating her.

"You may want to talk to her about it sooner rather than later. You deserve someone who's honest and not afraid to admit to the world she loves you."

Ouch. The truth hurt. Her mother's questions hit Kate like a ton of bricks.

After their conversation, Kate began to fear the worst. *What if Angela never wants to end her fake marriage with Jason? What if she does intend on living a charade forever? Then what?* Kate hadn't really thought about it. She was so madly in love with Angela that, up until now, she didn't care if they had to sneak around for the rest of their lives.

Angela had told Kate about the ultimatum her lover, Kristan, gave her. At the time, Kate thought it was selfish of Kristan to have put that burden on Angela, knowing she couldn't possibly go public about their relationship. Now she was beginning to understand why Kristan did that.

Kate decided she had to have a conversation with Angela about their future. They'd been together for over four months now. No one, except her mother, knew of the relationship. Her best friends, Marisol and Jamie had no idea why Kate had been too busy for them in recent months.

Marisol was perplexed by Kate's disappearances that she asked her if she was doing drugs.

"Are you nuts? Of course I'm not doing drugs. I told you I've been busy with work," Kate informed Marisol as they strolled on the beach in Malibu.

"We used to spend more time together. It seems you're always busy and never home. Are you seeing someone?"

"No. I'm just busy. Trust me." It killed Kate to have to lie to Marisol.

"You're not seeing Tami again, are you?"

"Hell, no. Do you think I've totally lost my mind or something just because I've been taking on more assignments? I haven't had any contact with Tami since I filed the restraining order against her." After Kate and Angela's first date, Tami continued to call and email her. On one occasion, Tami revealed that she knew Kate was seeing Angela and shared places in which they were seen together.

Kate knew the only way Tami would know this information is if she were following her. Kate denied having a relationship with Angela—that their meetings were of a professional nature. The next day, Kate petitioned for a restraining order, which was granted immediately after Kate showed the police officers her cell phone log and Tami's emails. Kate hadn't heard from her since.

Tami was furious she was served with restraining order papers instructing her to stay away from Kate. She blamed it all on Angela. *Kate would never do this to me. Angela must have put her up to this.* Tami had a gut feeling from that first night Paul followed Kate that the two had something going on, though Paul reported back to Tami nothing of the sort.

After a week of Paul tailing Kate, Tami told Paul that if Kate and Angela were indeed seeing each other as her intuition told her, she wanted a photo to prove it.

"I'll give you $50,000 if you get a photo of those two bitches together," she offered Paul. "And it has to be a photo that screams out the two are more than friends. Got it?" Tami knew she had to make this enticing for Paul. Paul was the type of low life who would forego telling Tami that Kate and Angela were seeing each other just so he could get paid by a tabloid. She was no dummy.

Paul practically foamed at the mouth. $50,000 could buy him a lot of coke. He thought about how this could lead to more opportunities to make even more cash. Once he received the $50,000 from Tami, he planned on getting much more by selling the photos to a tabloid—or maybe even tabloids. He could sell different photos to different tabloids. Or, he could get a large sum by dealing with one tabloid exclusively. He'd be calling the shots for once in his life. Goodbye to his pathetic driver's income.

When he wasn't driving Tami around, Paul spent every spare moment of his time stalking Kate and Angela.

He was getting impatient. It had been weeks and nothing. No photo of a kiss, a hug, or even a caress, though he saw Kate come and go from Angela's house every day.

Tami was growing impatient too.

"Angela, we need to talk," Kate said, turning toward Angela's side of the bed. It was morning and they'd spent the night at Angela's house, making love.

"What is it, honey?" Angela asked, lying next to Kate, twirling and toying with Kate's ponytail. Angela loved it when Kate pulled her hair up in a ponytail. It was sexy and cute at the same time.

"I need to know that someday you and me *won't* be a secret. I'm not giving you an ultimatum and promise I never will. I just want to know what your plans are for us." Kate felt a lump in her throat.

"I love you, Kate. My plans are to continue loving you and spending the rest of my life with you," Angela said.

"Do you think you'll ever come out?" Kate asked.

"I don't know."

"What are your biggest fears around coming out?"

"I guess it would be my parents. It would kill them. They still haven't accepted or dealt with the fact my brother Joe is gay."

"Then, it's not your career you worry about?"

"Well, of course I'm worried about that. The press would have a field day. Who knows where my career would go?"

"Do you think you could do it? I'm serious about this, Angela. Do you *ever* think you could be completely honest? To everyone? For me?" Kate sat up. She felt awkward having this conversation with Angela.

"I suppose some day." Angela paused, upset that she couldn't give Kate the answer she so desperately wanted and deserved to hear. "I'm sorry, Kate. I'm scared."

"You know you wouldn't be alone. I'd be there for you every step of the way…through it all." Kate wrapped Angela in her arms and kissed the edge of her ear.

"I know," Angela said, wishing her life was easier.

Angela thought about their conversation that entire week. Maybe she would come out. It would definitely be a huge relief on many levels. But then she thought about her parents' and the press' reactions and felt waves of fear swim through her veins. Coming out scared the shit out of her.

CHAPTER 26

"EXCLUSIVE: ANGELA MOORE'S Lesbian Affair!" The headline read on the cover of the tabloid. The photo underneath the heading showed Kate and Angela sitting in Kate's SUV, engaged in a passionate kiss. Inside was another photo of Angela and Kate holding each other in a passionate embrace, leaning on Kate's SUV.

Lindsey hand-delivered the magazine to Angela the morning it was published. "Who is this woman, Angela?" she asked, severe displeasure in her tone.

Angela grabbed the magazine. "What are you talking about, Lindsey?"

She looked at the magazine's headline and photo. She couldn't believe her eyes. She'd been outed to millions of people.

"Fuck," Angela said out loud.

"Yeah, that's right. You are fucked. We are fucked. More importantly, Angela, who the fuck is she?" Lindsey demanded.

"That's Kate," Angela muttered as she flipped through the tabloid's four-page spread of her and Kate in compromising positions.

"Who the fuck is Kate?" Lindsey's face was turning red and a vein was protruding from the side of her neck.

"Lindsey, I have no clue how they got this. I've been so careful." Angela was in shock as she held the magazine, staring blankly at the pages. It was surreal. This couldn't possibly be happening.

"Who fucking cares how they got it Angela? We need to figure out what you're going to say. How am I ever going to spin this one? It's impossible!" Lindsey screamed.

"I think....I'm going to say..." Angela was speechless.

"It's a lie. It's a doctored photo. That's what you're going to say," Lindsey ordered, obviously scrambling for an idea.

"Wait a minute, Lindsey." Angela felt like she had suddenly awoken from her state of shock. "I'm in love with this woman. It's time to just come out. This is the time."

"Are you nuts? Do you know what that could do to your career?" Lindsey paced the foyer. "Don't forget you're dealing with Jason's career too. Who knows what this could do to him."

"I don't know, Lindsey. Tell me. What will it do?" Angela was annoyed with Lindsey. "What the fuck will it do? What about me? What about the fact I'm in love with this woman and am sick of hiding it from everyone? I don't fucking give a shit anymore."

"Angela, I know what's best. You have to lie. You're out of your mind right now." Lindsey started to dial her cell phone. "I'm going to arrange a press conference for you to tell the world this photo isn't what it appears."

"No, Lindsey." Angela shoved the tabloid magazine into Lindsey's hands. "This time I'm not going to lie."

"How do you expect me to be your publicist if you won't take my advice?" Lindsey seethed.

"That's easy. You're fired."

Angela felt empowered by her decision to axe Lindsey. As soon as Lindsey stormed out of the house, Angela called

Mary and told her about the tabloid, firing Lindsey and that she'd need her to run interference with their parents until Angela was ready to talk to them.

"I can't believe you fired Lindsey. She'll probably sue you," Mary laughed.

"I really don't care. She can kiss my ass. I'm relieved to be rid of her. I just can't believe I'm going to go through with this. I'm so scared."

"I'll go to the press conference with you. It'll be o.k. Of course it's going to be difficult for the next month or so. Eventually, nobody will care anymore. It'll be old news."

Angela's swiftly hired a new publicist, Sheila James, who primarily handled gay clientele. Sheila arranged a press conference at her office in West Hollywood, carefully selecting a group of journalists she knew would go easy on Angela.

"I hope you're right. I just feel so bad for what Kate is going to have to go through. The press will hound her. And Jason. Oh, God, he's going to flip," Angela told Sheila.

"Have you talked to them yet?"

"I spoke with Kate. She wanted to go to the press conference to support me, but I insisted she stay at my house and chill for a little while. This is my problem. I'm going to deal with it. I'm going to talk to Jason as soon as I get off the phone with you."

"I can't imagine how he's going to react."

"I'm sure he'll fight me tooth and nail over this."

"Well, good luck."

"Thanks."

"Jason, I'm telling the truth and that's it," Angela said.

"You are out of your mind. Don't you know what this can do to me?" Jason was sitting in his bed, watching ESPN.

"It's over, Jason. The charade is over. I'm telling the press that I'm in love with Kate and you and I are over. I'll take all of the blame and be the bad guy." Angela paced alongside his bed, agitated and shaking.

"You need to sit tight for a minute. You can't jeopardize my career because you want to come out." Jason swung his feet around and placed them on the floor, next to the bed.

"Look, you knew what you were getting into when you married me. I love you, Jason, but I have to do this." Angela put her arm under Jason's underarm to help him stand up.

"What did Lindsey say?" Jason shooed her arm away and used the nightstand as leverage.

"I fired her." Angela stepped back to give Jason some space.

"You *what?*" after hearing this news, Jason lost his balance and nearly fell to the ground. He caught his fall by leaning into the bed and pushing himself back up to stand.

"Would you be careful?" Angela pleaded. "You're still recovering."

"Well this situation isn't helping me any."

"This has nothing to do with your accident. So don't put that on me right now." Angela was frustrated this conversation wasn't going well.

"I can't believe you fired Lindsey. You've totally lost your mind, Angela." Jason limped to the bedroom door.

"No I haven't. I'm not lying anymore. I can't deal with these lies. I'll never be able to have a real relationship. I deserve better." Angela walked over to the bedroom door and opened it for Jason.

"What about me and what I deserve? Does that matter?" He leaned against the door, out of breath.

"I'm sorry. I have to do this."

"Angela, I'm begging you. Please don't do this."

"It's over, Jason. I'm making a statement today."

"Please, Angela. For me," Jason pleaded.

222

"No. I'm finally doing something for *me*, Jason. I love you, but I have to do this."

Kate overheard Angela and Jason argue as she waited down the hall in Angela's bedroom. Kate drove to Angela's house immediately after Angela called her with the news about their photo in the tabloid. When Kate arrived at the gate to Angela's house, there were a few rogue photographers she recognized. As she drove past them, they snapped a flurry of photos.

She sat in Angela's room, waiting for the argument to be over and wondered what she could possibly do to help Angela. She felt terrible for her. Coming out is like turning your entire world upside down. Well, actually, it's like turning it right side up—the way it was always meant to be.

Angela entered the bedroom and immediately embraced Kate with a hug. She was crying. "He is such an asshole. All he can think about is his career," Angela wept.

"He's scared, Angela," Kate said, holding Angela tight.

"So am I. I'm petrified. Look, I'm shaking like a leaf." Angela held out her hand to show Kate her quivering hand.

"Oh, baby. I'm so sorry you have to go through this. You know, you don't have to do this now. You can always..."

"No," Angela interrupted. "Absolutely not. I'm ready. I'm not lying anymore. I love you and want the entire world to know." Angela cupped her hand to Kate's cheek and leaned in to kiss her.

The gate guard interrupted by announcing over the intercom that Mary had arrived and was entering the driveway.

"My ride is here," Angela said. "Guess it's time to face the music."

"Just remember I love you and am so proud of you," Kate said.

***

"Are you ready, Angela?" Sheila asked. Angela was waiting in the office of Sheila's business partner. It adjoined Sheila's office, where the journalists were waiting.

"I guess." Angela was terrified. "I'm so nervous."

"I'll be next to you the entire time. It's going to be o.k., honey," Mary said.

"Let's do this," Angela announced.

"O.k. Follow me," Sheila said as she led Angela and Mary out into the hallway.

There were five journalists: one from the LA Times, another from Variety, and three representing various entertainment television programs. Photo flashes lit up the room as Angela made her way to the end of a very long conference table. Mary sat next to her and held her hand under the table.

"Each of you will be permitted one question. After you've all had a chance to interview Ms. Moore, the press conference will end," Sheila instructed the eager-looking men and women.

Sheila called on the first journalist from the LA Times.

"Angela, is this you in this photo, kissing another woman?" he asked.

"Yes. That is me in that picture, kissing my girlfriend," Angela said. The journalists whispered to each other, obviously savoring every minute of this confession.

"What is the status of your marriage to Jason Saunders?" the journalist from Entertainment Tonight asked.

"Jason and I have been separated since before his accident. I have stood by him during his recovery period." Angela hesitated to swallow what felt like a lump in her throat, and then continued, "We remain very close and amicable. But, I must admit that our marriage is over and has been over for some time now." Angela found that difficult to say. They weren't close or amicable at this point. He was furious with her.

"Who is this woman? The woman you are kissing in this photo?" the next journalist asked.

"I don't think it's necessary for me to divulge who I'm seeing. Revealing her identity or intimate details of our relationship is not why I'm here. I'm here to be truthful about the status of my marriage and that I am in a committed and loving relationship with another woman."

"Have you always been a lesbian, Angela?" an attractive blonde reporter asked.

"All I can say is that I am currently in a relationship with a woman. I don't feel the need to define myself or discuss my past."

"How long have you been seeing Kate Ashford?" the last journalist asked. Angela was taken aback by the mention of Kate's name.

Rather than deny it was Kate or pussyfoot around, Angela said, "Kate and I have been seeing each other for around four months."

"That's it everyone," Sheila announced as Angela and Mary arose from the table.

As they were leaving, the journalists made a last ditch attempt to gather more information.

"How did the two of you meet?" "What does Jason think?" "Do you think this will hurt your career?" were just some of the questions asked.

"I can't believe they mentioned Kate's name. I was a fool to ever think she'd be safe from these vultures," Angela told Mary as they entered the elevator to leave Sheila's office.

"It was bound to happen. You can tell it's her in the photo. They know her. She's a colleague," Mary said.

"I know. I just feel so bad for her." Angela thought she'd

feel relieved after coming out. This was not the case. She felt disgusted by the media and even more worried for Kate and Jason.

"You did the right thing, Angela. I'm proud of you." Mary hugged her sister. Mary was so supportive. Angela felt lucky to have such a wonderful sister.

"Thank you for being there for me, Mary. It means so much."

"Hey. I've been waiting for this day to come for a long time. No more lies."

"Too bad you're going to have to deal with mom and dad."

"They should be the least of your concerns right now. I'll handle them. I'm sure I have voice mail messages waiting for me at home."

"I just can't deal with them yet. Thanks for everything. I'm so grateful to have you in my life, Mary."

CHAPTER 27

THAT EVENING, NEARLY every local and national news station in America covered the press conference and tabloid story of Angela and Kate. The following day, the story made headlines in nearly every major newspaper.

Since Angela's mother wouldn't stop calling, she decided to return her phone calls.

"What happened to you and Jason?" her mother asked, sobbing.

"Nothing happened, mom. This is just the way it is," Angela said matter-of-factly.

"Was there something your dad and I could've done?" her mother whimpered.

"Mom, this has nothing to do with you or dad." Angela couldn't wait to get off the phone. Having lived through her parents' revelation that her brother Joe was gay, Angela knew the only cure for dealing with her mother would be time. Nothing she said to her mother at this point would make a difference.

"First Joey. Now you. What did we do wrong? We brought you up in a nice Catholic home." Her mother was trying to lay the guilt on thick.

"Mom, I'm not going to listen to your religious guilt trip. You either accept this like you had to with Joe, or don't call me." Angela felt a huge weight lift from her body. Finally, she felt strong, and refused to take her mother's subtle abuse.

"How can you say such a thing to your own mother? That poor Jason. I'm sure he is heartbroken."

"He's fine, mom. You need to know that this isn't about you or Jason right now. This is *my* life," Angela said, angrily.

"We are so disappointed. We had such high hopes for you and Jason. Don't you ever want to have children, Angela?"

"Mom, I can't talk to you right now. Call me when you've gotten over this and can have a conversation without judging me or shaming me." Angela hung the phone up. She was angry with her mother for being so self-righteous. She knew if she continued to talk with her, she'd surely go insane.

Angela and Jason's house and cell phones rang non-stop. It seemed as though everyone they had ever known, including fellow actors and minor acquaintances, were trying to contact them to see if they were ok or needed anything. Publicists, agents, and divorce and entertainment attorneys were calling to get a piece of the action as well.

Though his publicist encouraged him to make a statement, Jason refused to make a public comment. The press, with nothing to go on from Jason's point of view, portrayed him as the unfortunate victim of Angela's deceit.

The paparazzi were camped outside the gate of their home morning and night. Angela felt like a prisoner of her own home and decided she and Kate needed to leave L.A.

"We have to get out of here. Billy Marshall, the producer of my last movie, offered his private jet. We can leave tonight," Angela informed Kate.

"Where are we going?" Kate asked.

"I don't know."

Kate paused, and then said, "I have an idea. We can go to Australia to stay with my mom. Her place is in a very remote area. We won't be bothered. Plus, she would love to meet you."

"That's a great idea." Angela lit up. "I want to meet her too."

Angela made the necessary phone calls to arrange the flight and began packing. She was glad she didn't have to worry about taking a commercial flight. It would've been too easy for the press to follow their every move.

To throw off the paparazzi, Angela came up with a plan to use Mary as a decoy. Angela found a wig similar to her current hairstyle in her closet from a movie she'd acted in. Angela figured if Mary wore the wig everyone would think Mary was Angela.

Angela recorded a statement on a small tape recorder for Mary to play when she exited the gate.

"Get a life you jerks. Don't you have something better to do?" Angela yelled into the tape recorder.

"That's exactly something you'd say to them," said Kate, laughing.

"I hope this works," Mary said. "Both of you deserve a break from this."

When Angela and Kate were ready to leave for the airport, they packed their suitcases in the back of Angela's chef, Evan's SUV. Next, Mary got into a hired limo and instructed the driver to slowly drive to the gate. As Mary drove away, Kate and Angela climbed into the back of Evan's SUV and waited for Mary's phone call letting them know it was clear for Evan to drive them to the airport.

As the limo exited the gate leading to the road littered with paparazzi, Mary cracked the window to the limo and played the tape Angela made. The limo pulled out onto the road and the photographers scrambled to get into their vehicles and follow her.

Mary immediately called Angela. "All clear. They fell for it," Mary told Angela.

"Thanks. Make sure you take them on the longest wild goose chase of their lives," Angela said, snidely.

"Do you think I should bring them to Malibu? It's in the opposite direction of LAX," Mary suggested.

"Yes, I love it. Don't forget to flip them off occasionally," Angela laughed.

"Will do," Mary agreed.

Angela hung the phone up and gave a thumbs-up signal for Evan to start driving.

The plan worked.

Evan deposited Angela and Kate safely at the airport, sans any paparazzi. In the meantime, Mary arrived in Malibu and had the limo park in front of a coffee shop. She waited for the paparazzi to surround her, then exited the limo, ripped off her wig and gave the middle finger to onlookers.

Mary returned to the house to check on Jason.

"I can't believe she's done this to me," Jason told Mary.

"Jason, you've got to put yourself in her shoes. Let her be happy. My God, you act like the two of you really were married," Mary said as she brought Jason a pillow. Though his recovery was coming along at a miraculously swift rate, he still spent the majority of his time in bed, in pain.

"You don't understand, Mary." Jason had to tell someone about his feelings for Angela. He couldn't keep it to himself any longer. "I have to tell you something important."

"What is it, Jason?" Mary sat on the side of Jason's bed.

"I think I fell in love with Angela," Jason admitted.

"Jason, that's impossible. What are you talking about?" Mary reached out and took Jason's hand in hers.

"I don't know. The night I got into the accident, I went out for a drive. I was pissed off at Angela because she was going out on a date with Kate. I turned the music up and drove really fast. I was so angry. That's why I got in the accident."

"Oh, Jason. I'm so sorry." Mary held Jason's hand tightly. "You have to accept that Angela is in love with Kate."

"I know. I don't know what I was thinking. All of a sudden, I felt like I didn't want to be a bachelor anymore. I wanted a real wife and kids. I started having these fantasies that Angela could be that person. I guess I was out of my mind," Jason said, shedding a tear.

"I would have to agree with you on that," Mary snickered. "My sister has always been gay. There's no chance in hell you two could ever be more than friends."

"You probably think I'm a jerk now, don't you?" Jason asked.

"No, Jason. Not at all. I still think you're a great guy. You'll meet that woman to share your life with. It's just never going to be Angela."

"Yeah. I know that now," Jason said. "I can't wait to feel better and get back to work. That'll take my mind off all of this."

Angela and Kate were thrilled the press didn't figure out their get-a-way plan. Besides the small crew, they were the only passengers on the private flight to Australia. They were able to cuddle next to each other without being harassed by anyone. It was the most peace they'd experienced since the photos of the two were released.

Fifteen hours after departing Los Angeles, they arrived in Melbourne, followed by, a two-hour drive to the Grampians region of Australia. The Grampians region, located in the south eastern Australian province of Victoria, boasted breathtaking mountains, ancient volcanoes, deep gorges, rivers and quaint mining towns. The koala reserve was located in the town of Halls Gap, situated at the foot of the Wonderland Range and at the center of the Wonderland Forest Park.

As Angela and Kate approached Halls Gap, they were amazed by the awe-inspiring sight of the mountains and rock formations that rose from the flat plains below. Kangaroos roamed freely and koalas could be seen perched in trees in the distance.

Sharon resided in a modest cottage adjacent to the reserve. It was the perfect place for Kate and Angela to relax and enjoy each other, which was a far contrast from the craziness of L.A. Halls Gap was a laidback sort of town where Australians traveled from all over to come to relax on vacation.

Angela bonded immediately with Sharon. Kate and Angela spent their first evening together in Australia listening to Sharon share her stories of the koala bears, lemurs and other animals she'd dedicated her life to. She told them of how chlamydial disease, a common condition in koalas, lowered their reproductive rates, resulting in their endangerment.

"Of course, chlamydia wasn't the only precursor to koala endangerment," Sharon said. "There are other factors that threaten them, like deforestation, human settlement and hunting."

Angela felt like she could listen to Sharon talk for hours about the koalas and her work with animals.

Sharon spent much of her time at the reserve treating the animals, while her conservationist colleagues focused on saving the koala's habitat from destruction. After a few days of relaxation and sightseeing, Angela and Kate went straight to work helping the conservationists mulch old gum tree branches, plant new trees and prepare extra cages for injured wildlife.

Their evenings were spent watching the sunset, chatting with Kate's mother, and making love in their private room.

"Will you come and live with me?" Angela asked Kate while they lied in bed one evening, the full moon beaming through the window.

"What about Jason?" Kate asked. "I'd rather we had our own place."

"You're right. As soon as we get back, we're going house hunting," Angela said.

"Well, be prepared to downsize, with my salary."

"Don't do that Kate. We are a couple now. What's mine is yours. Let me worry about the cost of the house. I want us to be together. Forever."

"Me too."

Ten days had gone by and not a photographer in sight. It was pure bliss. However, bliss would not last. Sharon's phone rang and everything would change.

CHAPTER 28

"HEY GIRL," ANGELA said, excitedly. Sharon had informed her that it was her sister Mary on the phone.

"Hi." Mary didn't sound excited. "We've gotta talk Angela." Mary's tone was very serious.

"What's going on? Everything o.k.?" Angela was concerned.

"Well, no. Jason just received a letter. I mean, you received a letter and Jason accidentally opened it."

"What did it say?" Angela sat down on Sharon's front porch swing.

"The person who wrote the letter claims Kate is the person who leaked the photographs of the two of you to the press," Mary revealed.

"That's crazy!" Angela blurted.

"The letter was signed by a reporter at the tabloid. I don't think it's fake. It's on letterhead."

"Give me the phone number. I'll call the reporter myself," Angela demanded.

Mary gave her the phone number.

"Is everything else o.k.?"

"Yeah."

"How's Jason?"

"He'll be fine. I mean, he's fine."

"I have to call this person and see what this is all about," Angela said. "I'll let you know what happens."

"Don't jump to any conclusions. I just thought you should know sooner rather than later."

"No. I'm glad you called me. Love you," Angela said, hurrying off the phone.

"Love you too. Bye."

Angela put the phone down.

This is ridiculous, Angela thought. Kate would never do anything like that. Someone must be playing a horrible joke on them.

She hesitated before she dialed the number Mary gave her. She wondered if she should even bother. Maybe it was trick to screen the call and locate her. Then she remembered having seen Sharon's phone number listed on Kate's cell phone's caller id as "Private".

Angela quickly punched the numbers on the phone. It rang twice, and then a receptionist with a valley girl accent answered.

"Hi, I'd like to speak with Mike Jones. He's a reporter there," Angela said.

"Hold on. I'll transfer you," the whiny receptionist said.

"Hello," Mike said, into a speakerphone.

"Hi. This is Angela Moore."

"Yeah, right." He let out a deep chuckle.

"No, it really is. I received a letter from you," Angela pleaded.

"You did? Then tell me what it says. Maybe I'll believe you," the reporter said, inquisitively.

Angela recited what Mary told her was written in the letter.

"You got it. Kate Ashford sold me those photos," he proclaimed.

"What? Are you joking?" Angela couldn't believe what she was hearing.

"Nope. I'm not joking."

"Why are you bothering to tell me this?" Angela asked. "Why would you even care to send a letter to me about this? Don't you reporters have some sort of code where you have to respect your source?"

"Thought I'd be a good samaritan. Wouldn't you rather know?" Mike was nonchalant. Angela could hear him chewing on something, maybe food or a big wad of gum.

"Of course I would want to know. Anyone in their right mind would want to know." Angela was in shock. Angela paused for a moment and decided she couldn't trust this person. "Why should I believe you? I shouldn't even bother talking to you. I know you're lying to me. You just want a story."

"Believe what you want." His chewing became louder. "But I got proof."

"How can you prove this?" Angela demanded.

"We gave your girlfriend half a million. It was a record payout for our tabloid. I have all the paperwork here. She had to sign documents to prove the photos were authentic in lieu of the payment."

"I'll need to see those documents when I get back."

"Where are you?"

"I'm not falling for that one." Angela hung up.

She sat on the swing and couldn't believe what had just transpired. How could Kate betray her? Why would she? She could have anything of Angela's she wanted. She didn't need to sell the photos. Angela felt faint.

"I just spoke with Angela. She wants to see documents proving Kate did it," Mike Jones said.

"Then create the damn things," the caller said.

"I'm not sure I should go through with this. If my boss finds out, I'll never work in this town again," Mike said, worry in his tone.

"I'm giving you $250,000," the caller said. "If you get fired, you can live on that for a while."

"I don't know. I'm rethinking this. That money will only last a couple of years. I'll still need a job. This is getting out of hand."

"If you're trying to get more money out of me, forget it. Now go and figure out how to concoct those documents. If you don't, you won't get the rest of your money."

"All right. But I'll need something with Kate's signature on it."

"What's the matter, honey? You look like you saw a ghost," Kate asked.

"My sister just called," Angela said in a depressed tone.

"What is it? Is everyone o.k.?" Kate was worried that someone was hurt or dead.

"No, everything's not o.k., Kate. A reporter from the tabloid sent me a letter claiming you sold him those photos of us together," Angela struggled with her words.

"That's insane. You know that could never be true." Kate was adamant.

"I called him. He said it was true and he'll show me the documents you signed." Angela started to cry.

"No, baby. Don't believe him. Someone's trying to tear us apart. I would never do anything like that. You have to believe me. I love you so much. You are the love of my life." Kate grabbed Angela and held her tight.

"I want to believe you. I'm just very confused right now," Angela sobbed.

"We'll get through this. Don't worry. You'll see he's lying. Everything will work out." Kate tried to assure Angela.

Angela trusted what Kate was telling her was true. She needed to make sure, though, that Kate was being a 100% honest with her. She decided to let it go for now until they returned to L.A. in a week.

The first thing Angela did when she returned to L.A. was call the reporter, Mike Jones, to arrange a meeting with him to see the documents supposedly implicating Kate. Kate insisted on going with Angela to the meeting. They made plans to meet in a park near Malibu later that day.

"Why don't you tell her the truth right now, Mike? I didn't sell you those photos," Kate demanded. She knew Mike from special event assignments. He was a major slimeball.

Mike, a short balding man resembling Danny Devito, sat alongside Kate and Angela on a park bench, manila envelope in hand. "Let her see for herself, Kate," he said, reaching into the envelope.

He pulled out documents and handed them to Angela. She immediately went to work reading them. The documents, which consisted of affidavits, letters, and a receipt, validated Mike's accusation—that Kate supplied the tabloid with the photos and in turn received $500,000.

"Is this your signature, Kate?" Angela asked. "It looks identical to your handwriting."

Kate grabbed the papers and couldn't believe what she saw. It was indeed her signature, or a very good likeness thereof.

"Yes. I mean no." Kate was bewildered.

"What are you talking about? Is it your signature or not?" Angela asked, with anger in her voice.

"Someone must have scanned my signature into this document or copied it somehow. I never signed this document. I swear to you Angela," Kate pleaded.

"It is Kate's signature. It couldn't be anyone else's. She's the only one who sold the photos to us," Mike snickered. "Sorry, Kate, you got caught."

Kate jumped up and kneeled in front of Angela, grabbing on to her arms. "Angela, you have to believe me. He's lying. Someone wants to ruin our relationship. He's a tabloid reporter for Christ's sake. Think about it. You're too smart for this bullshit," Kate pleaded.

"These look like copies of an original. Can I keep these?" Angela asked Mike, referring to the documents.

"Sorry, can't do that. These are the property of the magazine," he said.

"Then, here." Angela handed the documents back to Mike. Angela arose from the park bench and began walking back to her car, not saying a word.

Kate immediately followed her, the entire time pleading her innocence. When Kate tried to open the passenger side door, Angela said. "I can't be around you right now. Get a ride with your buddy, Mike."

"Angela, you have to believe me. Please. Don't believe that slimy troll's lies. Please. I'm begging you. I love you. I would never hurt you. Ever." Kate began crying. She couldn't believe she was being set up like this, and that Angela was falling for it.

"I don't know what to believe right now, Kate. I'm in shock. I just feel really fucked up and confused. Two weeks before the photos were printed, you were talking to me about coming out. You have to understand what I'm going through right now. I need some time." Angela got in the car, slammed the door and sped off, leaving Kate at the side of the road with Mike.

Kate turned to Mike and furiously shouted, "Listen you motherfucker. I'm going to get to the bottom of this. And when I do, you won't be able to get a job reporting for a high school newspaper."

Angela was horrified by what had just occurred. She was trembling. Her hands could barely keep a grip on the steering wheel. Deep down, a part of her knew without a doubt that Kate would never do this to her. Then her mind would err to the side of caution. The proof was right there on paper. She thought about it and wondered who on earth went to such lengths to try and break them up?

As she drove home, she thought about calling her old dealer and getting some pills to ease her pain. The emotional pain she felt was growing. She wanted to take something that would numb her. She wished she could use drugs safely and in moderation. However, she'd been clean a long time and knew that one pill would eventually turn into hundreds. She didn't want to feel all of these emotions right now. Taking a pill would change that. She hated feeling this way. It reminded her of when Julie left her and Ted died.

"Tami. I know you did this. You set me up with the tabloid. I know you did this," Kate shouted into her cell phone.

"What are you talking about, Kate?" Tami asked.

"You know what you did. You better make things right or I'll make sure you regret it," Kate warned.

"Kate, I honestly don't know what you're talking about. You're crazy."

"Fuck you, Tami. This is exactly what you wanted. Why don't you admit you did this?"

"Did what? *What* are you talking about?"

Kate couldn't stand to hear another word out of Tami's mouth, so she hung up the phone. Kate was so angry it frightened her. She was so mad that she felt like killing Tami.

"I can't believe she'd do something like that. Are you positive?" Mary asked Angela.

"I saw what I saw. That's all I know," Angela replied, pacing the length of her house's rear patio.

"Are you two broken up now?" Jason, seated on the couch next to Mary, asked. Mary shot Jason a "don't even go there look".

"Duh! Of course we are," Angela replied sarcastically. "Happy?"

"Jason, Angela needs our support," Mary instructed Jason.

"I *am* being supportive. I was just wondering," Jason defended himself.

Angela stopped pacing and looked out to the garden. "I loved this woman more than I've ever loved anyone. I can't believe this is happening to me. I thought I'd finally found the woman I wanted to spend the rest of my life with. I came out to the whole world for her."

"It doesn't seem like something Kate would do, Angela." Mary stood and put her arm around Angela.

"I know. That's why this is so hard. I don't know who to believe or what to think. One part of me knows this is complete bullshit. The other part of me is apprehensive and doesn't trust her."

Jason got up and headed into the house.

"Where are *you* going?" Mary asked Jason.

Jason turned around and said, "I'm sick of all this. Does anyone care that my life is pretty fucked up too right now? Every tabloid has me at the center of this lesbian triangle. Depending on which one you read, I'm either a pathetic bystander or a stupid idiot."

"I'm sorry, Jason. I really am. I never planned to screw your life up like this," Angela said, apologetically.

"Well, it sucks." Jason left the two women and entered the house, trying unsuccessfully to slam the screen door, which gently flapped back open.

"How did it go?"

"I'm pretty sure Angela believed me. She took off in her car without Kate. She was definitely not a happy camper," Mike Jones said.

"Good. I'll give you the remainder of your payment. Just stick to your story," the caller said.

"What if Angela goes to the publisher and wants a full investigation? Then what? Any expert will be able to tell I doctored the documents and signature." Mike felt like he was about to have a panic attack. He hadn't had a panic attack in years and worried that he was mentally relapsing.

"She's not going to bother wasting her time on that. Don't worry about it. You did your job. And you're a richer man because of it."

Kate was devastated over the allegations and invited Marisol and Jamie to her house for support.

"I'm so sorry Kate. We know you would never do anything like this," Marisol said, putting her hand on Jamie's.

Kate, curious about this intimate sign of affection and asked, "Are you two together now?"

"Yeah. We didn't want to tell you in case it didn't work out. We've been seeing each other for the past two months," Jamie said, gazing lovingly into Marisol's eyes.

"We're in love," Marisol professed, returning Jamie's gaze.

"Well, I'm happy for the both of you," Kate said, with torment in her voice. "I'm glad there's a couple who's happy in this world."

"Can't you demand copies of the original document and have them tested for authenticity somehow?" Jamie asked, clenching Marisol's hand.

"I never thought of that." Kate's eyes lit up. "I'll call the publisher tomorrow. He knows me. I've sold him photos in the past."

"Well, if you supposedly received a half a million dollars for this, wouldn't there be a cancelled check or something?" Marisol added.

"You're right." Kate felt a surge of energy. She now had some hope there would be a solution to this horrible dilemma. She would find proof and show Angela she was telling the truth.

"I think you should invest all of your time making this right. I mean, I know it's hard to understand why Angela wouldn't believe you, but think about it," Jamie said.

"Yeah. I guess I can't blame her for feeling betrayed and confused. Damn that Mike Jones and whoever set him up to do this," Kate said.

The next day, Kate stormed into the publisher of the tabloid's office, ignoring the receptionist's plea to stay in the waiting area. Kate demanded to see the originals and a copy of the cancelled check. The publisher said he didn't know anything about Kate having sold the photos. Finally, she felt assured this whole ordeal would finally be resolved.

"Mike told me someone, who wanted to remain anonymous, delivered the photos. We didn't pay anyone as far as I know. Here, let's go talk to Mike." The publisher dropped a paper he was reviewing prior to Kate storming into his office and led Kate to Mike's office, which was actually a cubicle located at the center of over two dozen other cubicles.

"Hey Mike. Got a minute?" the publisher asked, while Kate stood next to him.

Mike stopped typing on his computer keyboard, "Sure. What's this about?"

"Could you tell me what's going on?" the publisher motioned his head in Kate's direction.

"Yeah, Mike. Tell your boss how you set me up," Kate said, angrily.

"I don't know what you're talking about, Kate. What's going on?" Mike innocently responded.

"You know exactly what's going on. Give me those documents so I can show your boss." Kate's face was beet red. She was losing patience with him.

"What documents, Kate?" Mike asked, acting dumbfounded.

"You know. The documents you forged my signature on."

"Listen, Kate. You're mistaken." He turned to the publisher. "I honestly don't know what she's talking about."

The publisher told Mike the story Kate had just shared with him moments ago about the photos, the money and Angela.

"Look, I don't know what you're trying to pull, Kate. If you're having problems with your girlfriend, don't get me involved." Mike looked into the publisher's eyes. "I honestly don't know anything about this. I received the photos anonymously, like I told you."

"I'm sorry, Kate. It seems we don't have what you're looking for. I think you need to heed Mike's advice and solve your own relationship problems," the publisher said, apologetically. "We'd be glad to take a statement on the record if that will help."

"Yeah right. Like I'd fall for that. I had no problems until this weasel created them. I think it's only fair, Mike, that you call Angela right this minute and tell her I didn't sell you the photos and this has been one huge mistake," Kate instructed.

"Wo wo wait a minute. I told you. I am not getting in the middle of your lover's quarrel. I'm not calling her. You're setting me up for career suicide here. I'll never be able to get an exclusive from her again," Mike reasoned.

"Oh, please. You blew that already. Just do it. Call her right now," Kate demanded.

Mike looked at his boss and said, "Could you please have her removed? This is insane."

"Kate, I can't have these disruptions. This is a place of business. Mike's right. You should leave now." The publisher grabbed Kate's elbow to try and lead her away from Mike's cubicle.

Kate shook his hand off of her and screamed at Mike, "I promise you Mike. Your short, fat, bald ass will never work in this industry again."

"Please leave now or I'll call the cops," the publisher warned.

Kate threw the large cup of iced coffee she bought earlier at Starbucks in Mike's face and briskly exited the office.

Kate had no idea what she was going to do now. She had to tell Angela what Mike said. She called Angela's cell phone. There wasn't any answer. The voice mail had reached the capacity of allotted messages. She tried Angela's house phone next and was able to leave a voice message.

"Angela, I have to talk to you. It's important. I went to the tabloid and talked to the publisher. Mike told him I didn't sell the photos to him. I don't know what's going on. None of it makes sense. I love you, Angela. We should be going through this together, not apart." Kate began to cry and said good-bye.

Later, while Angela was in bed, she listened to Kate's message three times before deciding to call her back.

"Hi, Kate. I got your message," Angela said, feeling unsure about having a conversation with Kate.

"Thank God you called me back. I was set up, Angela.

You have to call Mike. He'll tell you everything. I don't know what's going on. Someone's trying to keep us apart." Kate was breathless from the excitement of hearing Angela's voice for the first time in days.

Kate told Angela about her encounter with the publisher and Mike.

"I'll call him now," Angela said. Maybe this will put an end to her feelings of doubt and prove this was a huge misunderstanding.

"Honey, I miss you so much. I love you Angela. I would never do anything to hurt you or us. Call him now," Kate said with desperation in her voice.

"I love you too. I'll call you back."

Angela immediately called Mike at the tabloid.

"Hi Mike. Kate told me about her meeting with you and your publisher. Can you tell me who gave you those photos?"

Fuck. Mike thought. *Now what do I do? I've totally fucked this whole thing up.* To get the $250,000, he still had to play along about Kate providing the photos. Unfortunately, now his boss was involved and his job and reputation as one of the best tabloid reporters was on the line. He had to continue the charade. He needed the dough.

"Kate's reaching for straws, Angela. She's desperate to cover up what she did. I already told you and proved it to you. Kate sold me the photos. It was a private deal between me and the silent partner who owns part of the paper. The publisher didn't know about the deal we made with her. He just gets a paycheck like everyone else. This deal went over his head." Mike was convincing.

"What about the documents you showed me? She said you told the publisher they didn't exist." Angela was dumbfounded.

"I told him that because Kate ripped them out of my

hands and took off with them after you drove off yesterday. It was the only copy I had. I'm trying to cover my ass here with the silent partner. I can honestly tell you that she gave me those photos."

"So you're telling me there were no other documents? What about the originals?"

"The silent partner has them. He won't get involved, believe me. He has more important things to do than get involved with your personal drama, unless of course he can make money off of it. And, you'll never in my lifetime know the identity of the silent partner. So, Angela, just give up and accept the fact that Kate isn't who she appears to be. I've known her a long time in this business. She can't be trusted."

Angela hung the phone up. She couldn't stand to hear anymore. Now she was even more confused than ever. Deep down, she wanted to believe Kate. After all, Mike was a sleazy tabloid reporter. But now a shadow of doubt cast over their relationship. She needed more time. She needed time away from Kate.

"Angela, I don't know what more I can do to convince you I'm telling the truth," Kate pleaded through tears.

"I just think it's best we take some time to digest all of this," Angela said.

"Someone is doing this to us intentionally. Someone set this whole thing up. Don't you know that?" Kate felt like she was losing control of her entire life.

"Why on earth do you think that?" Angela asked.

"I think it may be Tami Montgomery."

"Tami Montgomery? Why do you think that?"

"Don't you remember me telling you about the woman I dated? The crazy nutcase I dated before you and I got together? It was Tami Montgomery. I had to get a restraining

STANDING NAKED IN PUBLIC

order against her. She was out of her mind. She is so crazy.
I can see her concocting something like this to get back at
me."

"I highly doubt it. All of the evidence was there. Why
would the reporter care about lying to me about it? He has
nothing to gain."

"Unless she's paying him off."

"This is getting way out of control, Kate. I have to go."

"This is killing me, Angela. I love you so much and would
never do anything to hurt you."

"This is killing me too. One minute I thought I found
the love of my life. The next, I'm faced with this shit. I feel so
fucked up, Kate." Angela started to cry. "I need time."

"Well, I'm not giving up on us," Kate promised.

"Good-bye, Kate," Angela responded.

"Wait," Kate said. Angela had already hung up.

Kate threw her phone into her handbag, grabbed her
jacket and car keys and headed off to Tami's house. She sped
the entire route, weaving in and out of lanes, cutting cars off
and nearly causing several major collisions. She was in a fury,
determined to confront Tami.

"Open the door, Tami!" Kate screamed, as she pounded on
the door of Tami's mansion.

Tami opened the door, wearing a pink terry robe. "Kate,
you know I can't have any contact with you," Tami said,
referring to the order of protection. Kate brushed passed her,
letting herself into the house.

"You bitch!" Kate yelled. "How could you do this to
me?"

"What are you talking about?" Tami asked, completely
bewildered.

"You paid Mike Jones to say I sold those photos of Angela and me to him. Don't pretend you don't know what I'm talking about."

"I did *what?*"

"You need to call Angela right now and tell her the truth," Kate ordered.

"I don't know what you're talking about. I had nothing to do with that. I was as shocked as everyone else to see those photos," Tami said, which was a complete lie since she had Paul stalking the two lovers for the very purpose of exposing their relationship.

"Fuck you, you lying bitch. You'll do anything to get me back." Kate grew more furious the more Tami denied knowing anything about the photos.

A pretty, blonde woman with a short, pixy hairstyle came running down the spiral stairs to where Kate and Tami were arguing.

"What's going on?" the attractive blonde asked Tami.

"It's nothing, Suzanna. She's leaving," Tami said, trying to cajole the woman.

"I'm not fucking leaving until you call her, Tami." Kate ignored Suzanna's presence.

"Who the fuck are you?" Suzanna asked Kate.

"None of your fucking business," Kate said as she gave Suzanna a side glance. "This is between Tami and me."

"I think it *is* my business. Tami's my girlfriend and she wants you to leave." Suzanna stepped forward, positioning herself between Kate and Tami.

"Tami, call her now." Kate ignored Suzanna and pushed her cell phone in front of Tami's face.

"Kate, you need to leave. I really don't know anything about this. I've been seeing Suzanna for the last three months. I really don't give a shit about you and Angela," Tami said, in a calm but persistent voice.

"That's right," Suzanna said, pointing to the door. "Now leave, bitch."

"I don't believe you." Kate pushed Tami—not very hard—but just enough for Tami to step back, then miss her footing and tumble to the floor.

Suzanna grabbed Kate's arm and started to drag her to the front door. "That's it, you're leaving," she said.

"Get your hands off of me," Kate said as she pushed Suzanna off of her.

Suzanna retaliated by tackling Kate to the floor, thrashing her fists at her. Kate fought back, trying to wrestle Suzanna's fists from hitting her.

Tami found a sense of delight and pride in witnessing Suzanna's valiant effort to defend her. Regardless, Tami panicked when she spotted blood. "Stop it you two. You're going to kill each other," Tami pleaded.

She couldn't identify which woman was bleeding, but knew now was the time to call her security guard.

Moments later, the guard entered the house and broke up the fight. Kate left with a bloody nose, bruises all over her body and a huge shiner around her right eye. Suzanna didn't fare much better. The fight was a draw.

CHAPTER 29

CATHERINE ERICKSON WAS drunk. No, she was plastered. She had just attended a charity ball at which she guzzled over a dozen martinis, mojitos and cosmopolitans. Her third and current husband, Howard, hated when she got drunk. It was bad enough that she irritated him to no end when she was sober. However, when she was drunk, she was completely out of control, obnoxious and verbally abusive.

Tonight, she was so hammered she couldn't walk. Howard had to carry her from the car and place her into their bed.

"Ya know what?" she slurred.

"What, Catherine?" he asked, irritated and disgusted.

"I di' it," she mumbled.

"You did what?" Howard prayed she'd pass out again. He hated engaging in these sloppy conversations with her. He was sick of her.

He couldn't wait to have her served with divorce papers. Unfortunately, he had made the ultimate Hollywood-husband mistake of signing an iron-clad prenuptial agreement. Therefore, prepared for the worst, he knew he had to retain a successful and high profile divorce attorney. Howard got lucky and found a real shark—an attorney who was willing and able to take on Catherine and her so-called iron-clad prenup. He spent that morning with his new lawyer; and reveled in listening to his attorney describe the tricks he had planned and loopholes he found in the prenup. Catherine would be in for a big surprise.

"I go' Angela Moore back," Catherine mumbled.

"What?" Howard was convinced she was dreaming or hallucinating.

"I gave the tabloid the photos of her and her girlfriend." Suddenly, Catherine became coherent. "She thinks her girlfriend sold them. But I know what really happened."

"You do? What's that, Catherine?" Howard was interested. He was trying to get dirt on her for the divorce. She sang like a canary when she was drunk. He needed to keep her awake by continuing to talk with her.

"I ruined their lil' happy party." Catherine let out a snort, which sounded as though it was meant to be a giggle.

"How'd you get the photos?" Howard pried.

"Paul. Our new driver. He's a doll. Then I paid the reporter to lie and tell Angela that Kate sold the photos to him." Catherine started laughing and snorting uncontrollably.

Howard knew his wife was a cold hearted bitch who hated Angela Moore with a passion, but this took the cake. He wondered how he could've ever been attracted to this vindictive lush.

Even though he had heard all of the rumors of her being a major bitch, Catherine was rich, drop-dead gorgeous from countless plastic surgery procedures, and well-connected in Hollywood. She would be his lifeline to a successful career in screenwriting. How bad could it possibly be to be married to her?

After a million dollar, star-studded wedding, Howard learned quickly how bad it could be. He spent his wedding night babysitting a very drunk Catherine, who belittled him the entire evening and refused to have sex with him. She told him he was a terrible writer and that he had a little dick. When he confronted her the following morning, she claimed that she didn't remember saying any of the awful things he recounted to her.

Since the day he married Catherine, Howard felt as though he had descended into hell. The only reprieve he'd get from her abuse was when she'd get called away to work on a movie. Occasionally, however, she'd insist he be there right by her side between takes, which infuriated him. On these occasions, Catherine treated him like a slave. "Get this, Howard." "Get that, Howard." "They fucked up my sandwich Howard, go get me another one." Howard hated going on location with Catherine. At least back in L.A. he had excuses to escape. He kept himself busy with screenwriter meetings, charity work, and golf.

"Just go to sleep," Howard whispered in her ear. *Yeah, you little witch. Go to sleep and you'll wake up with divorce papers in hand. I'm leaving you for good. This is our last night together.* He joyfully said to himself.

Catherine's evil laughter subsided and quickly she was snoring.

Howard reveled in Catherine's confession. One thing he knew about Catherine was that when she was drunk, she said what was on her mind—what she really thought. Alcohol was like truth serum for Catherine. Tonight's confession may become a necessary bargaining tool in his upcoming divorce proceedings.

Paul was having the time of his life spending his newly acquired small fortune. He was in Las Vegas, hosting a wild party in his Palms hotel suite. He had an endless supply of drugs, gorgeous women and money to gamble.

As he sat in a retro 60's style chair, taking in the festivities, he thought about how smart he had been to have gone to work for Catherine Erickson. Tami Montgomery was a major bitch. When he couldn't produce the photos of Angela and Kate for her in a timely enough manner, she canned him.

Paul's friend, who worked as a driver for Catherine Erickson, informed him that she was looking for a second driver. Paul had read in the tabloids about Catherine and Angela's contempt for each other and concocted a proposition for Catherine. During his private interview with her, Paul told Catherine about his idea to "out" Angela. Catherine listened intently and asked what he wanted as compensation. Paul responded that he would need $100,000 for photos of the two women, plus a guarantee in writing that he'd be employed as Catherine's driver for the next two years at $50,000 a year.

Catherine nearly choked on the amount and terms he demanded. Eventually, after a few days of scheming to figure out how badly she could ruin Angela's life and career, she accepted Paul's offer, only under the condition that she would have all rights to the photos and sales thereof. His plan to profit from the sale of the photos in addition to Catherine's payment was now off the table, which disappointed him. He decided he couldn't complain about $100,000 and guaranteed employment. He ultimately accepted Catherine's offer.

Paul felt like he was on top of the world. *Maybe I could do this for a living?* He thought. *Maybe I could fuck with celebrity's lives on a permanent basis and reap the rewards.*

His game plan would have to wait. Right now, he needed to get laid. He was sick of drinking and doing coke. He needed sex.

He led a busty brunette, who was a popular porn star in the amateur circuit, into one of the suite's bedrooms. On the massive king bed was a man having his way with a famous heiress. This turned Paul on even more. He pulled the porn star onto the bed with him and started to undress her.

The other couple clearly didn't mind their new companions. "Want to play?" the heiress asked.

"Sure." Paul and the porn star said eagerly in unison. They undressed and joined the other couple in a flurry of kissing, touching, and probing. Paul knew he was fucked up. He felt, though, as long as he could sustain a hard-on, he didn't have to worry about his sexual performance. The two women made out and positioned themselves into a sixty-nine position to devour each other's pussy. The other man started pleasuring Paul. Paul had never been with a man and had always been homophobic, but this guy knew how to make him happy. As the women brought each other to orgasm, Paul reached climax. It was the best night of his life.

Paul awoke the next morning and went into a tirade, kicking everyone out of the suite. He had a massive hangover and was a nightmare to be around when he was coming down from coke. After spending a week in Las Vegas, he decided it was time to drive his brand new convertible Mustang back to L.A. Paul had fifty grand left, but the money was running out quickly. He needed to come up with a plan to con more money and secure his future.

Angela decided to leave L.A. for some R&R and to visit her brother, Joe, in New York. Along with donating a small investment to help Joe upgrade and pay off all of his loans on his drag-themed restaurant, Angela had also purchased an apartment in SoHo for him. She purchased the three bedroom, two and a half bath penthouse apartment three years prior for the bargain price of $750,000 as it was in need of many improvements. Now, similar properties were going for five times what she had paid.

While being driven to Joe's house from the airport,

Angela took in the sights, sounds and smells of New York she'd missed so much. The last few times she'd been in New York, she was doing the press junket thing for her latest film and didn't have time to visit downtown or enjoy the city as she used to know it. She hadn't taken the time to enjoy New York since visiting Joe's grand opening of his restaurant several years ago.

Still, it was like she'd never left the city. She felt a piece of her heart was suddenly put back into place. *I really did get caught up in the whole Hollywood thing, didn't I?* She thought. *I love you New York. I'm home.*

Joe greeted Angela at the front door of his building. "Hey baby girl," Joe gushed, opening his arms to welcome Angela.

"You look incredible," Angela commented. Joe was tall, dark, fit and handsome with bright blue eyes like Angela's. Joe was any gay man's dream come true.

Joe released his embrace to check Angela out. "Honey, you look like you've been to hell and back. Sorry, but you do."

"Believe me. You're not telling me anything I don't already know."

"Come on. Enriquo can't wait to see you." Enriquo was Joe's lover. They'd been together nearly five years and hoped that someday soon they could legally get married.

Angela followed Joe to the private access elevator that brought them to the penthouse apartment. Angela gasped in amazement when the elevator door opened to the grand space, consisting of a large open living/dining room combination and kitchen with a ceiling that boasted an ivy-covered skylight that flooded the apartment with sunlight. Beyond the kitchen were doors leading to a terrace offering spectacular views of the Hudson River. The last time Angela saw the apartment it was in the middle of renovations. The result was magnificent.

Joe and Enriquo had performed a miracle on the apartment. They gutted most of it, installed mahogany hardwood and marble flooring, modernized the kitchen and decorated and painted the apartment with a flare only a New York City gay male could accomplish. Modern art hung above African statues and alongside imported tapestry. The rooms were bright, painted with hues of vibrant yellows, oranges and reds.

Since Joe's restaurant had become one of the most successful gay restaurants and bars in Manhattan, Joe and Enriquo lived a very comfortable lifestyle. They recently purchased a condo in Miami, where Joe planned to open another drag-themed restaurant in South Beach.

"Enriquo!" Angela exclaimed, running over to where he was sitting on a suede, burnt orange couch. She opened her arms to initiate a hug.

"Angela. You are beautiful, but sad. No?" Enriquo hugged Angela. Enriquo was from Ecuador and like his partner, tall, dark and handsome. His skin was smooth and dark tan.

"Well, I'm here to get happy again," Angela proclaimed.

"You stay with us as long as you need to, honey," Joe offered.

"Let me get you some herbal tea, or, we have Perrier." Enriquo headed for the kitchen.

"Some Perrier would be great. With lemon if you've got it," Angela said.

"Coming right up," Enriquo said, while rummaging through the enormous Viking stainless steel refrigerator.

"While he's doing that, let me show you to your room. Let me take those bags," Joe said, carrying Angela's luggage.

The guest room was decorated in a Tibetan/Asian motif. It was peaceful, with floor pillows, various buddha statues, candles, incense, spiritual books and asian art. "This doubles as my meditation room," Joe said.

"I'm sorry for imposing on your space, Joe. Where will you meditate now?" Angela asked.

Joe laughed. "In theory, this is a meditation room. You know Enriquo and me. Can you honestly see us taking the time to meditate? For God's sake, I'm too busy with the construction of my new restaurant. I walk into this room, take it all in, then exit, convinced I've meditated."

Angela laughed. "Ok. I don't feel so bad now."

Joe continued, "Just promise to make the bed and pick up every day in case a miracle strikes me and I actually do feel like meditating."

"No maid?" Angela joked. "Whatever will I do?"

"Here you go, sweetie." Enriquo delivered Angela's Perrier with a wedge of lemon.

"Thank you, Enriquo," Angela said, accepting the drink. She took a sip, then placed the glass on a nightstand and began unzipping one of her suitcases.

Assuming that was a hint that Angela wanted to unpack, Joe jabbed his elbow into Enriquo's side, "We'll let you get settled in. Right, Enriquo?"

"Of course," Enriquo replied.

Angela sat alone on the bed. Tears came flooding to her eyes. Angela missed Kate. Her visit with her brother and Enriquo felt bittersweet. Thoughts about Kate and her alleged deception chattered in her head. She felt torn. Her stomach ached from the emotional pain. It felt like her guts were being wrenched. Angela sobbed, wondering if she should call Kate and tell her she loved her—that she didn't care what the reporter had alleged. She believed Kate and knew she'd never do anything like this. It wasn't in her nature. She just wished she had some sort of sign that Kate definitely, beyond a shadow of a doubt, didn't deceive her—one sign of proof.

As an actress, she had many experiences of people getting close to her only to profit somehow from her fame. She wished she were a normal person. It was a double-edged sword being a famous actress. Angela loved her work, the income, and glamour. However, she was noticed everywhere she went and privacy was impossible to accomplish.

Angela's stomach continued to flip flop. She felt sick and ran out of the bedroom seeking the bathroom. She found a bathroom next to her room, entered and shut the door. She gagged over the toilet bowl, retching through dry heaves, until; finally, she released the knot from her stomach. The sour liquid came pouring out of her mouth as tears dripped into the brown, chunky water.

Joe came running into the bathroom, "Are you ok Angela?" he asked, worry in his voice.

Angela, spitting bile from her lips, replied, "No. I miss Kate. I love her so much. It hurts so bad."

"Oh, baby. I'm so sorry," Joe said as he handed Angela a towel and started to rub her back, offering comfort.

"I thought she was the one—the woman I'd spend the rest of my life with," Angela said, while trying to catch her breath from crying so hard.

"Angela, I've been thinking. I don't even know Kate, but from what you've told me, it sounds like she loves you and this is a huge conspiracy. Every wonderful thing you've told me about her leads me to believe this was a big mistake."

"That's why this is so hard. I want to believe her. I just don't know 100% that she didn't sell those pictures." Angela stood up and ran the water from the sink faucet, waiting for it to get warm. She washed her face and hands with soap and took a swig of mouthwash to mask the bitter taste in her mouth.

"I think you should go with your gut. Hollywood is so cruel. Don't let them break you apart."

Joe was gentle, caring and nurturing. Angela was glad she decided to stay with him.

"I know. You're right. I just need time."

"Well, like I said. You stay as long as you need to. Enriquo and I are here for you. We love you, sweetie."

"Thank God for you and Mary. I just wish mom and dad were more understanding."

"They are the way they are. There's nothing we can do to change them. I learned that with time it got better. Of course, they're still not accepting of Enriquo and me. It'll be o.k."

"What a surprise. How are you doing today?" Mary asked Jason. Jason was able to drive now and showed up, unexpectedly, at Mary's house.

"I'm feeling good today, not too much pain. It feels good to be out of that house. Unfortunately, I can't go anywhere in public without the paparazzi attacking me with questions about Angela and me."

"Screw them. By the way, Angela just called to tell me she made it into New York safe and sound."

"That's good. I really feel awful for her," Jason said, taking a seat at the breakfast nook bar stool alongside Mary's kitchen island. "I've been such a jerk, not supportive at all."

"Well, that's understandable. Your life has been turned upside down, too, not just hers." Mary said as she chopped onions for fajitas on the butcher block island in her kitchen. The kids loved when she made Mexican food.

"I want her and Kate to work this out. Angela deserves to be happy," Jason said.

"Wow. I'm surprised to hear you say that." Her eyes began to tear from the onions.

"I realize now how much they love each other. I'm happy they found each other. It killed me to see Angela in pain. She was a mess the morning she left for New York."

"I'm glad you've come to your senses, Jason." Mary threw the chopped onions into a deep skillet on the Jenn-Air stove and started cutting a green pepper into slices.

"Mary, I really don't think Kate sent those photos," Jason surmised.

"I don't either. But, I agree with Angela's decision to separate herself from Kate. Angela has every right to want proof Kate isn't responsible for the photos. I would feel the same way if I were her."

"True." Jason hesitated for a moment, then said, "Mary, I came over to tell you thank you for all you've done for me."

"You're welcome, Jason. No matter what happened between you and Angela, you'll always be my brother-in-law."

"Yeah. I feel the same way about you. It's weird. This near death experience shit. It forces you to take a hard look at your life. I think I'm going to take more time enjoying life in different ways than I did before. I'd like to spend more time with you and the kids. They will always be my nephew and niece. I told my agent I don't want to do that film with Catherine Erickson and to not book me for any other projects right now."

"That's great, Jason. What else do you want to do?" Mary was happy for Jason. It sounded like he was getting back on track.

"Well, for one, this." Jason stood up from the bar stool, stood next to Mary, cupped her cheek in his hand and kissed her softly on the lips.

Mary pulled back slowly and asked, in a soft tone, "Jason. What are you doing?" She was in complete shock and didn't know what to make of her feelings. She wanted to kiss him back and wasn't sure exactly why. It was a very awkward moment.

"I realized that everything I've ever wanted has been right here in front of me all along. You are a beautiful, smart, caring and incredible woman. You were my angel when I was at my worst. I love you, Mary," Jason said in a serious tone.

"Wow. I don't know what to say." Mary sat on one of the bar stools and put her hands to her face.

"Mary, I'm serious," Jason said, sitting next to her, rubbing her back. "I love you. I've always loved you. I was just too stupid to comprehend what I was feeling."

"I think you've been on those pain meds too long. You're my brother-in-law. It isn't right."

"No, Mary, I am not your brother-in-law. Don't look at us that way. I want to kiss you. I want to take care of you, make love to you, have kids with you, spend my life with you," Jason said.

"I-I need some time." Mary stood up and began pacing, her arms folded over her chest. "This is so weird. I don't even know what exactly it is I'm feeling. I think I'm in shock."

"I'll give you time to think. I just hope you feel the same way I do. I love you, Mary."

Jason sensed Mary's feeling of being uncomfortable. He said goodbye and left.

Mary was dazed over what had just happened. When Jason kissed her, her first urge had been to kiss him back, harder and longer. Regardless, she didn't want to be another one of Jason's conquests. She was glad she made the decision to pull away and not give into her feelings of lust. She'd always had a slight crush on Jason. After all, he was one of the most gorgeous men in the world. Alternatively, he was also a playboy and her sister's husband. He had definitely been off limits. Until now.

CHAPTER 30

"MY GOD! WHAT happened to you?" Marisol gasped, looking at Kate's bruised arms and black-eye.

Kate went to Marisol's house immediately after the fight that took place at Tami's house. "I got into a fight with Tami's new girlfriend, Suzanna."

"Get in here. Let's get an ice pack for that eye," Marisol said in a motherly way.

Marisol brought an ice pack from her freezer and handed it to Kate. "Tell me what happened."

"I went over to Tami's insisting she call Angela to tell her I didn't give those pictures to that magazine. Tami kept telling me she didn't know what I was talking about. Then, before I knew it, her girlfriend pounced on me, throwing punches." Kate applied the ice pack to her swollen eye. Her entire body ached. She felt like she got ran over by a truck.

"Wow. A real cat fight," Marisol said.

"Ha ha," Kate responded, sarcastically.

"Do you still think Tami did it?"

"I don't know. She really didn't seem to know anything about the photos. I may have made a big mistake."

"Then who else would do this to you?"

"I have absolutely no clue. Tami was the most logical

choice. But, unless she's a really good actress, I have my doubts now that she did it."

Kate decided to respect Angela's request for time to herself and didn't call or try to contact her. Kate was deeply depressed. She missed Angela tremendously. She couldn't bear to accept the fact that she and Angela may never reunite.

Kate knew the only logical way of dealing with this was to go on assignment somewhere. It was the best solution to get her mind off of Angela. She didn't feel like pursuing this game of lies with Mike Jones anymore. He obviously was not going to budge from his make believe story. Someone must be paying him to say these things.

If Tami didn't do this, then who? She wondered.

Kate wanted to runaway. She missed photojournalism. Working would take her mind off of everything. She emailed and called every journalism contact she had in her blackberry. Within an hour, she received a call back from a major news magazine asking if she'd be interested in covering a story on Liberian refugees in Ghana, Africa. Kate didn't hesitate. She accepted the assignment on the spot.

Angela spent her time in New York reading, shopping and walking around Manhattan. With sunglasses, frumpy clothes and a baseball cap, she was able to elude roving photographers much of the time. Occasionally, she'd go to the corner kiosk to buy the New York Times or New York Post, and would peruse the latest tabloid headlines.

This week, it was alleged that the real reason for Angela's lesbian affair and the breakup of her marriage to Jason was Jason's philandering and partying. The latest headlines said that Angela became a lesbian out of revenge. Angela couldn't help but laugh, but then felt sad that Jason was now the one being raked through the mud as the bad guy.

She tried anything to distract herself from thinking about Kate. She occupied her evening time by helping her brother at his restaurant and reviewing the Miami restaurant plans with him. Her favorite thing to do was her morning shopping trip to a nearby, outdoor flower shop. She'd take her time hand picking selections for the bouquets she'd bring back to the restaurant and apartment. Her favorite flowers were the enormous gerbera daisies and sunflowers. They were so huge it looked like they'd been fed growth hormones or were grown on an island of giants where everything was much larger than normal.

Though she tried to busy herself, she still obsessed over thoughts of Kate and realized she needed something more meaningful to occupy her time and engage her full attention.

One sunny afternoon, she strolled down a street in the midtown theatre district and noticed a sign seeking actors for an upcoming play. The playbill signs in the window brought back fond memories of when Angela was a struggling stage actor. She missed the challenge and intimacy of acting before a live audience.

When she returned to the apartment, Angela contacted her agent, Larry, asking him to look into theatre auditions on Broadway. Larry wasn't entirely thrilled with Angela's ambition to become a theatre actress again. It would mean a much smaller commission for him. Again, when Larry attempted to push a film project on her, Angela made it clear that she wasn't ready or interested in doing film work for a while. She wanted to act on stage again.

After Angela threatened to hire an agent in New York who specialized in representing theater actors, Larry conceded and agreed to find her a theatre role. Something was better than nothing.

Prior to ending their conversation, he reminded Angela

that she was contractually obligated to promote the release of her film "Battleday", which was scheduled to premiere in two weeks.

Angela forgot about this commitment and groaned, "Of course, Larry. I know. Once you and Sheila finalize all of the appearances, email them to me," she said.

Within a couple of days, Larry had secured three theatrical leading role auditions for Angela.

Angela was nervous. She wondered if she could still pull off acting on stage as it had been nearly a decade since her last stage performance.

The first audition flopped. She didn't feel a connection with her character at all. At the second audition, she found out from another actor that the casting director already had another actress in mind for the role. At the third audition, she felt she gave the best audition of her career. She loved the character, Laura, a woman recovering from a nervous breakdown triggered by the death of the love of her life. She definitely related to her character's woes.

The next day, she received a call informing her she'd been offered the role of Laura.

Kate was on her way to Ghana.

"Sorry, but we're out of tomato juice. I do have a can of bloody mary mix," the flight attendant offered.

"That will do," Kate accepted.

She felt a flutter in her stomach as the plane hit an air pocket. She liked to fly, but hated air pockets and turbulence. She had always thought of the worst scenarios, like the plane was going to blow up in mid-air or suddenly lose power and do a nose-dive.

This time was different. When the plane jostled and tipped slightly to the right, Kate didn't feel anxious. She was calm and hopeful, looking forward to meeting the refugees and help them tell their stories to the rest of the world.

Kate would be in Ghana for a month. She hoped in that time, some divine intervention would take place to reunite her with Angela. Till then, she found comfort in knowing she was needed by people who were unable to help themselves.

CHAPTER 31

CATHERINE WAS LIVID after having been served divorce papers. She swore to Howard that he wouldn't get a penny of her money.

"You don't have a leg to stand on, Howard. Our pre-nup is impenetrable," Catherine hollered into her bluetooth.

"I think it's time to take a walk down memory lane, Catherine." Howard, comfortably situated in a rented suite at the luxurious Hotel Casa Del Mar in Santa Monica, decided now was the time to begin his plan of manipulation and blackmail.

"What are you getting at? You have nothing on me," Catherine responded adamantly.

"When you were drunk, you told me all about what you did to Angela Moore and her girlfriend—the sale of the photos, setting up Kate, you told me everything," Howard proudly stated.

She remembered nothing, surmising that she must have blacked out during her confession to Howard.

"Catherine, not only did you want to ruin Angela's career by exposing her as a lesbian, you went one step further to break them up. Do you really want that information out there for all to know?"

For the first time in their marriage, Catherine was speechless.

Howard continued, "I would love nothing more than to expose you to the world for who you really are." He relished in this dialogue with Catherine. For once, he had the upper hand and was in control.

Catherine hesitated in responding. She was in a precarious situation. Should she kick Howard to the curb without a dime of her fortune? Or, should she fess up to her little scheme with the tabloid? Her furor for Howard definitely outweighed her desire to keep mum about the photos. He broke her heart and certainly was not going to benefit monetarily from it. Her fans would forgive and love her no matter what.

"I don't care, Howard. Do what you want with the lie I told you. You aren't going to blackmail me. I'll just tell everyone you're a gold digging liar and it's not true," Catherine countered.

Howard was furious. He thought for sure she'd want to save face. "You know it's not a lie, Catherine."

"Whatever, Howard. Tell that bitch your story. She's never going to believe you."

Howard couldn't wait to inform Angela about Catherine's deception. Catherine would get hers in the end.

Angela had a magnificent opening night for her role as Laura. Rave reviews abounded. "Brilliant acting on the part of Angela Moore," was the consensus from the theater critics.

Just as she was enjoying her reawakened career in theater, Sheila emailed her the agenda for the promotion of "Battleday". Angela would have to attend the premiere in one week and participate in media interviews with the other leading cast members.

Angela wished she could lie and say she never received

the email—that she was completely oblivious of the premiere and interviews. However, the likelihood she could get away with this fantasy was nil. After all, Larry and Sheila would call her a dozen times to discuss interview protocol and establish a set of responses to reporter and talk show host questions.

When she returned home to Joe and Enriquo's apartment after her fifth night of playing the part of Laura, she found comfort in hearing a voice message from Jason.

"Hi Angela. Congratulations on the great reviews. I'm so proud of you. Hey, on another note, Catherine Erickson's husband, Howard has been trying to contact you. I think you should call him. He said he has information about the tabloid photos and that Kate didn't sell them. His number is..."

Angela wrote down the number and continued to listen to his message. "Look, Angela, I'm sorry I haven't been supportive of you. I think coming out was the right thing to do. I really need to talk to you about some things. Call me."

It had been nearly a month since she and Jason last spoke. She hesitated calling him as she figured he was still mad over her decision to come out. It was good to hear his voice, especially since he didn't sound bitter.

Angela called Jason. "Hi Jason. How are you?" Angela asked.

"Angie. It's so good to hear your voice. I'm feeling great," Jason said, sounding positive.

"It's good to hear you too. I miss you." Angela was relieved to hear Jason's voice on the other line. She was worried about him and missed his friendship.

"I'm really sorry I've been an ass." Jason's voice became serious and apologetic. "I have something I need to talk to you about."

Angela wondered what was so important. "It's ok, Jason.

You had every right to be concerned and angry. I feel awful, like I've ruined your life in so many ways."

"No. You did me a huge favor. I decided to take some time off of work. I've been realizing a lot about myself since the accident. There must be a reason why I survived."

"You are lucky to be alive. That's for sure."

"I really don't know how to say this..." Jason hesitated. "I'm in love with Mary. I went to her house last week and told her."

Angela's heart raced. She was shocked by Jason's confession. "Wow, Jay. I don't know what to say." There was silence for a moment. Angela continued, "How long have you been seeing each other?"

"It's not like that. We haven't even been on a date. I went to her house, told her I was in love with her, kissed her, and then left. I haven't heard from her since," Jason recounted. "Has she called you?"

"Come to think of it. I haven't talked to her in a few days. Our conversations have been short. She's always in a hurry to get off the phone. Now I know why," Angela concluded.

"Oh no. I probably freaked her out."

"Maybe she feels the same way as you. She's probably in shock, like I feel right now. Jay, this is definitely weird."

"Thanks a lot. You're real encouraging."

"Well, think about it. You were married to her sister." Angela laughed. "How did this happen, anyway?"

"She was taking care of me and one day I realized I wanted to be with her."

"Are you sure? I mean, you've been through a lot lately." Angela continued to laugh. "Maybe you have a traumatic brain injury the doctor's missed."

"Ha. Ha. Ha. Very funny. I'm being serious. And, no, my brain is fine."

"I'm sorry. I'll try to behave myself."

"I'm positive about this. I want to be with Mary."

"I just don't want to see Mary get hurt." Angela's tone became serious. "She's been through so much in her life."

"Believe me, Angela, I'm sick of my old lifestyle and am in love with her. I started having thoughts about settling down before the accident. Like a dumb idiot, I actually thought for a moment that you would be that person to settle down with."

"Are you crazy, Jason?"

"I *was* crazy. Not anymore."

"I just want to know that you really care for her. I don't want to see my sister get hurt. She deserves better than a player who will cheat on her."

"I've totally changed. I swear. The accident was the best thing that happened to me. I'm in love with Mary. I won't let you or her down. I mean it," Jason pleaded.

"Ok, Jay. I'll call her and see what's going on. In the meantime, we really need to get a divorce and make it final. I'm going to stay in New York for a while. Do you want the house in L.A.?"

"I'd like to start fresh. Let's sell the house. I can take the pets until you get your own place."

"I'm all for it. I'm really liking it here, staying with Joe. I didn't realize how much I missed New York and loved living here. I may move here permanently. Plus, the paparazzi aren't as bad here as they are in L.A."

"Sounds like a plan. I'll contact my lawyer and real estate agent tomorrow."

"Ok. I'll call my lawyer tomorrow too. I have to call Catherine's husband now. I wonder what he wants."

"He sounded serious and a bit desperate."

"Great. I can't wait to have a conversation with psycho Catherine's nut job husband. I'll talk to you later. Love you."

"Love you too."

Angela called Howard immediately after hanging up with Jason. The phone rang and went to voice mail.

"Jason informed me that you may have information about the tabloid photos. Please call me." Angela gave him her cell phone number and hung up. Angela didn't trust anyone close to Catherine, but figured she'd give it a shot, especially since it involved the photo situation with Kate.

Catherine contacted Howard minutes before he was about to return Angela's message.

"I've been thinking. Maybe we can work out a deal," Catherine said. She had given it much thought and realized that Angela was a powerful Hollywood player who could potentially ruin her career. "As much as I despise the thought of you getting a cent of my hard-earned money, I'm sure our lawyers can figure something out. That is, if you haven't told Angela my little secret yet."

"You're in luck. I was just about to call her."

"Good. You're in luck. My lawyer will contact yours and we'll settle this."

"You better not be stalling, Catherine. Your lawyer better have a decent offer and contract drawn up by the end of this week." This gave Catherine and her lawyer three days to come up with a reasonable offer.

"That is not enough time and you know it," Catherine fired back.

"You can do it. I have faith in you." Howard reveled in having control of the situation.

"Fine. I can't wait to be rid of you." With that, Catherine hung up the phone.

CHAPTER 32

KATE FELL IN love with the Ghana refugees and admired the volunteers who helped on behalf of several different relief organizations. The refugees living in makeshift camps fled to Ghana after rebel factions opposing the government ransacked towns and villages, murdering anyone in their path. Many of the refugees were orphaned children, brought to Ghana after their parents were killed in Liberia.

Kate photographed and interviewed the refugees from early morning till late at night. She worked tirelessly on this project, wanting the world to know about the refugees' desire to return to their homeland and the horrible bloodshed that occurred.

Her assignment was slated for completion after a month. With Kate's tenacity, she was able to provide a final copy of her photos and article to the news magazine's publisher in three weeks.

The night before she was to return to the United States, she was awoken by the sound of gunfire. The gunfire wasn't far in the distance. Kate knew something was wrong.

After she left the voice message for Howard, Angela called Mary.

"Hi Mary. I just spoke with Jason."

"Yeah?" Mary answered, curious to know what Jason had discussed with her sister.

"Why didn't you tell me he's in love with you?" Angela asked.

"He told you that?" Mary sounded annoyed.

"Actually, you should've trusted me enough to tell me. I can't believe you haven't mentioned this to me."

"I'm not sure how I feel, Angela. I wasn't ready to tell you. I'm still in shock. I have feelings for Jason, but I'm not sure why."

"Mary, I believed Jason when he told me how much he loves and cares about you. What's so wrong with that?"

"It's making me feel crazy, like it's wrong."

"Mary, it's not wrong. What *was* wrong was Jason and me. Don't waste this chance at love. I wasted mine." Angela thought about Kate and felt a wave of sadness come over her.

"You could always call Kate and make the decision to believe her," Mary suggested. "I thought all along you should trust her. It's just not in Kate's nature to do something like that. You *do* have enemies, Angela."

"Speaking of enemies, Catherine Erickson's husband, Howard, called me."

"What the hell did he want?" Mary asked, surprised.

"He left a message with Jason, something about the photos and that he knows Kate didn't do it. I left a message for him, but he hasn't called me back."

"See. He probably knows who did this. It was probably Catherine. I could totally see her pulling something like this."

"Well, hopefully he'll call back."

"Call Kate. Please Angela. It's time."

"I know. You're right. I just don't know if I'm ready. I still have this stupid premiere crap for the film release. I dread having to do those terrible interviews."

"You'll get through it. After that, call her, Angela."

"Under one condition."

"What's that?"

"You'll give Jason a chance."

"I can't believe I'm saying this, but, it's a deal."

Paul had no money. He was flat broke. Less than two months ago, he'd received a check for $100,000. He did have $20,000 invested in a real estate deal his cousin set up, but spent all of his disposable income. Most of the money was spent on gambling, drugs, women, hotels and his new mustang. He also gave away money to his so-called friends, who, now that he was broke, were nowhere to be found.

He needed money.

He craved coke.

He had an idea. He would ask Catherine for more money. Then he quickly remembered how much of a bitch she was and doubted she'd give him a dime. Then he thought that maybe Angela would. Maybe he could get some cash out of revealing the truth to Angela. After all, he got his money from Catherine and owed no allegiance to her. *She* was the one who signed a contract to employ him for two years. *He* owed her nothing and could walk away at any time. He decided he'd tell Angela, under the condition she paid him first for this information. How, though, was he going to contact her? He was a nobody. Paul suddenly remembered he used to party with Angela's agent Larry's son, Austin.

Paul called Austin, who answered his phone on the second ring.

"Yo, Paul. Where you been? I heard you came into some big money and have partying it up without me," Austin said.

"Yeah man, it's been a while. I came into some money, but there' more money to be made if you can do me a huge favor."

"What d'ya need?"

"Angela Moore's phone number, preferably her cell phone." Paul knew it was a huge request and expected Austin to tell him he was crazy.

"Well, my dad's her agent, but I don't have access to her number. What d'ya need *her* number for?"

"I can't tell ya. Let's just say, she owes me some money for some work I did," Paul lied. "If all goes well, you'll be the first person I call to go to Vegas and party down."

"Here's what I'll do, man. I'll sneak into my dad's room when he's sleeping and look her number up on his cell phone."

"Perfect. Call me later with the number." Paul ended the call.

Howard reviewed the proposed settlement. He was pleased with the terms and happily signed every piece of paper placed in front of him by his attorney. He would receive a one-time payment of ten million dollars set up in a trust account that he would have limited access to. The money would be doled out like an allowance. He would have access to two million dollars immediately.

In return, Howard agreed to a confidentiality clause that required him to never discuss anything regarding Catherine—and that meant anything. If he violated this clause, he'd lose the money in the trust and have to pay back any monies he already spent that culminated from the divorce settlement.

Their lawyers met, papers were signed and filed, and Howard became an independently wealthy man who would never mention Catherine's name again.

Angela went to the premiere of "Battleday" with Joe. She lucked out with the premiere taking place in New York City and not L.A. She told Sheila that she would only participate in premiere interviews in New York. Angela had no desire to return to L.A. no matter what the reason.

Since most of the major Hollywood reporters would already be in New York for the premiere, they were amenable to this stipulation. In addition, Angela had Sheila inform the press that she would immediately end any interview that attempted to delve into her personal life. All interviews had to focus on her new movie. Naturally, the reporters did not like this stipulation.

The red carpet for Battleday wasn't that bad. Not one reporter dared bring up Kate or Jason. They were more concerned with wanting to know which designer gown she was wearing and who Joe was.

The news and talk shows that followed the premiere were a different story. These reporters delicately probed into her present status in a passive-aggressive manner.

"How are you doing Angela?" one talk show host asked, acting concerned, while placing her hand on Angela's shoulder.

Another boldly asked Angela, "What has happened to your relationship with that woman?"

Angela stopped the interview immediately. She didn't leave the interview immediately and chose to answer the question under the condition the reporter stop asking anymore personal questions.

"I'm taking time to be with me. I'm enjoying getting to know Angela," she responded.

The truth was that Angela still ached for Kate.

Kate heard the gunfire getting closer to the camp. She arose from her cot and exited the tent she had called home for the past three weeks. A relief worker, who looked terrified, scurried to her.

"We have to leave," he demanded.

"What's going on?" Kate asked. She felt like she was in a dream, bewildered and sleepy.

"We have to leave *now*! Rebels are looking for one of the Liberian government's generals. They think he's hiding here at the refugee camp."

"That's absurd. The only people here are children and families," Kate protested.

"I know. But we have to get out of here. I have a U.N. jeep ready to bring us to the airport. We have to go now," the relief worker insisted.

"This is wrong. They can't just come in here and slaughter these people. They've done nothing wrong," Kate implored.

"Kate, we can't do anything about it. We have to go. Otherwise, we'll be killed." The relief worker was losing his patience.

"Can't we call someone at the U.N.?" Kate hoped there was something someone could do to prevent the slaughter of these innocent people.

"This is a civil war. You know that. There's nothing we can do. Now get your stuff and come on," the relief worker shouted.

Kate returned to her tent to obtain her belongings. She felt guilt like never before in her entire life. It was as though she was a privileged traitor, who didn't deserve the luxury of escaping this battle. She didn't want to leave the refugees behind to be murdered. She wished there was something she could do.

The relief worker opened the flap of the flimsy tent's opening. "Come on," he insisted. "What's taking you so long?"

Kate looked at her camera, hanging from a hook by her

cot. "I came here to do a story. This is a story the world should know about."

"You're crazy, Kate," he said, baffled by her stubbornness.

Kate threw her duffle bag to him. "Here, put this in the jeep. I'll be there in a minute."

"If you're not there by the time the rebels enter the camp, I'm leaving without you," he warned, and then quickly ran to the jeep with Kate's duffle bag.

Kate wandered outside and realized it was too dark to use her camera without a light source. She'd have to use a bright flash, which would draw attention to her. She saw a group of rebel fighters making their way to the camp. Without hesitation, she quickly attached the bright flash and started taking pictures of the gun-toting madmen.

Immediately, the rebels began shooting at her. Kate turned and ran for the relief worker's jeep. She could feel bullets brush pass her as she ran, shoeless, on the dirt road.

She reached the jeep and opened the passenger side door. As she settled into the jeep's , she felt a sharp pain in her leg.

"Go! Go! Go!" Kate shouted. "They're right behind us!" Bullets riddled the rear of the jeep as they tried to drive away. The clutch seemed to break loose, which made the jeep buck and stall. The relief worker repositioned the hand gear and eased up on the clutch. The jeep bucked forward and began to speed away from the camp.

Kate looked back to see the gunmen and the camp disappear from sight. The relief worker must've been driving at sixty miles an hour on the narrow dirt road. She feared they'd get into an accident.

That thought soon dissipated as she reached down and brushed her hand over the area of her leg where the sharp pain radiated. She was horrified to feel the area was wet and sticky.

"I think I've been shot," she exclaimed.

"You can get medical assistance at the airport. We can't do anything about it now," the relief worker said, unsympathetic.

Kate realized she felt pain elsewhere. Her shoulder ached. She reached back to feel that it too was wet and sticky. Kate feared she'd never make it back to the United States alive. She'd never have the chance to reunite with Angela. She started to feel woozy. Everything became dark.

"Kate's been shot, Angela. She's in a hospital in France," Marisol relayed to Angela. She was able to get her cell phone number by rummaging through Kate's apartment.

"Where? How? Is she going to be ok?" Angela panicked.

"She was in Ghana doing a story on refugees when a gun battle broke out. She lost a lot of blood, but will be ok."

Angela couldn't believe what she'd just heard. Suddenly the photo sale allegations meant nothing. *I can't believe Kate could have died. I let this separation go on way too long and should've called Kate a long time ago.* Angela's thoughts wouldn't stop. Angela grew frantic by the second.

"Are you there, Angela?" Marisol asked, after a brief moment of silence.

"Yes," Angela said, trying to process all of the thoughts passing through her mind. "I just can't believe this happened." She suddenly wondered what she should do. Should she go to Kate? Should she stay and wait till Kate returned to the U.S.?

"She will be flying back to L.A. in a few days. That's as long as she continues to do well and the doctors clear her.

So, there's really no reason to go over to France now. If that's what you were considering," Marisol said.

"I don't know. I mean, we haven't been together. I don't know what I should do." Angela hoped Marisol would make a decision for her.

"Angela, I know you don't know me very well. The entire time you and Kate were together, I thought Kate was on drugs or back with Tami. I had no clue you were seeing each other. Trust me when I tell you that she kept your relationship a complete secret," Marisol took a deep breath and went on. "Please don't take this the wrong way, but you're insane to think for a minute that Kate would ever sell those photos to a tabloid or betray you." Marisol's growing anger and frustration reflected in her voice. "I've known her for over ten years. She's the most honest and decent person I know. And for you to believe some crackpot reporter at a tabloid is a terrible shame."

Angela felt the need to defend herself, "What was I supposed to think? I'm given this evidence against her. It's been terrible. I love Kate. I also know there are people out there who only want to capitalize off of my fame."

"Well, I can promise you that Kate is not one of *those* people. If you really took the time to get to know Kate, you'd know beyond a shadow of a doubt she's a good person. Instead, you abandoned her when she needed you most. I've never seen her in love like this before. She would never do anything to hurt you," Marisol said in a scolding tone.

Angela was speechless. Though there were two sides to this story, Angela surrendered to her debate with Marisol.

"I guess I've said everything I needed to say. It's just a shame you don't know the Kate I know. Otherwise, you'd have never doubted her." Marisol awaited Angela's response.

"I appreciate you calling me, Marisol," Angela said, accepting defeat, feeling ashamed. "If you could, please fax

Kate's flight itinerary and hospital information to my agent. The fax number is..."

After the curt phone call from Marisol, Angela questioned her response to the entire photo/tabloid allegations. She suddenly felt horrible that she hadn't believed Kate. Marisol definitely spoke the truth about Kate. Kate was an honest and loving person. Angela questioned how she could have been so confused. She needed to go to Kate, to the hospital in France. Angela decided she couldn't wait for Kate to return to the U.S. She had to go to her now.

Angela called the director of the play and informed him that she needed to take a week off to tend to Kate. The director, a very hyper worrywart-type, wasn't pleased with Angela's news. He would need to prepare Angela's understudy and, worse, ticket holders would undoubtedly demand refunds as most of them purchased the tickets to see Angela in person, on stage.

Angela was relieved her agent included a clause in the contract stating that if there were injury or illness of a family member, close friend or significant other, she would be entitled to the same rights as anyone else under the family medical leave act.

Next, she contacted her travel agent to book a first class flight to Paris. The earliest flight, direct from New York to Paris would be leaving in three hours and there was one seat left on the entire flight. Angela gave the go-ahead to book it.

Angela hurriedly threw a few pieces of clothing and essentials into a carry-on bag. She figured she wouldn't be gone more than a day or two, according to Marisol's remark of when Kate was scheduled to return home.

Once she boarded the plane, Angela realized she neglected to find out at which hospital in Paris Kate was a patient. As the plane began taxiing the runway and the flight attendant instructed all electronic devices to be turned off, Angela realized she'd have to wait until she arrived in Paris to contact Marisol for this information.

CHAPTER 33

KATE WAS FLOWN to the Pitie-Salpetriere hospital in Paris from Ghana. The gunshot wounds weren't serious enough to warrant she stay in Africa for emergency, invasive treatment. Fortunately, the bullets entered the muscle, by-passing any major veins or arteries. However, she certainly wouldn't make it back to the U.S. without a short hospital stay to control the bleeding and remove the bullets lodged in her right calf and left shoulder blade. Kate had also lost a considerable amount of blood, which required a blood transfusion.

Upon news of Kate's injury, her mother, Sharon, booked the earliest departing flight to Paris from Melbourne, Australia and arrived a day and a half after Kate's admission to the hospital. Sharon made Kate's hospital room her lodging accommodations. Insistent upon not leaving Kate's side, she slept in a reclining chair next to Kate's hospital bed every night.

Five days after arriving at the Paris hospital, Kate was cleared to return home in two days, which was much earlier than anyone expected.

Kate was weak, but looked forward to returning home to see her friends Marisol and Jamie. Sharon planned to join Kate on her flight to L.A. and assist in caring for Kate once they returned to Kate's home. Kate wondered how Angela was doing and if she should let her former partner know that she had been wounded. Kate decided against it. It was a lost cause.

Once the plane landed in Paris, Angela tried to contact Marisol and couldn't get her cell phone to make an outgoing call. She realized she must not have international calling features on her new phone or plan. Worse, Marisol hadn't faxed the hospital information as Angela requested of her to her agent. She decided she'd have to call each hospital at random to figure out where Kate had been admitted.

After wandering around aimlessly for fifteen minutes in Charles de Gaulle airport, she found a policeman. Angela did not know a lick of French and suddenly wished that she'd paid attention in high school French class. In English, Angela asked him if he could help her find the phone numbers of all the major hospitals in and around Paris. He understood her, agreed to help, and asked her to follow him to the business center. Along the way, the police officer commented that he recognized her from the cinéma.

"I love your feelms," the police officer commented. "You are...how do you say? Beeg star here."

At the business center, an attractive young Parisian woman sitting behind a desk greeted the officer. They exchanged a short conversation in French.

"Thees eez Mademoiselle Lourdes," the officer said, introducing the two women. "She will eesist you, Mademoiselle Moore. Enjoy your stay in Paris."

Lourdes greeted Angela, "Bonjour Mademoiselle. I love your films," she said, speaking impeccable English.

"Thank you. I mean. Merci." Angela, for the first time, was extremely grateful to be a visible movie star. This was definitely helping her effort to locate Kate.

She downloaded a list of hospitals with phone numbers from her computer. Lourdes offered to call the hospitals, which was a relief to Angela, considering the language barrier.

"Merci. Merci. Merci." Angela made a gesture as though she were bowing to Lourdes in worship.

"Mademoiselle Ashford is at Pitie-Salpetriere hospital", Lourdes said. Pitie-Salpetriere was the second hospital she'd called.

"Merci beaucoup!" Angela exclaimed, clapping her hands together.

Angela raced through the airport to the ground transportation area. She refused to wait in the long line for a taxi so she proceeded to offer fifty euros to anyone allowing her to get ahead of them in line. Her scheme worked like a charm. Angela made her way to the front of the taxi line in no time. When it was her turn, she ordered the taxi driver to hurry as fast as he could to the Pitie-Salpetriere as she shoved a hundred euros in his face.

Angela was on her way to see Kate to tell her she loved her and that she was sorry about everything. Marisol's words were ringing in Angela's head. Marisol knew Kate very well and Angela decided she must believe Marisol when she said that Kate would never do anything to betray Angela.

Sharon pushed the wheelchair Kate was sitting in to the exit door of the hospital. "The hospital said there'd be a taxi ready for you, but I don't see it. Let me check with the front desk to see when it'll arrive," Sharon said.

Kate was happy she was on her way home. She thought about the photos she'd taken of the rebel attack. Though she had been losing blood and was falling in and out of consciousness, Kate managed to unload her camera. Before she was airlifted to Paris, she handed the film to the relief worker, along with strict instructions on where to send the film to the magazine publisher. She hadn't heard anything about the photos or film, which deeply upset her. She would have to follow up with the publisher once she returned to the U.S.

Sharon returned. "The taxi will be here in a few minutes," Sharon informed Kate.

Angela couldn't believe her misfortune. The taxi she was riding in had a flat tire and subsequently careened out of control, slamming into a parked car just three blocks from the hospital. Eager to see Kate, she decided to run the rest of the way. She handed the taxi driver a fistful of U.S. money as she had no euros left. Pleased to see a few hundred dollar bills in his hand, he pointed in the direction of the hospital, instructing Angela where to go.

When she reached the hospital, she proceeded to the front desk. Angela was dismayed when the woman behind the desk informed her that Kate had been discharged. "I was told she would be here another day. Are you sure she's been discharged?"

"Yes. She was discharged an hour ago."

"Merci," Angela said. She walked out the front door and took a seat on a nearby bench. She felt defeated. *Serves me right*, she thought.

Angela slowly walked to the exit. She sat on a bench outside and began to cry.

Just then, she heard a familiar voice.

"Angela?" It was Kate's voice. She was in a taxi.

Angela quickly stood up and approached the vehicle. She couldn't believe her luck.

"What are you doing here?" Kate asked.

"Marisol called and told me what happened. I am so

sorry, Kate, for everything. I was so worried about you. They told me you had already left the hospital and…"

Kate interrupted and said, "I can't believe you're here, that you came all this way to see me."

"I love you Kate. I understand if you don't want to talk to me. I just had to come here and make sure you're all right," Angela said, excitedly. Her heart was racing and her stomach had butterflies.

"Of course I want to talk to you, Angela. But my flight leaves in two hours," Kate said, ecstatic to see Angela for the first time in over a month. "Where are you going?"

"I guess wherever you are going," Angela replied.

"Then get in." Kate opened the door for Angela to join her.

Angela entered the taxi. "I'm so sorry. I don't ever want to be without you again. I was so stupid to not believe you. I was out of my mind, confused. It was ridiculous. I know I can trust you. Please forgive me for being such a fool," Angela pleaded.

Kate carefully thought of her reply while Sharon looked on. "This is going to be really hard, Angela—you and me getting back together." Kate hesitated. Angela developed a worried look. "And yet, I know we can get through this if we commit to trusting each other and really communicating, not running away."

Angela, relieved by Kate's willingness to heal their relationship and move forward, said, "You are the love of my life, the best thing that's ever happened to me. I'm willing to do anything for us."

Kate turned to Angela and kissed her. Angela put her arms around Kate to hold her. "Ouch!" Kate screamed. "You're pressing on my wound," Kate said.

"I'm sorry, baby. I just love you so much," Angela said, loosening her hug.

"It's ok. Just be careful. I'm very fragile right now," Kate said.

"I want to take care of you. Can I come home with you?" Angela asked.

"I would love that," Kate answered.

Back in L.A., Angela called the director of the play to inform him she'd be taking a month off. He completely flipped out after hearing her decision. Since Angela's absence, the play's attendance was half the full house Angela's presence commanded. He was also in a bind as the first understudy came down with whooping cough and Angela's second understudy was now in the lead role.

The director screamed and yelled obscenities at Angela and demanded for her to return to New York. He threatened to sue her. Angela apologized profusely and promised to return to acting in the play once Kate was feeling better. She instructed him to contact her lawyer in the meantime if he wanted to pursue a lawsuit. Otherwise, there was nothing she could do.

Angela wasn't concerned about a lawsuit. She would pay a million dollars if it meant she could spend time with Kate. Nothing would tear them apart ever again. There was no way in hell Angela was going to leave Kate's side. So much time had passed since they had been together. She didn't want to lose Kate forever. From now on, Kate came first, acting second. Angela wasn't going to make the same mistake as in past relationships. She would never again put stardom before love.

Angela spent most of her days and evenings tending to Kate, sitting on the balcony of Kate's Malibu bungalow, watching sea animals play, taking in the beautiful Pacific sunsets with Kate by her side. Marisol and Jamie dropped by every day to visit Kate, occasionally bringing groceries, a magazine or a book for Kate. This gave Angela the opportunity of getting to know Kate's closest friends. Marisol and Jamie enjoyed getting to know Angela. She wasn't the high strung, over-the-top actress they had read about in tabloid magazines. She was just like them in so many ways.

About a week after returning to the States with Kate, Sharon felt assured Kate was being taken care of and decided to return to Australia to tend to her koala bears.

CHAPTER 34

"I'LL GET IT," Angela yelled to Kate, referring to the ringing telephone. Angela hesitated to pick up the phone as the caller id displayed a private number. She usually allowed private callers go to voice mail. For some reason, she felt a burning desire to answer this call and find out who the caller was.

"Hello?" Angela asked.

"Is Kate there?" the caller's voice sounded familiar, but Angela couldn't pinpoint who it was.

"She's not available right now. Can I tell her who's calling?" Angela politely asked.

"It's Tami. Tami Montgomery," Tami revealed.

Angela immediately felt uneasy and jealous. "Hi, Tami. It's Angela. What do you need to talk to Kate about?" Angela asked, tersely.

"Oh hi Angela." Tami obviously hadn't realized it was Angela who initially answered the phone. "It's not what you think. Don't worry. I'm calling because I have some very important information about those tabloid photos." She said this very quickly as she sensed that Angela was about to hang up on her.

"What is it Tami?" Angela asked, in a bitter tone.

"Do you remember my limo driver, Paul?"

"Yes." Angela wondered what Paul had to do with anything.

"Well, he just told me something I think you need to hear."

Tami proceeded to recount Paul's version of his and Catherine's involvement with the photos and her intent to ruin Angela's career and relationship.

"Oh my God," Angela blurted. She was hesitant to believe anything that came out of Tami's mouth. "Are you making this up, Tami?"

"No. I swear to you this is the truth," Tami responded.

"I'd like to talk to Paul myself—and with Kate, of course," Angela said.

"Well, unfortunately there's a catch. And, believe me when I say, I have nothing to do with it," Tami said.

"What is it?" Angela asked.

"He wants money. Apparently all of the money Catherine gave him has run out. He's desperate for cash and said he won't give you all of the details unless you fork up some cash for him."

"Why should I waste a cent on him? He could be making this up. Or better yet, you could be making this up to vindicate yourself, Tami."

"No. That's definitely not true." Tami said. "Look, you can either listen to what he has to say or not. I really don't give a shit either way. I just want to clear myself and move on. You can reach him at..."

Paul was devastated when Austin told him that he couldn't get Angela's phone number. Apparently Austin's dad used special code names for all of his clients.

"Sorry man. I tried, but her name isn't in my dad's contacts. He's got all these weird names in there, like Ruby Red and Green Goddess. He obviously uses code names for his clients," Austin apologized.

"Fuck. I really need to get a hold of Angela."

"Why don't you ask Tami. Didn't you mention to me that they used to fuck?"

"Tami and I haven't spoken since she fired me. Plus, I'm sure Angela's phone number has changed five times since then. That's what those celebrities do. They have to change their number all the time because their always leaked."

"Well, good luck man. Let's party some time. Call me."

Paul ended the call and realized Tami actually could help him get in contact with Angela. He remembered Catherine mention that she had heard Kate thought Tami pulled off the photo scam. Catherine was very pleased that no one suspected her involvement. *This must mean that Kate confronted Tami and the shit probably hit the fan between the two of them.* Paul thought.

Paul promptly called Tami.

"Hey Tami. It's Paul," Paul said nervously.

"What the hell do you want?" Tami answered.

"I know we parted in a bad way, but I have a proposition for you. Please give me a few minutes to explain."

"I'm listening," Tami responded.

Paul went on to provide details of Catherine's scam and his involvement with everything.

"That fucking bitch Catherine!" Tami exclaimed. "Kate came over here and got into a fight with my new girlfriend Suzanna over this shit. Kate and Angela still think I did it."

"I have an idea to redeem yourself and help me out financially," Paul said.

"Ok. I'm actually open to whatever crazy scheme you have in mind—but only because I've changed. Suzanna actually thinks I framed Kate and Angela, which isn't good."

This conversation led to Paul visiting with Tami and

Suzanna to explain in detail everything that happened with Catherine and that he needed $100,000 to confess to Angela. Tami thought the amount was ridiculous, but would leave that up to Angela to decide, whether that amount was too high.

Angela relayed Tami's conversation to Kate. Kate told Angela that after her interaction with Tami, which resulted in the fight with Suzanna, she was convinced Tami had nothing to do with the photos.

"I wonder if this is a scam," Angela shared.

"I guess there's only one way to find out and that's to call Paul," Kate reasoned.

"I'll call him right now. Won't hurt any, right?" Angela suggested.

Angela wanted more than anything for this Paul guy to explain everything and provide closure on this entire saga.

She contacted Paul, who told Angela he was part of the photo scheme and received money for taking the famous tabloid photos. Then he went into great detail about how he needed more money and was willing to provide her with the information. The only catch was that he wanted $100,000.

"Are you crazy? How do I even know what you'll tell me is true?" Angela was ready to hang the phone up.

"Look, I guarantee this information is 100% true. I'll even tell you the story first and then you can pay me. It will all make sense. Believe me," Paul said.

"Let me think about it. I'll call you back," Angela said.

Angela was dying to know what this guy Paul allegedly knew. He must know something. Only those close to Kate and Angela knew Kate was accused of selling the photos. This scandal, surprisingly, did not make it into the tabloids.

Kate and Angela discussed Paul's offer and decided to negotiate with him.

"Angela, I'm not vengeful, but I would love more than anything to expose that reporter Mike and have him fired," Kate said.

"And I'd like to know, just for peace of mind, what exactly went down and who was responsible for this," Angela said.

Angela called Paul again. "Ok. I thought about it. I'll give you $50,000 if I believe what you say is true."

"$75,000 and nothing lower. I guarantee what I have is the truth," Paul countered.

"Ok. But your story better make sense or prepare to get nothing," Angela said.

"Meet me at the Sunshine Diner on Wilshire Blvd. tonight, with the check," Paul instructed.

"Ok. I'll have bodyguards with me. So, if you have an ulterior motive, I suggest you bow out now," Angela warned.

"Don't worry. All I want is the money. All you want is the truth. Bring whoever you want," Paul said eagerly. He couldn't wait to get more money. He was craving a line of coke.

Angela was understandably suspicious of Paul. He looked ragged, like he hadn't showered in a few days. His hair was matted in some spots, sticking straight out in others. He had large, dark circles and puffy bags under his bloodshot eyes. He was a mess.

Angela and Kate were glad they decided to bring two of Angela's occasional bodyguards with them. Paul just didn't look right.

"Show me the check," Paul requested as the two women sat down in the booth across from him.

"Show him the check," Angela directed the six foot nine inch muscular bodyguard seated at the table next to her.

The bodyguard held up the check for Paul to view. Satisfied with what he saw, Paul proceeded to tell his story. First, he told them about his initial involvement with Tami, which led to his scheme and employment with Catherine. He told them about how he'd stalked them until he finally got what he needed—photos of the two women engaged in a kiss. He shared about having overheard a conversation Catherine was having with the tabloid reporter, Mike Jones, in Catherine's living room. He overheard the two discussing how they would frame Kate as the person who sold the photos of Kate and Angela to the tabloid.

"Catherine hates you, Angela. She wants you to be miserable, like her," Paul revealed.

Angela was shocked. Paul had reiterated so many details that made sense. "How can I truly know this is factual?"

Paul produced a copy of the cancelled check Catherine had given him for producing the photos. "Why would she give me this? I was just a driver." Paul also showed Angela and Kate a document containing Kate's signature that Catherine used to scan into the false documents. He'd fished it out of her garbage "in case" he needed it someday.

"Thank you, Paul," Angela said. "Give him the check," she instructed her bodyguard.

"Get me Catherine Erickson's private number, now," Angela demanded of her publicist, Sheila.

"What for?"

"I'll tell you all about it later."

Sheila called Angela back with the number after making some phone calls.

Catherine didn't answer her phone, so Angela left a message providing bits of the story Paul had shared, but didn't mention his name.

Later that evening, while Angela and Kate were in bed together, Catherine returned Angela's call.

"Who told you this? Was it Howard?" Catherine asked, furious.

Angela remembered that Howard had tried to contact her about the photos. "I'm not telling you who it was. I just want to know why you did this?" Angela demanded.

"These are complete lies. My ex-husband needs to be reminded of the confidentiality clause in our divorce agreement." Angela could picture Catherine on the other end of the phone, looking crazed.

Maybe that's why Howard never called her back: a confidentiality clause, Angela thought.

"Catherine, you are a scumbag. I can't believe you did this to me. I'm going to file a report with the police for fraud. Then I'm going to sue you. And by the way, Howard wasn't the person who ratted you out." Angela hung up.

Angela put the phone down. She threw the cordless phone on the floor, turned to Kate and said, "I am so sorry I didn't believe you. I just never thought there was someone like Catherine out there who hated me so much. I was so stupid and naive. Will you ever forgive me?" Angela pleaded.

"Angela, it's ok. You didn't know," Kate consoled. "I would've had my doubts too."

"I just can't believe how fortunate I am to have someone like you in my life. I should've believed you. I should've never doubted you." Angela wrapped her arms around Kate and pressed her body up against hers.

"It doesn't matter anymore, honey." Kate lightly kissed Angela on the forehead. "I love you."

"I love you too," Angela murmured.

EPILOGUE

A MONTH AFTER KATE and Angela reunited, Kate was
well enough to accompany Angela to New York for
Angela's return to the stage. The two women agreed they'd
make New York City their permanent home. It was much
easier to live a somewhat normal life in New York than L.A.
There were paparazzi, but they were a completely different
type of paparazzi, much less invasive. Plus, it was easy to
blend in to the overpopulated New York City streets.

Angela purchased a historic Greek Revival townhome
in Greenwich Village, not far from where Joe and Enriquo
lived. The three-story home was a steal as it was a foreclosure
property. Since Angela would have occasional business on
the West Coast, she convinced the owners of Kate's Malibu
bungalow to sell her the property.

Kate officially retired from her job as a celebrity photographer and accepted a teaching position at the Tisch School
of the Arts at New York University. In the fall, she taught
photography and imaging to freshmen and in the spring
taught photojournalism to seniors. During the summer
months, she traveled on photojournalism assignments, and
brought Angela along.

Kate's photos and firsthand account of the Ghana refugee
camp and Liberian rebels made the front page of the popular

news magazine. Her story was disseminated worldwide and contributed to the United Nations stepping in to help the refugees reclaim their homeland.

Angela, feeling the need to be more charitable, founded an acting program for disadvantaged and at-risk youth in the Bronx. She devoted time to working with the kids hands-on as often as she could while continuing to act in lead roles on Broadway. She has also arranged her schedule so that she was able to travel with Kate on her photojournalism assignments.

Kate and Angela returned to L.A. for the Academy Awards. This time, as Angela's date, Kate was a celebrity walking the red carpet with the paparazzi photographing her. Kate joined Angela for every photo opportunity and broadcast interview, and was overjoyed to see her buddy Andre.

"Now I know why you wouldn't go out on a date with me," Andre snickered.

"If I wasn't gay, I would've said yes," Kate said, with a slight chuckle.

"I'm proud of you girl. You deserve to be happy."

"Yes, I do Andre. Yes I do."

While Kate reveled in her new role as red-carpet walker, Angela wasn't thrilled with having to attend the public event. She enjoyed her new low-key life in New York. However, she was nominated for Best Actress in "Battleday". She didn't care much about winning. She felt like she had already won the greatest award possible. She had Kate.

When Angela's name was announced as the Best Actress winner, she realized she hadn't even prepared a brief speech. She thanked her agent, publicist, the movie's production crew and director, her family, and of course Kate.

"I especially want to thank the love of my life, Kate Ashford. You have shown me that it is not only ok to tell the truth, but most importantly, to live the truth. This is for you baby!" Angela said as she held up the golden statue.

Her Oscar statue remains in a box in the brownstone's guestroom closet, next to the kitty litter box.

A month after the Academy Awards, Kate and Angela held a commitment ceremony at Joe's new restaurant in Miami, surrounded by their friends and family. Angela's mother and father and Kate's father attended, which was a huge surprise to the couple. In their vows, the women agreed they would never believe a tabloid report or rumor ever again and professed their eternal love for each other. A year later, they made their commitment official by getting married in a very private ceremony, alongside newlyweds Marisol and Jamie, on the beach of their Malibu bungalow.

Kate and Angela are now going through the process of adopting a child from Indonesia. The tabloids are still reporting on Angela and, in true tabloid style, making things up as they go along.

After Mary confessed the feelings were mutual between her and Jason, they began spending every free moment together. Both were convinced that everything must have happened for a reason for them to end up together. For the first time in his life, Jason was committed to someone and never so much as looked at another woman.

Mary sold her home in Orange County and moved with the kids into Jason's newly purchased mansion located in the Hollywood Hills. Jason kept Angela's dogs and Lucinda, their maid. Angela didn't want the dogs to be cooped up in her New York home all day when they could run around the vast yard of Jason and Mary's new home. And, when Angela and Jason asked Lucinda if she'd rather work in New York or remain in California, she quickly responded, "I don't do snow and cold. New York get crazy snow. I don't like that."

A month following Kate and Angela's commitment ceremony, Mary and Jason wed in Santa Barbara. Jason didn't renew his contract for his hit television show. He wanted to devote his time to Mary and the kids and their newest family addition Mary was expecting. Rather than have to deal with the long hours of television production, he carefully selected film roles and acted in no more than two movies a year. The tabloids continued to pester him, concocting rumors about Mary and his relationship. Mary and Jason could care less what the tabloids made up and rolled their eyes at the paparazzi.

Catherine and Angela privately settled a civil suit Angela brought against Catherine for the Kate/Angela photo scheme. The out of court settlement ordered Catherine to pay two million dollars to Angela and granted Angela a restraining order against Catherine. In turn, Angela agreed that she wouldn't expose Catherine's scheme publicly, under the condition Catherine abided by the terms of the settlement. Unfortunately, not being able to expose Catherine also meant that Angela couldn't prove what Mike Jones, the sleazy reporter, had done to her.

Catherine was thrilled to find out that Angela was taking a hiatus from moviemaking. She was even happier that Angela moved to New York. *Good riddens*, Catherine thought.

Putting on her phony face, Catherine applauded and smiled for Angela when she beat her out of the Best Actress Oscar. Inside, Catherine was steaming mad with thoughts of murdering Angela. *I must put an end to her. She deserves to die.* Catherine was actually contemplating putting a hit out on Angela. She had a brief relationship with a mob guy that ended amicably. The last thing he said to Catherine was, "If you ever need something taken care of, you know where to go sweetheart."

Catherine was still convinced that Howard spilled the beans about her involvement in the photo scheme, though Angela insisted he didn't tell her anything. To this day she hasn't been able to prove it. Howard continues to exercise the privilege of withdrawing from his trust account and is dating a nice, attractive young heiress addicted to Kabbalah.

Tami left Suzanna for a famous lesbian talk show host. Suzanna was so irate she tried to burn down the talk show host's house. Suzanna turned out to be a terrible criminal. The neighbors of the talk show host called the police after seeing a woman dressed in black attempting to build a fire next to the talk show host's sunroom. Suzanna was arrested for attempted arson and is on probation.

Tami cleaned up her act and no longer uses drugs or alcohol. She and her new lover are cohabitating and spend much of their free time advocating to overturn Proposition 8 in California.

Paul cashed Angela's check and overdosed on a combination of heroin and cocaine, commonly referred to as a "speedball". His body was found next to a garbage can in Venice Beach.